BOOK TWO

THE BLACK SIGIL OF NAPHAL SERIES

PAIGE ALEXANDRIA

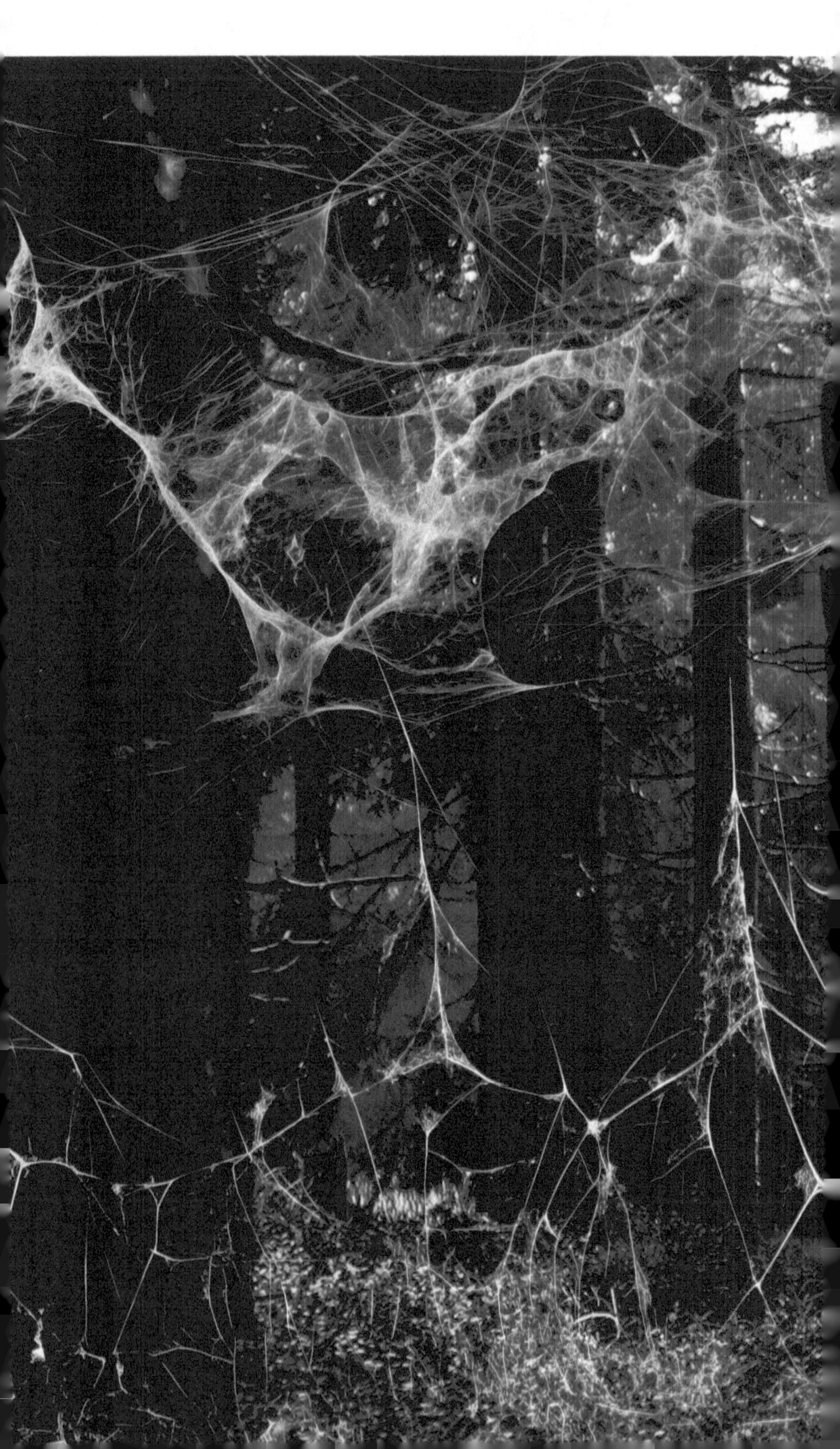

IN
REICH
AND
RUIN

TRIGGER WARNING

This novel contains dark themes and mature content that may be distressing to some readers. It explores trauma recovery, psychological manipulation, ancestral burdens, and morally complex relationships.

Please read with caution.

Trigger Warnings Include:

- Psychological abuse, manipulation, and gaslighting
- PTSD symptoms, panic attacks, dissociation, and trauma responses
- Emotional abuse, fear-based conditioning, and survivor's guilt
- Coercive environments, captivity elements, and loss of autonomy (non-sexual)
- Violence and injury (non-graphic), including off-page torture and ENA-related harm
- Familial secrets, betrayal, and distressing revelations about ancestry
- Cult dynamics, indoctrination, and ritualistic belief systems
- Religious trauma or ritualistic coercion
- Forced loyalty / indoctrination punishments
- Threats of harm, pursuit by dangerous individuals, and constant surveillance

• Explicit language & sexual content (BDSM elements, power imbalances)
• Power imbalances within relationships and institutions
• Mentions of past abuse and implied past trauma
• Trauma-induced memory issues or distorted perception
• Themes of abandonment, dependency, and psychological unraveling

This is a dark romance intended for mature audiences only (18+).

Reader discretion is strongly advised.

For the ones who stay even when hope isn't enough.

This book continues directly after the events of Epilogue Two in Sage Haven and concludes Sage and Reich's story, though they will appear in later books within The Black Sigil of Naphal series. This is the only installment that begins after a significant period of time.

PROLOGUE

REICH

This shouldn't be happening.

She shouldn't be here.

But she was.

Curled in the farthest corner, barely more than a shadow. Just some fragile, broken thing. Someone who would have been forgotten, had I not shown up.

The night pressed in around us, thick with the scent of damp earth and a rusty beatdown hatch. I told myself to move, to breathe, but my pulse hammered in my throat and my body locked in place as I looked at her—*really* looked at her.

Bones too sharp beneath bruised skin. Clothes torn and stiff with grime. Hair matted, tangled with dried blood but those same eyes.

The ones that belonged to the girl who haunted me since I left Providence.

Sage.

I wasn't supposed to even be here.

I told myself that I was going to pass this new job on to someone else. Because whatever was buried beneath the place, where I once rescued her and executed Klay and his psychopath brother, was better left untouched.

I asked myself why would I travel back to Providence?

To the past that had already swallowed enough of me?

To the girl I never wanted to leave but had to protect?

But the truth was, the past never let go.

And neither had she.

I reached for her, slow and careful, like she might disappear if I wasn't gentle.

Her breath beneath my touch was a whisper, fragile as a dying ember. I barely heard it over the roar in my ears, and the weight of this moment that seemed to press down on my ribs making breathing seem next to fucking impossible.

I didn't know if her breaths were real or if I was just hallucinating life into an already lifeless body.

My fingers brushed against the edge of her wrist, and a pulse—*weak but present*—left beats beneath my touch.

Alive.

Relief surged through me, sharp enough to hurt.

"Wildflower," I murmured against her skin. The old nickname was barely more than I could let out.

Yet, I said it like a prayer.

She flinched. Just a tremor, but it sent a crack through me all the same. Her gaze flickered, as her eyes opened struggling to focus, like she wasn't sure if I was real or just another ghost that had come to haunt her.

Then, finally, she spoke.

"...You."

I swallowed hard. "I came back."

A humorless breath—half a laugh, half a sob—escaped her lips. "Too late," she whispered.

Two words—shattered and accusing.

She was right and I didn't argue because I couldn't.

Three years.

Three years since I walked away.

Since I left pieces of myself with her. I thought I had known what it was to feel hollow before, but I hadn't, not truly. Not until I left her behind.

But I knew that I had to.

Every part of me wanted to stay.

That's how I knew I couldn't.

I couldn't let her be a part of this.

Castor and I had to keep a low profile when we left. He wasn't happy about it even though I found out later he brought Sam along for the ride without my knowledge. Still, he played off a resentment that simmered beneath his silence, though I tried to convince him that, in the long run, this would all be worth it. If we pulled off what we talked to Keenan and Nael about... the treasonous plan—we'd finally be free.

The odds were next to impossible.

But impossible was still something.

And I had to believe we were that slim chance.

No matter how bleak it was beginning to look.

Because I wanted to be someone else. Because of her.

And to do that, I had to launch myself into my life's warzone in hopes of attaining peace. It was going to be a brutal battle, but I was going to fight for it.

For her.

For *all of us*.

The air in this underground place was thick and heavy. Like it had been waiting for something or maybe, someone.

And as I stared down at Sage, hovered in the corner, I felt it for the first time.

A flicker of something deep inside of me.

A shift beneath the skin on the back of my neck where my mark sat.

It was barely there, a whisper of warmth where there should be nothing, but my breath stuttered. Instinct told me to move, to look away from her but I couldn't.

I cupped her cheek when it came fast—sharp and hot, like a livewire hitting my hand.

A pain that I hadn't felt before. I jerked back before I even realized what was happening. The sensation faded instantly when I stayed back.

I flexed my fingers, staring at my palm like I'd find something burned there.

Nothing.

But when I glanced at Sage, she was present, her expression showed concern.

"Are you okay?" she murmured; voice rough from disuse.

Here she was. Barely holding on, asking me if I was okay.

I wanted to laugh at the reality of it but something in her tone made my stomach twist.

Like she had felt it too.

I shifted closer, reaching for her again, in shock as I was able to move my hand through her hair with shaking fingers.

No pain this time... just her perfect skin.

Before I knew it, all I could think about was the fact that she was alive.

Somehow, she was alive and here.

Her eyes locked onto mine, and something in her expression started to crack wide open.

"Sage, come with me..." I said, my voice softer now than it had been before.

She didn't move.

Didn't reach for me.

Just stared back at me.

And as the silence stretched between us, thick and suffocating, I realized something about her.

She wasn't afraid.

She wasn't even broken.

She just wasn't sure if she wanted to be saved.

But in that moment, I didn't care about her feelings, because I wouldn't leave her like this.

So, I pulled her into me.

Into my arms.

Her breath was uneven, and her body felt rigid against mine. I didn't know what to say. Didn't know if I even had the right to say anything at all.

But when her fingers curled into my shirt, clutching onto me like I was something steady in a world that had swallowed her whole—*I knew.*

If I kept touching her, I'd never loosen my grip.

Because letting her go once almost destroyed me and I wouldn't survive it twice.

Chapter One

REICH

I thought I was prepared for that moment—for the possibility of her reappearing in my life like a ghost refusing to stay buried. But nothing could have prepared me for the reality of it.

For *her*.

For realizing it was actually her in that place.

She was thinner now, her body hardened by whatever hell she had endured in the time we'd been apart. Shadows clung beneath her eyes, and her skin was paler than I remembered, but it was her. Undoubtedly her.

I was going to stay away. Hand off this task to someone else.

I had told myself that when I got the tip—an anonymous message about a girl who had been found, who needed shelter.

I wasn't expecting it to be her.

I wasn't *ready* for it to be her.

But once she was in my arms again, once I felt the weight of her against me, the soft, perfect edges of her body pressing into mine, I knew.

Leaving was never an option again.

Her recklessness was what led me to her.

Hell, it always had. Just like that night we met.

But for two years, I watched from the sidelines. Watched her move on. Watched her rebuild. She was broken at first—six months of misery and barely getting by, then her resilience kicked in, just as I knew it would.

She had always been a force all of her own, something untouchable and unbreakable. Not even I had managed to keep her buried for long when I left.

After she picked herself back up, she spent a year and a half bouncing from one suitor to another.

That was the worst part. Seeing guy after guy go after her.

None of them worthy of her, though she pretended otherwise. I told myself she was happy. I told myself she was free. But deep down I think I knew better.

But I still watched, every agonizing moment.

Every time someone touched her, I learned how close I was to the monster I'd always been.

I hated seeing the way they looked at her.

Hated even more when she reciprocated.

But nothing—*nothing*—compared to the first time I saw her actually fall for someone else.

Mark was his name.

I almost ended him when she kissed him.

I did... but that came later.

She was only with him for a few months, but I convinced myself that it was her future. That she had found something steady, something I couldn't give her.

But it didn't last and that's when she disappeared from my watch.

A year. No trace. No way to find her, though I searched. Though I burned through every contact I had, every connection I could use.

And now, by some cruel twist of fate, she was here.

And I had to find a way to get through to her again, just like I had before.

IN REICH AND RUIN

She hadn't said much since we left the hideout where I had found her.

She wouldn't let me help her up initially, wouldn't even let me carry her back to the bunker.

She just let out quiet, measured breaths and the occasional sharp inhale when she moved wrong. I didn't need her to tell me she was in pain. I could see it in the way she held herself and the way her fingers twitched but never quite curled into fists.

Stubborn as ever.

Thankfully it was a short walk, about a mile away on the outskirts of Providence.

I pulled the door shut behind us, the metal groaned against the frame and just like that, we were cut off from the rest of the world.

The bunker was always cold, but somehow Sage seemed colder.

She swayed, just a little. It was quick, barely there, but I caught it.

She was injured. I could tell.

I exhaled through my nose and nodded toward the nearby cot. "Sit."

"I'm fine." She stated.

She wasn't.

I didn't argue. Instead, I moved toward the cabinet in the corner and pulled out a medical kit, setting it down beside me before I turned back to her. "Then keep yourself steady while I help and then once I am done you can get some rest."

Her glare was sharp, but she sunk onto the cot anyway.

Silence settled between us as she watched me wet a cloth and press it against the wound at her ribs she kept holding onto. She sucked in a sharp breath, her body tensing beneath my touch.

"Didn't know if I'd ever see you again," I said, quieter than intended.

She scoffed. "Didn't know if you wanted to."

I stilled. Just for a second. Then I got back to work, wrapping the bandage around her ribs, securing it with a knot.

The way she looked at me—it was different now.

"You didn't used to be so... hardened," I murmured.

A dry, humorless laugh escaped her. "...your wildflower grew thorns."

I met her gaze, taking her in—the fire in her eyes, the steel in her spine, the quiet defiance written into the way she now held herself.

"Good," I said. "You'll need them."

CHAPTER TWO

SAGE

I TRIED TO REST but sleep wouldn't come easily. Not when my body kept startling itself awake.

I told myself it was the cold, or the bruises, or the feeling earlier of Reich breathing too steadily beside me as he fixed my wound.

But none of that was what kept my eyes open.

It was the dark... and the fact that there was no window in this place.

It reminded me of the place I had just been.

Trapped and cut off from the world.

The bunker was silent, but my hands felt like they were shaking loudly.

This place felt too small. The walls were pressed in, and the cold air was unforgiving against my skin, but it wasn't the draft that made it hard to breathe. It was *him*.

I turned over and saw him.

Reich.

He sat in the chair on the other side of the room before he met my eyes and stood up.

His arms were crossed as he moved towards me, his hazel eyes unreadable. Always so damn unreadable. He barely spoke after he patched me up, and the silence had become suffocating.

And now he just watched me. I didn't even know for how long, but I knew he saw the jolt that woke me up.

"Were you watching me this whole time?" I asked.

Nothing.

"You've been seriously watching me this entire time?" I continued to ask.

Nothing.

Now I was getting angry. Three years of pent up frustration came crashing down all of a sudden.

"Really? You have barely said a word since you brought me back here and ordered me to bed and now you are going to stare at me like you don't know what to say?"

My voice had come out colder than I meant it to be, but I continued, "Go on. Say whatever it is you're holding back... You've had three years to practice. There has to be something you want to say after leaving me behind with nothing but a copout excuse for a note."

His jaw tightened. "You already know what I'm going to say."

"Do I?" A bitter laugh escaped before I could stop it. "Because I feel like I don't know anything when it comes to you.... I thought we were on the same page and then you just... left."

He let the silence do the damage for him.

No clever comeback. Just *nothing*.

His silence was infuriating.

I got up from the cot and stepped closer to where he was standing before I could think any better of it. My chest was tight, my pulse hammered beneath my skin, but I ignored it. "You act like you don't care, but I see the way you still look at me, Reich..."

I said his name on purpose, remembering what it once did to him.

He exhaled, slow and measured, but his grip seemed to tighten where his hands rested on his arms.

"Sage." My name came out low and strained from his lips, like a warning.

I ignored it.

"Why won't you give me something... Hell you can tell me to leave... Just like before." My voice wavered, but I didn't back down. "... tell me you don't feel this and I will... Or better yet, leave again. *You seem to be good at that.*"

His eyes darkened but he didn't step back. Didn't push me away.

"You make it sound so damn simple," he murmured.

I moved back towards the cot and sat down.

"Isn't it?" I scoffed.

For a long moment, neither of us moved. The tension was thick and electric, and I hated how badly I wanted to close the distance between us. To chase the warmth that I shouldn't need.

Reich moved first. Not away but closer. Until he was sitting next to me on the cot.

His fingers brushed against my wrist, barely a touch, but it sent a spark through me anyway. Something I hadn't felt in years. My breath caught, my skin burning where he lingered, and I knew—*damn it, I knew*—that I should move away. That I should pull back before this goes somewhere dangerous.

But I didn't.

Because even in the frustration, even in the anger, the passion was still there. It always was.

And right then I didn't want to fight because truthfully... I just missed him.

I hated that he still had that power over me. Hated that after everything—after the agony of searching for him, the nights spent cursing his name, the weight of every unanswered question—I still *wanted* him.

I couldn't stop staring. His eyes were the same shade of dark hazel that I remembered, sharp and unreadable, but there was something beneath them now.

Something almost *hidden*.

His breath was shallow, his lips parting like he wanted to speak but the silence stretched between us, thick as smoke.

"Say something..." I demanded, my voice shaking. "Anything."

He exhaled, his hand lifting slightly, like he wanted to reach for me but wasn't sure he still had the right. "There's nothing I can say that doesn't make this worse."

"...Tell me you never thought about me. Tell me I don't mean anything to you anymore. Tell me... that you forgot about me."

His jaw tightened, the muscles there clenching, and for a moment, I thought he would. That he'd give me the clean break I should want.

But he didn't.

Instead, his fingers ghosted along my arm, barely there, like he was testing to see if I was real. The touch was light, but it burned within me, and I hated that I still reacted to him. That even after everything, he could still cause my breath to catch in my throat.

"You think I forgot you?" he murmured, low and rough. "You think I didn't wake up every damn day with your name in my head?"

I should have moved away.

But instead, I grabbed the front of his shirt, fisting the fabric.

Give in. Talk later. Sounded like a good plan to me.

"I hate you," I whispered, even though it was a lie, even though the way I was gripping him told a different story.

He let out a sharp breath, like my words cut him, but then suddenly—*finally*—his hands were on me, and everything shattered.

His lips crashed against mine, raw and desperate, and I didn't stop him. I should, but I didn't.

Because this was what I wanted. What I ached for these last three years.

I pressed into him, my hands sliding up into his hair, my body molded against his like I belonged there. His grip tightened at my waist, pulling me closer, and I could feel the way his breath stuttered, the way he was holding back like he was afraid of breaking me.

Like he was afraid of breaking himself.

But I didn't want careful. I didn't want restraint.

All I wanted was *him*.

So, I bit his lip, just enough to draw a sharp inhale from him, and it was like something snapped.

He backed me up against the wall that the cot was butted up against, in one swift movement, his body caged mine in, his mouth devoured me. His hands roamed—gripping, mapping, memorizing—and I knew, *I knew*, that neither of us would walk away from this untouched.

"You have no idea," he growled against my lips, "what it's done to me...not having you." His teeth scraped my bottom lip, sharp and possessive. "And now you're here."

I was already trembling, my body betraying me, arching into him with a need I hadn't been able to kill. Not after everything. Not after all this time.

His hands tore at my clothes—no finesse, no patience. The sound of dropping fabric filled the air, but I didn't care. I wasn't sure I could care about anything but the feel of his skin burning against mine.

I gasped as he pressed me harder into the wall, one hand sliding between us, fingers rough as they found me. He groaned low in his throat, a vicious sound that made my pulse stumble.

"Fuck, Sage... Somehow I knew you'd still be mine." He rasped.

I wasn't sure if it was a question or a demand or if I even still was, but I answered with what I thought he wanted to hear anyway. "I've always been yours."

His breath hitched, but his fingers didn't falter. They slid inside me without warning, and I bit down hard on his shoulder to keep from crying out. He cursed, shifting his hips against me, grinding the hard length of him into my thigh.

"If you scream, someone will hear… this isn't like Providence." he said, voice tight.

I wanted to tell him I didn't care. That I wanted the whole world to know he was here, as close as he could possibly be to me after all this time.

But I didn't say anything. I nodded instead, my fingers clawing at his back as his thumb circled that spot right above that made me shudder. His pace was merciless. There was no slow build. No teasing. Just Reich—ruthless, raw and desperate.

I came undone in his hands, biting his skin hard enough to leave a mark because it was the only thing keeping me from screaming his name.

But he didn't stop.

Before the tremors faded, he freed himself and lined up without a word, holding me pinned with one hand while the other guided him inside me in one brutal thrust.

I choked on a sob. My nails dug deeper. His mouth swallowed the sound with a kiss, rough and punishing.

"You made a mistake looking for me," he snarled. "Because I don't know how to leave anymore."

He moved then—deep, relentless strokes that shook my whole body. I couldn't breathe, couldn't think. Could only feel.

His rhythm stuttered when I clenched around him. His breath hissed through his teeth, his forehead pressing to mine.

We shattered together, locked tight, his name a silent scream on my lips as his body tensed, pulsing inside me. He held me there, shaking, both of us wrecked and ruined and still wanting more.

When he finally pulled back enough to look at me, his expression was unreadable. But his thumb traced my cheek, gentle and reverent.

Now came the hard part.

CHAPTER THREE

REICH

THE AIR BETWEEN US was thick— cloaked with everything we hadn't said and everything we shouldn't have done.

Sage laid beside me, her skin still warm from where we collided and came undone in a way that solved nothing but dulled the ache for one brief, hollow moment. I watched as the sheets stayed tangled around her hips, clinging to her. Her breathing was slow but uneven, the kind of quiet that wasn't restful.

The kind that seemed to be holding something back.

And the silence I knew was about to come between us now?

Would be even sharper than before, edged with the same frustration, the same fury, that drove us here in the first place.

I stared up at the ceiling for a long moment, as I felt the weight of her beside me like an untended wound. Then as I turned my head, I realized she was already watching me.

Her gaze was level. Guarded. But underneath it, there was something else.

Something *waiting*.

So I bit the bullet and gave her what she wanted.

"Are you ready to talk?" I murmured.

Her lips pressed into a thin line, her expression shuttered tight as she responded, "Are you?"

"I asked first." A humorless smirk tugged at my mouth but I couldn't make it reach my eyes.

She exhaled, dragging air loudly through her teeth as she rolled onto her back, staring up at the imperfections in the steel ceiling. Her hair fanned out against the pillow in dark tangles, still damp with sweat and steam from our earlier entanglement.

Like this—*us*—what we had just done was some half-forgotten thing that she wasn't sure she wanted to remember.

"What is it that you really want me to say, Reich?" she asked. Her voice was brittle, held together by threads that I could see unraveling the longer we did this.

She continued, "That I regret coming to look for you? That I regret this?" She gestured between us, her hand slicing through the charged space like a blade. "Because I don't. But I also know it doesn't change anything because... you still left."

Something twisted in my chest. A slow, grinding pain that was too familiar by now.

"No," I said quietly. "It doesn't change anything."

The silence stretched between us again. Long. Heavy.

And I let it.

Then, almost on instinct, I reached for my phone. Scrolling without looking. The speaker hummed softly on the nightstand, filling the space with something quieter than our breathing.

The slow pull of music spilled into the room, barely there—like it was bleeding through the cracks in us instead of the speaker.

I didn't think either of us was listening though.

Not really.

I dragged in a breath, slow, steady.

And then I made the first move.

I always do, even back when I was begging her to give me answers which seemed like a lifetime ago at this point.

"I got a call," I said. My voice was steady, but lower now. Like I was pulling it up from some place I had buried. "An anonymous tip. Just another job on my list of a thousand other things I had to do."

I kept my gaze on her face, watching for any reaction, but her expression didn't shift.

So, I continued, "they said that they had found someone at an abandoned hideout."

Her breath caught faintly, but she didn't interrupt.

Didn't ask questions.

She just waited for me to keep going.

"I agreed without thinking much of it." I exhaled through my nose, the memory threading a chill that shot through my body. "When I opened the hatch door and saw you..." My jaw tightened. "Fuck, Sage."

I dragged a hand down my face, pulse thudding in my throat at the memory of it. "I thought I was seeing a ghost."

For a moment, something flickered in her eyes. Guarded. Like she was bracing herself for a hit that wouldn't come.

She shifted on the cot, fingers ghosting along the edge of the sheet like she was grounding herself.

"What is this place?" she asked, her voice quieter now—but there was steel wrapped through it. Her eyes darted around the space, wide with a mix of awe and suspicion. "This place is huge. There are at least ten doors surrounding us... and the uniformity—the way it's all set up." Her tone sharpened. "This is something else... isn't it?"

I hesitated. Because this—what I said next—would break every boundary I'd built between us. The truth I'd spent years burying. But she had already pried open the cracks. And I was too damn tired to keep holding them shut.

"You remember those rooms back at my house in Providence?" I asked.

Her brows furrowed. The faint light caught the tremor in her breath.

"The multiple rooms," she said slowly. "Like the one you kept me in. I saw them... that morning when I woke up in your bed for the first time."

"Yeah." My voice was low. "They weren't for me."

She froze as she waited for me to continue.

"The ENA uses me as sort of a... transitional housing unit," I said finally. The words felt foreign, even to me. "For the people they move between trafficking rings. Several come through here and always have. Even back in Providence."

She blinked, processing, her expression hardening with what looked like realization and disbelief mixed in one.

"How come I never heard them? Or saw anyone?"

"Because you weren't meant to," I said. "Each room is sealed with state-of-the-art security. Noise cancelation. Surveillance. They have everything they need in there. The ENA only comes once a year, when they've gathered enough people across different regions. They move them all at once—it minimizes exposure, lowers their risk. That's why I left... they stationed me here."

Her throat worked around a sound that wasn't quite a word.

"But..." she whispered, "you must have helped some of them, right? That's why those people contacted you about me... how you found me."

Not quite but I was going to let her believe that the people who told me about her had good intentions.

She didn't need to know that had it been anyone else that she would have been transitioned into the ring and never heard from again.

I nodded once. "Yes, I helped a few but only a few and it was quietly. Off record. Cas knew, but we never talked about it—not to anyone. It would've put them at risk. The ENA couldn't know. They still don't."

IN REICH AND RUIN

Her breath hitched. I watched the realization settle over her—slow and heavy, like dust on untouched glass.

"And that's why no one knew... not even me... that's why you kept it from me," she murmured.

It wasn't a question. Just an echo of comprehension breaking her open.

I said nothing because there was nothing else to say.

This was a risk. Saving her was a risk.

But I was willing to put my life on the line to do it.

After a long silence, she exhaled shakily. "All those years ago... I wondered. But I never asked."

"I chose to keep it a secret."

Her jaw tightened as she dragged in a breath. "But you're telling me now?" Her gaze cut to mine, sharp, as she continued, "After you stumbled across me by sheer coincidence?"

I held her stare. "I don't want to keep secrets from you anymore."

Even though I seemed to keep doing that.

She scoffed. A rough sound, full of all the broken things we hadn't said yet. "That's rich, coming from you."

I breathed through the frustration twisting in my gut.

If only she knew what I was risking... especially after the way she kept walking into danger like she was invincible.

"Don't act like I am the only one who's been keeping secrets, Sage. Where did you disappear to this last year?"

Her body went rigid. Her fists curled in the sheets. "If you understood, you'd walk away," she muttered.

"Try me."

For a moment, I think she won't.

I think she'll let the silence devour us both. But then— "I tried to move on," she said. The words come out of her stiff. Like they hurt to speak. "After you disappeared. After Sam was just... gone."

She swallowed hard, her throat working around the weight of it. "It had been two years that I tried to pretend you didn't exist. That none of it mattered. That my best friend didn't just up and disappear at the same time you left."

I nodded slowly, "I know."

Her head snapped toward me, fury flashing beneath the hurt in her eyes. "You know?" she repeated, her voice jagged.

I held her gaze steady.

"I watched," I said quietly. "From a distance... I just needed to know you were okay."

Her breath shuddered. "I was a pretty fucked-up definition of okay," she whispered.

I didn't argue. I didn't apologize. Because we both knew there was nothing that made this right.

And once she found out Sam tagged along with Castor... I knew I was going to have to answer for why I didn't bring her along with me.

She swallowed again, like she was forcing herself to keep going. "I couldn't do it," she said. "I couldn't let go." Her fingers brushed against my wrist, light and absent. "So, I went looking for you. Hoping I would find you. Hoping you would help me find Sam."

My pulse jumped every time she mentioned Sam, but I didn't move.

"I remembered the mark," she continued. "The one on the back of your neck."

I went still. Every instinct I had tightened like an invisible noose ready to strangle me.

"I searched for it," she said, her voice almost distant. "Looked for anyone else who had it. But I couldn't find anyone. Except... I remembered Klay."

She glanced at me. "Klay had the same mark as you and Castor. But I never saw him again after that night. Because of you. Because you, Nael, and Keenan ended it. I didn't have to wonder if he'd come back for me."

"So," she said, "I went to where Klay spent most of his time. Back in Sanele."

My hands flexed against the sheet.

"Sanele," I echoed.

"Yeah," she said but there was something dark in her tone.

I forced myself to breathe evenly. "Where?" I asked.

"The Bloodwine," she said.

Of course.

"That's how you ended up in that hideout," I murmured.

She nodded. "I followed the thread. Started asking questions. But …. that's also when I found something else."

She hesitated.

And for the first time, I could see fear crack through her eyes.

I reached for her, tilting her chin up with my fingers. "What?" I asked.

Her gaze flickered.

"My mother," she whispered. "She was involved with the ENA. Before she left me and my father... Before she vanished."

I went still. Completely still.

"So instead of really looking for you...I spent a year trying to chase her shadow," she continued. "And then... I got too close."

I didn't have to ask what happened next.

I already knew.

They took her.

I exhaled hard, dragging my hand over my face. "Fuck, Sage."

She pressed her lips together. And for the first time tonight, she looked drained. Empty. Like the weight of it all was hollowing her out from the inside.

The music was nearly gone now. Just a ghost of a sound in the background. But the damage was already done.

I watched her carefully. Then I asked, "Why didn't you tell me any of this before?"

I realized it was a stupid question when I heard her bitter laugh.

"You weren't exactly available for deep, heartfelt conversations, Reich." Her gaze cut through me, as she continued, "Let alone available at all."

I didn't argue, because she was right.

I shifted, sitting up, my hand braced against my knee as I tried to process the pieces that she had just handed me. The fragments of a truth I wasn't ready for.

She watched me. Cautious and wary.

I had to give her something, so I gave her the answer I knew she really wanted.

"I went to look for the remainder of Klay's brothers... The ones I failed to get rid of." I stopped, as I raked my hand through my hair before continuing, "... and I found them."

I still never found out what went wrong, who the men were that impersonated the brothers and why.

I always wondered if it was ENA interference.

But knew if that was the case, I'd be dead by now.

I wasn't supposed to go after the Ovitts because of how the ENA valued them. They were "soldiers" in their eyes. But they were sick and after what they did to Sage, I was overjoyed to serve them the same kind of hell they made her go through... but worse.

I couldn't help but smile at the memory of what I did to them. The *real* brothers. It wasn't a pleasant sight. But it was who I was... and it felt so fucking good to inflict my own special form of justice on them.

She looked at me, something reserved still in her eyes, but she thanked me.

"You didn't have to do that... go after them... But thank you. I always wondered if that was why you left." She said softly before her tone shifted. "Although, I still don't understand why you didn't bring me along... especially after everything we went through with Klay.... Why?"

I looked at her. Really looked at her.

"You know why, Sage." I said.

And when she looked at me, I knew she finally understood.

It was them. It was *always* about them.

The ENA.

And what they would do to her.

"Then what now?" she asked, her voice quieter, but not weak.

I met her gaze, taking in the exhaustion in her eyes and the quiet, fierce resolve beneath it. The part of her that was still waiting for me to break first.

I didn't.

I shook my head slowly. "Now," I murmured, voice steady, "we find out the truth about all of it ... including your mother."

Chapter Four

SAGE

Tʜᴇ ʜᴇᴀᴠɪɴᴇss ʙᴇᴛᴡᴇᴇɴ ᴜs eased when the silence broke at last. What once felt suffocating now felt lighter, as if each word we shared cleared the air, though I knew there were still questions that needed to be answered. But still, I could draw in a deep breath, and this time, it didn't burn. It steadied me instead.

"Now," Reich said, his voice low and certain, "we find out the truth about all of it... including your mother."

Reich's words hung there, suspended in the space between us, and they should have scared me. They should have made me think twice about everything we were about to do. But they didn't. Because I needed to know.

Maybe I always had.

I sat up slowly, the coolness of the room hit against my skin as the sheet fell loose around my hips. I pulled it tighter around me, but my body still hummed—still ached—from the way he touched me, from the anger and the hunger that twisted tight between us after all this time.

It wasn't just the heat of his hands that lingered on my skin.

It was the fury and the *need*.

Reich watched me carefully from where he sat at the edge of the bed, elbows braced on his knees, his eyes dark and steady. Waiting for me to push back.

Instead, I held his gaze as my throat tightened and my heart pounded against my ribs like it was trying to escape the cage I had kept it in for too long.

Because there was something that he didn't know.

"You don't know the full story of what I found when I was looking for my mother," I said quietly.

The warning was there. A line in the sand I should have drawn but I knew it was already too late for lines with Reich.

It always was.

His jaw ticked, and I saw the tension ripple through him like a storm waiting to break.

"Tell me…" he said.

I hesitated. Not because I didn't want to tell him. But because I didn't know if I could tell him without breaking myself open. Without bleeding the truth I'd buried so deep it hardly felt real anymore.

He shifted forward slightly, closing the space between us without moving more than an inch.

"Sage," he said, and it wasn't a question. It wasn't even a plea. It was an anchor.

It was hard to explain what it did to me when he said my name. Even just the way he said my name—low and so damn relentless—seemed to undo me in a way I never saw coming. Like he was calling me back to myself and had always been the only one that could do that.

I exhaled sharply, pressing my fingers against my temples, bracing myself for the unraveling and then I looked at him again.

He was still there. Still waiting. And I was just happy he was here in front of me again after all this time.

So, I gave him what he asked for.

Piece by jagged piece with no hesitation.

"I found a file," I said, my voice thinner than I wanted it to be. "At The Bloodwine. One I don't think I was supposed to see... It had my mother's name on it." The words scraped out of me like broken glass. "She wasn't just involved with the ENA," I continued. "She was a part of them or maybe one of their victims but it didn't look like she was there against her will. There were these photos... several of them... and she was walking into what looked like some sort of strange ritual willingly... The things around it were sick and twisted... malformed bodies and Frankenstein like corpses attached to different parts of animals... but she was still there, in all of the photos, looking like she enjoyed it. The film rolls showed her next to these young children... and I can't even begin to tell you what I saw, but Reich it was one of the most horrific things I think I've ever seen."

Reich didn't move. Didn't flinch.

But I saw it.

Something shifting.

The way his hands flexed where they rested on his knees. The way his pulse seemed to jump hard in his neck.

"Did it say anything about why she was a part of it?" he asked, his voice flat but dangerous. Tightly controlled. Like he already knew the answer wouldn't be enough even if I did know it.

"I don't know. There wasn't any explanation in the file."

The confession tasted bitter.

I swallowed against it. "I just saw her name. Listed. Like a signature on a contract." I dragged in a breath that did nothing to steady me. "It was dated... She signed it years before she met my father. Before she had me."

His entire body tensed, as his fingers curled into fists so tight, I half expected to hear something crack. I didn't have to look at him to know what was going through his head.

The calculations. The strategy. The slow, methodical way he was thinking through all the ways he could run through the people responsible. All the ways he could dismantle them piece by piece.

"I spent the last few months chasing her story," I continued, quieter now. "Following every breadcrumb. Every name listed in that file and every location I could find. I thought..." My breath caught, sharp and painful. "I thought if I found out what happened to her, I'd understand why she left and never came back all those years ago."

Reich was silent and utterly still.

I forced myself to meet his gaze again. "But then someone took me before I got any closer. Not that I made much progress anyway. But then this couple found me, told me they could help me and then ... well ... *you.*"

The words hung there, heavy and cold.

His hands flexed again, white-knuckled. His shoulders coiled tight, like he was barely keeping himself still. I could see it in his eyes—the fury, the hunger for revenge. But I could also see something else.

Something raw.

Something that looked like guilt.

But I continued, nonetheless, "Maybe I was closer to the truth than I originally thought ... and maybe they made sure that I knew it. The guy who took me certainly did."

The memory cut deep, cold and sharp.

The cell. The darkness. The whispers in the dark. What that man promised he would do to me. What they almost did. I'd be dead if it weren't for the couple that saw me. The ones who led Reich to me. I wonder if they somehow knew. Knew that we needed to see each other again.

But the idea seemed too unrealistic.

This was all just a coincidence, but it was a happy one.

I felt Reich move before I saw him.

A shift in the air that was heavier and closer than I expected.

And when I glanced at him again, his expression was unreadable but his hands weren't.

They were shaking.

Slight, but there.

"Who?" he asked.

A single word. Low and lethal.

And I knew what he was asking.

Who took me. Who hurt me. Who does he go after first.

But I didn't have the answers.

Not the ones that mattered.

"I don't know who took me," I admitted. "But I think I know where to start."

Reich exhaled hard, dragging a hand down his face like it was the only thing keeping him grounded and then his eyes were back on me.

Sharp. Clear. Focused.

"The Bloodwine," he said.

I nodded. "That's where I found answers first. I think there's more there." I paused. "Oliver—the owner—he helped me before because he was curious to know too. He might have more answers if I tell him what I've found."

Reich tilted his head back, staring at the ceiling like he needed the distance—like the only thing keeping him from moving right now was the thin thread of restraint he still had left.

When he finally spoke, his voice was quiet, but the edge was unmistakable steel.

"Do you trust him?"

"No," I answered honestly. "But... he seemed genuine."

A humorless smirk tugged at Reich's mouth, gone as quickly as it appeared. "Good. Then that's where we start. But after..." His jaw flexed, something dark breaking through. "I am burning it down."

I blinked. "Burning it down?"

"It's where your nightmare keeps starting," he said, eyes leveling with mine. "It's where they taught you fear... but I'm going to teach them something worse."

My throat tightened, but I nodded because there was nothing else to say—nothing else that would matter.

"And not just for you," he added, voice low. "For every innocent person who walks through those doors thinking they're safe, only to get caught in their web."

"Don't you think that's a little dramatic?" I tried, though even I didn't sound convinced. "Shouldn't we be keeping a low profile?"

Reich's laugh was soft, rough, and entirely humorless. "You haven't seen what I'm capable of when I stop pretending I'm good. This is what I do, Sage. It's who I am. You want in?" His eyes sharpened. "Then let me see those thorns you were talking about earlier."

I shrugged, trying for confidence I didn't fully feel. "I don't know if I really have them... but that doesn't mean I won't try."

Silence settled over us again—heavy, thick, but different than before.

Not hesitation. Not fear. Not all the things we kept swallowing down. This silence was full of something new.

Purpose. Resolve. And the first spark of revenge that was bright enough to burn.

I glanced down at my hands, at the bruises still dark on my wrists, at the faint scars that hadn't quite faded.

And then I looked at Reich, at the way he watched me, like he was waiting for me to crack or waiting for me to break apart.

I stood and my movements were slow but steady. "I think I need a shower," I said, voice level. I barely took a step before I felt him move.

His fingers caught my wrist, firm but careful, like he was testing how far he could go.

When I turned to look at him, his gaze was unreadable, but there was something hidden beneath it.

"Reich," I started, but he was already on his feet.

Already closing the space between us.

"I'm coming with you," he said. Quiet. Certain.

My pulse stuttered. "I can handle it myself—"

"I know you can." He interrupted. His voice was soft, but there was steel beneath it. "But I also know when I look at your eyes, that you won't."

And he was right because if I stepped into that shower alone—anywhere alone—I'd think too much. I'd *feel* too much.

And I wouldn't come out the same.

So, I didn't argue. I just nodded and let him lead the way.

I lingered behind but I followed slowly.

Hesitation gripping me in every step.

He moved quick, like a man on a mission and already had the water running when I stepped into the humid drenched, cramped bathroom.

I lingered and watched as the steam curled thick in the air, clinging to the walls as the mirror began to fog over. My fingers trembled as I reached for the hem of my shirt, and I didn't miss the way Reich watched me, patiently.

The way his gaze dragged over the bruises.

Over the scars. Over the parts of me that I've tried so hard to forget.

But these were for purpose. These scars and bruises had meaning this time, because I was fighting for something. Not just my life. But the *truth*.

He didn't say anything. He didn't look away. He just stepped forward, his hands finding the fabric of my shirt and helped me lift it over my head with a care that made me melt.

I let the rest of my clothes fall away, piece by piece, until there was nothing left to hide behind.

And then it was his turn.

He stripped his shirt off in one smooth motion, his muscles tight beneath the dim light. Old scars carved their stories into his skin—stories I had once asked about but never got the full truth. Stories I might never know. I traced them with my eyes, but not my hands.

Not yet.

When he was bare, he reached for me again.

Slower this time. Softer. Like he was waiting for me to say no.

But I didn't.

When his hand left my cheek, I stepped into the shower, the scalding water hitting my skin in a rush that stole the breath from my lungs. It burned, but I welcomed it.

I *needed* it.

I always needed something that hurt to make me feel alive.

Reich stepped in behind me, his hands finding my waist again as he steadied me. His mouth found the curve of my temple with his warm breath, even as the water hissed between us.

Neither of us spoke.

We didn't need to.

Because right there and then, the war outside didn't exist. The past didn't exist.

It was just me and him.

And for the first time in years, I didn't feel like I was drowning alone.

Chapter Five

REICH

Steam still clung to Sage's skin as she stepped out of the shower, droplets trailed lazy paths down the curve of her spine. They caught in the pitch of her lower back before sliding further, disappearing beneath the edge of the towel barely secured around her hips.

The room was thick with heat, the glass fogged and the air heavy. Her breathing was steady from the scalding water, but beneath it was something unknown I could feel in the space between us.

From everything unspoken still hanging there, filling the room like smoke.

I should have let her walk away.

Let her dry off and get dressed. Pretend that our moment of just being in each other's presence exposed under the hot water was enough to satisfy this thing clawing between us.

Pretend we both weren't hungry for more.

But I didn't.

Instead, I reached for the candle sitting on the sink. The one I had lit earlier in the day, when we first collided—before everything blurred into hands and mouths and that desperate, shaking need we kept pretending doesn't control us.

It was half-melted, wax cooled in long rivulets down its sides with the wick still burning low. The scent of it was warm and sweet in my nostrils.

Her back was turned to me, lazily wringing out her hair, eyes lost somewhere that wasn't here.

And when I moved, she didn't notice. Not at first.

Not until the faint scent of burnt wick curled through the heat-soaked air.

Then she stilled.

Her eyes found mine in the mirror, wide, dark and electric, like she already knew what I was thinking.

I stepped closer, slow and deliberate. My feet silent on the slick floor. Her breath hitched—just slightly—but she didn't move away. Not even when I was directly behind her.

"Really? After all this time?" Her voice was breathy, but it didn't waver. It was threaded with challenge and sharp at the edges. "I could barely handle it the last time..." She let out a light chuckle, "You're dangerous, Reich."

I smirked hard, with the corner of my mouth tugged upward as I leaned in. My free hand skimming along the damp curve of her waist, slow enough to feel the shiver ripple through her.

"And you," I murmured, lips brushing her temple, "... you keep choosing me. That one's on you, wildflower."

Her exhale was sharp and controlled. Her gaze flickered to the candle, then back to me, her throat working around something she wouldn't say. "Reich—"

I tilted the candle, just enough to let a single bead of molten wax drip free. It landed on her shoulder, tracing a path along damp skin.

She shuddered.

Her hands gripped the edge of the sink in front of her.

"Still here?" I asked, my voice low and rough.

Her lips parted, but nothing came out. Her throat worked, but her silence said more than words could.

I grinned, before I pressed my mouth to the crook of her neck. I could taste the sweet heat on her skin. She arched—*barely*—but enough. Enough for me to know she wasn't going anywhere.

Another drop slid down her shoulder blade, rolling like molten glass over the curve of her spine.

"You like this too much," she whispered.

But she was leaning into me now, giving in even as she accused.

"You let me do it too much," I countered, my breath hot against her ear.

I didn't hide the amusement in my tone.

I didn't have to.

She huffed a breath that might be a laugh as she tilted her head slightly, enough to catch my gaze again in the mirror. Her eyes were sharp, but softer than before. "Maybe I just missed this," she said.

I raised a brow, trailing my fingers along the hardened wax now cooled on her skin.

"The candle?" I asked, but I already knew the answer.

She smirked, but there was something honest in it. "Us."

It hit me harder than I expected. A tightness in my chest that had nothing to do with control.

Because I missed this too. *Us.*

The way she used to spar with me, never letting me win. The way silence between us was never empty—just full of everything we didn't need to say. The way we used to trade words like they mattered because they did.

I missed all of it and I didn't know how to tell her. I didn't know how to give her that piece of me.

Not when I could sense that something was coming. Not when I could feel how much harder things were about to get.

So, I didn't.

I pressed another slow kiss to the back of her neck instead and I set the candle down carefully on the counter.

My hand moved, smoothing along the path the wax made, feeling the way she shook beneath me.

I trailed my fingertips up her spine, slow and steady, until they found the curve of her neck again.

I stayed there a moment and then stepped back.

"Stop being a distraction, wildflower," I said quietly. "We should start packing."

I could feel her watching me in the mirror, something unreadable in her gaze.

As I turned and called out, "The Bloodwine isn't going to burn itself down."

Catching her eyeroll in my last glance—because it was easier than saying anything else for her—but she didn't argue. She grabbed a towel from the rack, wiping herself down with quick, efficient motions, before reaching for a pile of clothes scattered across the cot.

I watched her longer than I should. Longer than I could justify.

But I did it anyway. Because I was an addict when it came to her. And she was the only thing that made the noise inside my head quiet.

Which was so damn refreshing after these past few years. I could finally focus on something... which was her.

I forced myself to move. Pulled on a fresh shirt. Grabbed my bag from the floor and swung it up onto the nearby table.

Focused.

I was halfway to lacing up my boots when my phone buzzed.

The sound cut through the quiet like a blade.

I glanced at the screen.

Castor.

Of course, it was Cas.

Sage looked up, catching the hesitation in my body before I even knew it was there. She watched me like she was already putting pieces together.

I exhaled, dragging a hand over the back of my neck before answering. "Yeah?"

Cas didn't waste time. "So... you weren't going to tell me what happened, or did you prefer to make me play the guessing game?"

I pinched the bridge of my nose, as I felt the headache start low behind my eyes. "Tell you what?"

"That you found her." His voice was light, threaded with amusement, but there was something serious beneath it. Something sharp. "You sent a cryptic-ass text hours ago about Sage and how you were going to try and take her back to your bunker and then went completely dark. I figured you were either dead or busy."

Sage tensed. I felt it before I saw it.

She couldn't hear the other line, but it was as if she could.

Her hands went still where they were folding the pile of clothes. Her breath tightened.

"I'm always busy. And?" I asked carefully.

"And we're coming by. We are already on our way out to make the trek." Cas said it like it was nothing. Like he didn't just drop a grenade into my hands.

I went still. Every muscle in my body locked up.

Sage went even stiffer, like she already knew there was a conversation happening she was not part of. Like she knew something was about to crack wide open.

"Wait—" My voice was lower now.

But it didn't matter.

"No arguing," he cut in. "Sam and I will be there soon."

I felt like I stopped breathing.

Sage watched me closer, eyes narrowing as she read the shift in me.

"Really?" I asked, even though I already knew. Even though it was already detonating inside me.

"Yeah," Cas said, like it was the simplest thing in the world. "Me and you know... Sage's best friend. The one she thought was dead for the past three years. Ring any bells?"

There was a smirk in his voice. But it was a warning, and he knew.

He knew I hadn't told her yet.

My jaw clenched so tight, it was nearly painful.

"Ok... We will see you soon." I responded.

"See you soon, brother." Cas said before hanging up.

I lowered the phone slowly. My pulse hammered in my ears.

Sage was standing completely still, arms crossed. Her eyes sharp as knives. Waiting.

"Who was that?" she asked, voice low and calm.

Too calm.

I hesitated. Half a second too long.

Her expression shifted and hardened. She knew something was different just in the way I was standing. "Reich..."

I exhaled slowly, dragging a hand down my face, trying to find the words. "Cas..." I said.

"And?" Colder now. Quieter.

"And..." My voice scraped raw in my throat. "He's coming by."

She stared at me with confusion in her expression, trying to piece it together. "Oh ok... is there any reason why? Is it some ENA mission?"

I braced myself. I knew what was coming and it didn't matter how slow I went.

It would still break her.

"No... it's because he and Sam want to see you," I said.

Everything stopped. Like the air had been sucked out of the room. Like gravity just changed.

She blinked.

Once. Twice.

"Sam?" Her voice was barely a whisper, but it still cut through me.

I nodded then because my throat was too tight.

"Sam's alive?"

"Yes." I confirmed and that was all it took.

Her world fractured. And she didn't move. Didn't even blink.

She just stared at me like I was a stranger.

And then— "You knew?"

Quiet. Hurt.

I closed my eyes for a moment. When I opened them, she was still there. Still waiting. Hands shaking.

"Sage—" I started.

"You knew?" Her voice was louder now, almost breaking. Raw with betrayal.

I swallowed hard and forced it out, "Yes."

Her breath shuddered. Her lips parted, like she was going to yell.

But she didn't. She just laughs.

A hollow, sharp-edged sound that made my stomach twist.

She shook her head slowly, "That means that Castor took Sam with him all those years ago," she said. "And you—you just left me behind?" Her voice cracked at the end, and it gutted me.

Clean and deep.

"Sage," I said as I stepped forward. "It wasn't like that."

She laughed again, a bitter sound that sent chills across my skin. "Of course, it was. Are you going to tell me that Castor was ok putting Sam in danger? Because we both know that's a lie. You could have brought me ...And you didn't."

Then she turned and walked away. And slammed the bathroom door hard enough the walls shook.

And I stood there. Useless. Jaw clenched. Heart pounding with my hand still holding the phone like it could fix this.

I let her hate me.

It was easier than telling her I'd make the same choice again.

CHAPTER SIX

SAGE

I DIDN'T KNOW HOW long I stood there, gripping the edges of the bathroom counter, staring at myself in the mirror like I was waiting for something.

For answers. For the truth to look different. For the ache in my chest to stop feeling like it was digging its claws in deeper.

The glass was still slightly fogged from the heat of the shower, beads of condensation sliding in lazy streaks toward the bottom of the mirror. My skin was still warm from the water and my hair was damp where it clung to the sides of my neck.

But I couldn't feel any of it. None of it registered.

All I could feel was the sharp ache sitting heavy in my chest. The weight of something I wasn't sure I knew how to carry.

Sam was alive.

And Reich knew but hadn't told me.

Castor took Sam with him.

And Reich told me he would stay but left me behind.

I closed my eyes and pulled in a breath, through my nose, until my lungs started to beg for relief. I held it there, until the shaking quieted, until the air felt thin enough for me to breathe.

And then I exhaled.

Steady. Controlled. Or as close as I could get to it right then.

I didn't want to be angry. I didn't want this—*this thing*—to wedge itself between us like so many things already had.

But damn did it hurt. More than I was ready for.

A soft knock at the door cut through the haze.

I didn't move. Not at first.

"Sage," Reich said, quietly, almost careful.

I glanced at the handle I had locked.

I could leave him standing out there. I could leave the door closed, leave the words unsaid. But I knew Reich. I knew how he worked.

He wouldn't leave. Not until he said whatever he needed to say. And I wouldn't walk away until I heard whatever it was that he decided to give me.

So, I took one more deep breath, willing my hands to unclench from the counter. My knuckles ached from how hard I had been gripping it. I flexed my fingers, ignoring the sting as feeling rushed back to the tips, and reached for the handle.

I pulled the door open.

Reich stood there in the narrow hallway, shoulders squared but loose and his hands tucked into his pockets like he was trying to keep them still. His expression was unreadable, which would usually infuriate me, but not this time. This time, it felt like restraint. Like he was holding himself in check because he knew how close I was to unraveling.

He didn't try to touch me. Didn't try to step in. He just waited.

I crossed my arms over my chest, more to hold myself together than anything else.

"How long did you know?" My voice came out rougher than I expected, almost brittle sounding as I continued. "During the time you left? Before you left?"

His jaw tightened at that.

There was a flicker in his eyes, something quiet and sharp.

But he didn't answer right away.

And when he did, it wasn't with words. It was with the way his throat worked as he swallowed hard. With the way his hands twitched slightly in his pockets before going still again and I knew then that I had my answer.

I pressed forward. "Why didn't you tell me before you left?"

I clarified, "That she was going with you both."

He exhaled through his nose, dragging a hand down his face like it might scrub the guilt off. His fingers lingered for a moment against his mouth before falling back to his side.

"I didn't know for certain, but I suspected that was Castor's plan when we made the decision to leave Providence... and I knew if I told you what I suspected or came back and told you..." he said slowly, voice low and ragged, "...you would've tried to find her." He didn't blink. Didn't flinch. "And if you'd come looking—if you'd gotten anywhere near me or Cas or Sam—you would've been a target again. So, I kept you at a distance. When I found out about Sam, I kept her at a distance from you. You couldn't be back in this loop and involved again. Sam was already in too deep. You weren't. You could still live a life outside of all this."

I shook my head as I bit back the lump rising in my throat. "And yet here I am... You know that you don't get to make that decision for me, Reich."

"I know." He responded. His voice was soft. Steady in a way that cut more than it soothed.

"But I did." He continued, his gaze never leaving mine, "And I'd do it again and let you hate me for it."

The words land hard.

I let out a breath, short and bitter, turning away from him, staring down past the open doorframe he stood in front of towards the hallway, like I might find something out there that made sense.

"You left me behind." I commented.

"No," he said. And I felt him step closer. Closing the distance between us the way he always did—quiet and inevitable. "I chose your safety over your forgiveness."

I turned my gaze to meet his completely, anger flashing hot. "Safety?" I spat. "You call what I went through safe?"

His hands flexed at his sides, and for a second, I thought he might reach for me. But he didn't.

His throat worked around the words like they were knives. "You think I don't know how much I hurt you every time you look at me?" he asked, voice raw now, stripped of that arrogant confidence he wore like armor. "You think it didn't kill me to watch you with other men for two years? To see you trying to move on, to see you hurting, and not be able to do a fucking thing about it?" His voice broke on the last word, and I froze.

"I knew," he went on, quieter, "the second I let you back into my life you'd be dragged into all of this. And I couldn't let that happen."

I stared at him. At the cracks showing through all the places he was usually so composed. It was the rawest I'd seen him in years and it knocked the breath out of me.

My anger frayed at the edges. Unraveling into something softer. Something that hurt in a different way.

"Reich," I breathed, softer now.

His gaze flicked back to mine, searching, waiting for whatever came next. And I didn't know what that was. I didn't know what I was supposed to say. So, I said the thing that came easiest nowadays.

"I really do hate you," I whispered.

Just to see the way the corner of his mouth twitched. And it did. Just slightly.

He smirked. But when he spoke, his voice was quiet. "I know. I hate me too... but I'd do it again."

And just like that, I forgave him.

Not because it was easy. Not because I got it fully. But because I understood him. Because he did what he thought was right. Because deep down, he just wanted to protect me.

I reached for his hand, sliding my fingers between his, feeling the calluses and the scars. The quiet strength he never said out loud.

"You said Castor and Sam are coming," I said, not letting go. "We should probably get ready."

He nodded, as he squeezed my hand once and then let me go.

The knock came a day or so later.

Reich and I had been strategizing our plan for The Bloodwine while we waited for it.

Amongst other things we did together to pass the time.

I didn't realize how tense I was until I felt Reich's hand squeeze my shoulder briefly as he passed by, heading for the door. It was a grounding touch, but it did nothing for my pounding heart.

Reich opened the door and then there was a blur of movement.

Before I could process what was happening, I was hit full force with arms full of Sam. She crashed into me like a wrecking ball, knocking me back a step.

But I didn't fall.

I just held her because she was here.

She was alive.

"Oh my god, I missed you!" she shouted, and her voice was bright, vibrating with so much energy it made me laugh. It was shaky and unsteady, but it was real.

The first real one I had in a while.

I squeezed her back just as hard, fingers clutching at her jacket like I was afraid she might disappear if I let go.

"I've missed you so much, Sam, and … you're alive," I whispered.

She leaned back just enough to grin at me. "Damn right I am," she said. "You think I'd die before seeing you again? Please. I'm much harder to kill than that."

I laughed again.

There was a snort behind her, and when I looked up, Castor was leaning against the doorframe, arms crossed, a smirk pulled at his mouth.

"She's been insufferable since I told her." He said.

Sam rolled her eyes, flipping him off without turning around. "Shut up. You love me."

"Mmm," Castor hummed. "Jury's still out."

Reich shook his head, that faint, crooked smirk tugging at the edge of his mouth. And I realized suddenly that it felt normal. Like old times. Like not a day had passed between us.

Sam turned back to me, her grin wide and sharp. "So," she drawled, cocking a brow. "You really had to one-up me, huh?"

I blinked, caught off guard. "What?"

"You got kidnapped by a Davidian brother first," she teased, nudging me with her elbow. "I just had to see what all the hype was about."

Castor busted out laughing. Even Reich chuckled under his breath.

I groaned, dragging my hands over my face. "Oh my god."

"No regrets," she said, winking.

Castor slung an arm over her shoulders, glancing at me with a grin. "She's been waiting years to make that joke."

"I bet she has," I muttered, shaking my head.

Sam just beamed, nudging me again, gentler this time. "I missed you," she said softly.

I met her gaze, feeling the tightness in my chest ease a little more. "I missed you too."

"Till the bitter end?" I asked.

"Till the bitter end." She smiled.

And despite everything— despite the pain. Despite the questions that still hung between us.

Despite the war that was about to be waiting for me and Reich outside this bunker— I let myself have that moment.

Because we were all together.

And for now...that was enough.

Chapter Seven

REICH

I HADN'T SEEN SAGE smile like that since we were back in Providence and all together like we were now.

Not a faint, tight-lipped grin. Not the sharp-edged curve of her mouth she offered when she was holding everything else back.

This—this was *real*.

Unrestrained. The kind of smile that lit up her entire face, softening every line that had been carved there by grief and survival. Her laughter spilled out, bright and unguarded, as she kept her arms wrapped tightly around Sam. They were talking over each other now, voices overlapping, but I could hear the shape of the memories they were piecing back together, filling in the gaps left by too much time and too much distance.

For a moment, it almost hurt to look at her because I forgot that she used to look like that.

At least for a time back in Providence.

But truly content and at peace.

And I hated that I forgot. Hated that I let her forget how it felt.

I stood there, watching her, and I knew. I knew I made the right call letting Cas bring Sam here, though I wasn't sure it really was much of a choice. But I knew it was the right thing, no matter how much it cut to share her.

If I'd been smarter, if I'd been faster, I would've found a way to make sure Sage never lost Sam in the first place.

But I wasn't and she did, and we had both had been bleeding for it ever since.

Cas elbowed me hard enough to pull me out of my spiraling thoughts.

"You're staring," he said, voice pitched low, but smug.

"Shut up," I muttered, more reflex than anything, pushing open the door that led to the back room and stepped inside. Cas followed, but not before shooting one last glance back at them—*Sage and Sam*—still folded into each other's space like they were afraid to let go.

The door swung shut behind us with a muted click, muffling the sound of their laughter. The room we stepped into was dimly lit, dust caught in the thin shaft of sunlight that sliced through the cracks in the walls. It smelled like old paper, smoke, and something metallic—blood I cleaned up days ago but could still somehow feel sticking beneath my boots.

I crossed the room, grabbing my phone from where I left it on the table, and pulled myself into one of the chairs.

I nodded toward Cas. "Let's call them."

"I'm on it." He responded as he dropped into the seat across from me, already pulling his own phone free. He was casual about it—feet kicked out in front of him, back slouched low—but I knew better. His eyes were sharp. His fingers were slightly anxious as they dialed.

He was hiding something.

Call it brotherly intuition but I could feel it.

But before I could think too much longer about it.

Three rings. And then it was just Keenan's voice filtered through the small space in a low, rough and already annoyed tone.

"This better be good," Keenan growled. "I just stopped at Nael's place on my way back and we were in the middle of something."

From the background, Nael's voice came through, dry and unimpressed. "By 'we,' he means 'me'. *He* has been drinking."

Cas snorted, leaning back like he was settling in. "Keenan, it's barely noon."

"Time is a myth," Keenan answered without missing a beat. "How's paradise?"

I knew the next words were going to come as a shock, but I said them anyway as I leaned forward.

I rested my elbows on my knees, fingers laced tight enough to make my knuckles ache. "I found Sage in a hideout and now... we're moving in on The Bloodwine."

There was a beat of silence on the other end.

And then— "The Bloodwine?" Keenan repeated. He sounded sharper now. More alert. "Why the hell would you want to go there?"

I glanced briefly at Cas before answering, "Sage found out her mother was involved with the ENA," I said, keeping my voice even, though it was hard. "She thinks the club has information about what happened to her."

Another pause. Then Nael sighed. "Of course, she does."

My jaw tightened.

"I'll also be looking for information on the remaining families while we're there," I added, shifting gears, then continuing, "I figured we'd kill two birds with one stone. Dig into Sage's past. Tear a few more pieces off the ENA while we're at it."

Keenan hummed, low and thoughtful. "Well, good luck with that. You know how tight-lipped those club owner bastards are."

Cas grinned, sharp and bright. "Yeah, but they've never met me."

I looked at Cas, perplexed. *Did he just invite himself?*

Nael exhaled something like a huff. "They'll kill you before you get through the door."

"That's why Reich is going in first, sweetheart," Cas shot back without missing a beat.

Nael didn't dignify that with a response, but Keenan's muffled laughter carried through the device.

"Sage and I were planning on going alone," I said, cutting through the noise. "But apparently Cas and Sam are coming along too."

Nael made a noise like he was not surprised at all before rebutting, "And you're letting them?"

I exhaled, dragging a hand over my jaw. "Yes...even though I would prefer Sage and I go alone." I said simply.

Because that was the truth.

But I knew it was more important that Sage and Sam have more time together. I didn't want to keep them apart any longer than I already felt like I had.

Cas leaned forward, elbows on the table now, his smirk lazy. "Aw, you didn't want to share your alone time?"

I flipped him off without looking.

"Look at you, Reich," Cas said. "All grown up. Learning to share."

"Fuck off, *little* brother." I muttered, but it was mostly habit. And somehow it made the weight in my chest ease.

Just a tad.

Nael cut in before Cas could make it worse. "You need backup?"

I hesitated. Running through every scenario in my head.

"I don't think so," I said. "But we'll keep you updated if that changes at all."

Nael hummed. A sound of agreement, though I could tell he was judging me silently. "Keep your sound up."

"Try not to get shot, boys," Keenan added with mock cheer.

Cas grinned, wicked. "No promises."

Cas and I stepped back into the main room, boots heavy against the concrete, as the door closed softly behind us.

Sage and Sam were still deep in conversation, their heads close together in a way that made something sharp settle behind my ribs.

I didn't interrupt.

Not yet.

I let myself watch them for half a breath longer.

But Sam caught sight of us first, and she lit up like it was nothing.

"Oh, good," she said, smiling wide. "You're both back. I already told Sage we're going."

Cas busted out laughing like he knew that was coming. I just shook my head, but it wasn't out of annoyance. Not really.

"Of course, you did." He commented.

"Figured it was easier than waiting for you two to decide," Sam responded.

I huffed out a breath that might be a laugh.

"We just need to grab some things first," he said. "But we'll meet you halfway."

Sam grinned, bright and open, as she teased, "Wouldn't want to ruin too much of your *alone time*."

What a little eavesdropper.

I should have expected that one.

And I certainly should have expected Cas' remark immediately after.

"Yeah, brother… we did not mean to intrude on some of your most intimate relationship milestones. Disappearing for three years I am sure has led to a lot of character developments for you two… especially in the bedroom."

I glared, but it was weak. Sage groaned, covering her face with one hand, but I saw the smile underneath.

"I hate you both," Sage muttered jokingly.

Cas winked. "No, you don't."

I couldn't help but chime in, "I am going to file this under one of the thousands of unhinged things my *little* brother has ever said to me."

Cas looked at me and then looked down at Sam as he said, "Sam can attest that I am anything but *little*."

We all started to laugh and for the first time in years, it felt like everything was falling into place.

Not perfect. Not fixed. But better. Like maybe—just maybe—we had a shot at something more than just surviving.

Chapter Eight

SAGE

Tʜᴇ ᴅᴏᴏʀ ᴄʟɪᴄᴋᴇᴅ sʜᴜᴛ behind Castor and Sam, leaving a hollow sort of stillness in their wake. It echoed in the space between Reich and me, faint but distinct. Like the air had been holding its breath while they were here, and now it was waiting to see what happened next.

For a long moment, neither of us moved. We just stood there. And for the first time in years, I somehow felt... *lighter*.

The pressure that had been sitting heavy on my chest since the day I thought Sam was gone finally eased. The knots in my shoulders, in my ribs, in my throat—they loosened. And I finally just let myself breathe deep.

Sam is alive.

Safe.

And somehow, despite everything, we fell back into place like no time had passed. Like the distance between us had never stretched into something empty with this sort of longing absence.

I let out a slow breath and rolled my shoulders back, feeling the satisfying pull of tired muscles.

"That felt good," I admitted quietly, letting the truth of it settle between us.

Reich lifted a brow as he leaned his weight to one side, shoving his hands deep into his pockets. The hint of a smirk tugged at the corner of his mouth. "Yeah?" he drawled. "Seeing Sam, or making fun of Cas?"

I couldn't help but smirk back. "Both."

He huffed a quiet laugh, shaking his head like he was not even surprised. Then he pushed off the wall and strode to finish the packing that was interrupted by Cas and Sam showing up.

"Come on, wildflower," he said, his voice low and familiar in a way that made something twist in my chest. "We've got a long trek ahead of us. Let's get this packing finished up, so we can take off in the next day or so to meet up with our newly invited entourage."

I exhaled, but I was already moving. My fingers closed around the strap of the smaller bag on the floor, lifting it as I fell into step beside him. The rhythm of our movements was easy. Natural. Like this was what we do. Prepare to survive and just keep going.

But as I sorted through the supplies—rations, knives, water purifiers—I couldn't stop myself from glancing at him. Watching the way his hands moved, precise and sure, folding clothes with a kind of casual efficiency that shouldn't be attractive but somehow is.

"Are you really okay with Cas and Sam coming along?" I asked after a beat. My tone was light, but the question wasn't.

Reich didn't look up right away. His fingers moved unhurried as he folded a shirt, tucking it into the bag like it mattered where it fit inside.

"Doesn't matter if I am or not," he said.

I narrowed my eyes. "That's not an answer."

He stopped then; his hands stilled on the fabric. His gaze lifted to meet mine, steady and unflinching.

"You need time with Sam," he said simply. Blunt. Honest in the way he always is when he thinks it'll hurt less that way. "That's more important than me wanting you to myself."

His voice didn't waver, but something in his eyes...something flickered. Just like before.

It was enough to send a slow, warm ache curling through my stomach.

I cleared my throat and turned back to my bag, suddenly very interested in rolling up the last pair of clean socks.

"Well," I muttered, "try not to get too jealous."

His reply was slow. Teasing.

"Wildflower," he drawled, "I'm always jealous when I don't have you all to myself and unfortunately... I care about you too damn much to do anything about it."

The words made my pulse skip.

And when I glanced up, expecting to find his usual cocky smirk, what I got instead makes my breath catch.

He was watching me with that dark, unreadable intensity—the one that strips me bare. The one that makes it impossible to look away. It was dangerous.

I tore my gaze away before I could drown in it, focusing instead on zipping the bag.

"Speaking of Cas," Reich said, changing the subject, his voice still low, still threaded with something I couldn't name, "I should see where they want to meet us."

I nodded, forcing my hands to stay busy as he grabbed his phone from the table.

He dialed. Lifting it to his ear and waited.

The longer he waited, the heavier the silence became.

After several rings, he frowned.

"No answer?" I asked, glancing over.

Reich pulled the phone back, staring at the screen. His jaw flexed as he hit redial.

The second time felt longer.

When he lowered the phone again, his expression was tight.

"Nothing," he muttered.

I shifted my weight. "That's... weird, right?"

He hesitated then shook his head like he was convincing himself. "Probably nothing. Sam's probably talking his ear off or he's punishing me for not answering his incessant messages from earlier."

I snorted. "Sounds very much like a Cas thing to do."

He smirked at that, but the crease between his brows didn't disappear. He slid his phone back into his pocket with more force than necessary.

"I'll try again later," he said. "If I still can't get through, then I'll worry."

I nodded, trusting him to make the call, but the knot in my gut didn't seem to go away.

We went back to packing after that. Or at least... I did.

Reich stopped pretending to pack after a few minutes.

I could feel it, the shift in the air. Thickening. Like the weight of his gaze was something solid pressing against my back.

I pretended not to notice, but it was impossible to ignore the way the air felt heavier. The way I could sense him move behind me, close enough to feel the warmth of him. Close enough to make my skin hum with awareness.

"Reich," I said, warning in my tone.

He hummed, like he was amused. "Yeah?"

"You're not helping."

Another low chuckle, deep and quiet. "I think I am."

Before I could react, his hands were firm on my waist like he was grounding me. His fingertips slid beneath the hem of my shirt, slow and unhurried, calloused skin skimming along mine. And despite myself, a shiver rolled through me.

I hated that he knew what he was doing. Hated it even more that I didn't want him to stop.

I turned to face him, lifting a brow, hoping it hid the way my pulse was pounding.

"You're distracting me," I accused.

He tilted his head slightly, the barest hint of a smirk playing at his lips. "Am I?"

"Yes," I snapped, sharper than I mean it to be.

Because the truth was... I was about ready to crack.

And he knew it.

He always knew.

He leaned in a fraction closer, his voice dropping low enough that it felt like a touch against my skin. "You sound a little breathless."

I tilted my chin up in defiance, even as heat pooled low in my stomach. "You wish you had that much power over me," I said.

Something in his gaze darkened. Like a storm breaking on the horizon. Like the moment before lightning splits the sky.

"You think I don't?" he murmured.

I didn't have time to answer.

Because suddenly his mouth was on mine.

And I was gone.

The kiss was rough at first. Demanding.

But it shifted—slow and consuming, like he was making a point. Like he was showing me exactly how much power he had. And exactly how much I had already given him.

His hands slid lower, gripping the backs of my thighs, and before I could catch my breath, he was lifting me onto the table.

Effortless.

Like I weighed nothing. Like he had done this a thousand times in his head.

I braced my hands against his shoulders, fingers digging into muscle, trying to hold onto something solid as he leaned over me.

His eyes caught mine, dark and unreadable. And then he was kissing me again—deeper, slower. Stealing every last rational thought that I had left.

"Why do you always seem so reckless?" I managed.

He smiled against my skin, slow and deliberate.

"Because you're the only thing I lose control over."

Damn him. Damn me.

Because he was right.

And right now?

I didn't care about pretending to fight back.

Not even a little.

I let him tip me back onto the table, my hands tangled in his shirt, pulling him closer.

And somewhere in the back of my mind, I knew there was a world outside this room.

A trip we needed to make. A war we were already losing.

But not here. Not in this moment.

Here, it was just us.

Chapter Nine

REICH

WHEN I WOKE UP, I felt it.

A pain that lingered long after my night with Sage.

It wasn't like the dull, familiar ache I had grown used to—the steady thrum of discomfort that lived just beneath my skin since she came back into my life. I had carried that weight for a few days now.

No, this time…this time was *different*.

This time the pain cut deeper. Almost hotter. Like there was something sharp, burning alive inside me, crawling beneath my skin and clawing at the fragile boundary of my sanity.

This felt like actual fire. Like the brand at the back of my neck had come alive, with nerves of heat pulsing outward, searing through me from the inside out.

Why was this happening?

What was it even?

I sat up slowly, every movement tight and deliberate, careful not to wake her. My breath dragged heavy through my chest, uneven, catching at the edges like I was breathing in smoke. I pressed the heel of my palm against the mark at the nape of my neck. The skin there was fever-hot, feeling like it might split open beneath my hand.

It had never felt like this before. Never burned like this.

Not even the day they gave it to me.

I clenched my jaw until it ached, forcing myself to breathe through the pain. Forcing the memory away.

The dark room. The flickering candles that surrounded me.

The voice that scraped through the shadows, cold and knowing, telling me and Castor that we were to be bound for eternity.

The sound of my little brother's screams, and my own that followed shortly after.

I glanced at Sage.

She was still asleep, curled on her side, one arm tucked beneath her head. The blankets were tangled around her hips, leaving the curve of her bare back exposed to the weak morning light. Her breathing was steady. Calm. Lips parted slightly, her hair a messy halo across the pillow.

Peaceful. She looked so *fucking* peaceful.

She didn't know about this, and she couldn't know.

If she knew what I was going through—if she saw it, felt it the way I do—she for sure would be gone.

Not because she's weak.

But because she's smart.

Because no one in their right mind could stay when something this wrong with me was getting closer to the surface.

I felt like a dead man walking.

I exhaled slowly, dragging a hand down my face, wiping away the sweat at my temples.

My palm was still shaking when I reached for my phone on the nightstand.

The feeling hadn't left me.

That wrongness. The coil of it tightening around my ribs, like a rope being pulled, strand by strand, waiting until it snapped me loose and tore me apart from the inside out.

I needed to talk to Cas. I needed him to pick up.

I needed him to tell me I'm overthinking this, that I'm spiraling for nothing. That this pain I was experiencing was just phantom shadows from the past and they didn't mean anything.

I hit his contact and pressed the phone to my ear.

The line rang. And rang. And rang. *Nothing.*

I gripped the phone tighter, knuckles turning pale white. I focused on keeping my breathing even, my expression neutral, even though it was just me awake in this room, with Sage sound asleep next to me.

Cas had to be asleep. Or busy. Or being a dick.

Ignoring me because he knows I'll call again.

But it didn't feel fine. It felt wrong. It felt *off.*

I stared down at the phone screen for a second longer, thumb hovering over the call button.

Then I pressed it again.

The phone vibrated faintly in my hand.

Rang. And rang. Still *nothing.*

The uneasy feeling crawling through me sank deeper, lodging in the pit of my stomach like a stone.

I placed the phone onto the table with more force than necessary. It hit with a dull thud that sounded louder in the quiet.

It's fine. It's probably fine.

I told myself that, but I didn't believe it. Not when everything inside me was screaming that this was the beginning of something worse.

I glanced at Sage again.

She hadn't moved. Her breathing was still deep and slow. The only thing anchoring me right now was the steady rise and fall of her chest and the warmth of her body in this cold room.

She was here. She was *safe.*

And as long as she was, I could keep this together.

My brand started to burn again, but I still couldn't help but keep my focus on her.

I wanted to tell her what was happening.

I wanted to explain it all—*everything*.

But I couldn't.

Not when I didn't understand it myself. Not when I didn't know if I could keep it from pulling her under with me.

I wouldn't risk her like that. I wouldn't let her drown in this.

Not like I was. Not like I already did to Cas all those years ago.

I reached for the phone again, scrolling through my contacts. My thumb hesitated over Keenan's name before I hit call.

It rang twice before he answered.

"You better have a damn good reason for calling me at this ungodly hour," Keenan muttered. His voice was thick with sleep but edged with something sharper. He was always ready. Even half-conscious.

I let out a breath that almost sounded like a laugh. "Cas isn't answering his phone."

There was a pause. A shift. Like Keenan was sitting up, swinging his legs out of bed.

"You tried more than once?" He finally said.

"Yeah," I said, rubbing a hand over my jaw. "Nothing."

Keenan exhaled, and I swear I could hear the gears turning in his head. "Probably nothing. But I'll try him later. See if I get through."

I nodded, even though he couldn't see me. "Thanks."

There was a silence between us, not uncomfortable, but heavy.

I broke it first. "How's progress with Blythe?"

He didn't answer right away.

I waited.

I could almost hear him weighing the words. The truth. The exhaustion he never showed anyone.

"I think I pinned her location but I don't know... I just know that I won't ever stop," Keenan said quietly. "Not until I get her back."

The words settled heavy in my chest. I nodded again. "She's strong."

"The strongest," he replied without hesitation. "She'll make it through. And when she does, I'll be there."

Something sharp twisted behind my ribs.

I hated that I understood him. I hated it because while Keenan was fighting to bring Blythe back, I was here. Trying to keep Sage from meeting the same fate as *she* did and trying to keep myself from losing her as *he* did.

"I don't know how you do it," I admitted. My voice was quieter than before. Almost hollow.

Keenan chuckled softly, but it was a rough sound. Dry. "I don't...not really. I just manage." he said. He let that sit for a second, then added, "But you've still got Sage in your bed, Reich. Don't let the fear eat you alive."

I swallowed hard. My gaze drifted back to Sage, her sleeping form tangled in sheets, her face soft and open in a way she never let herself be when she was awake. "I'm trying."

"Try harder," Keenan said, voice firm. "Fear controlled me for too long. It made me hesitate. And that's how they took Blythe and honestly... probably why she is still gone."

The words slammed into me like a punch to the gut. I closed my eyes. My fingers tightening around the phone. I didn't say anything.

"Don't waste the time you do have," Keenan continued.

I let out a shaky breath. "Yeah."

"Yeah," Keenan echoed, softer now. "Get some sleep. We'll check in tomorrow."

I murmured a quiet thanks and ended the call.

The silence after was suffocating.

I stared at my phone for a long time before setting it back on the nightstand. My hand lingered there, fingers brushing the cold surface, before I finally turned my attention back to Sage.

She was still sleeping. Her hair was messy against the pillow, her breathing even and deep.

She was beautiful in a way that hurt.

Like something I didn't deserve and something I'd already ruined.

I shifted carefully, lowering myself back onto the mattress, close enough to feel her warmth. Close enough to breathe her in.

I let my arm rest lightly across her waist, my hand resting against her stomach. Her skin was warm beneath my touch.

For the first time since I woke, my body started to relax. The burn at the back of my neck dulled to a slow throb and the fire eased.

I didn't know what was coming. I didn't know what this mark meant. I didn't know why the whisper in my head was getting louder, or why the pain was getting worse.

But Keenan was right.

I had Sage now. I had *this*.

And I'll be damned if I wasted a single second of it.

I pressed my face into her hair, breathing her in.

Letting it ground me. Letting it keep me human. For as long as it could.

CHAPTER TEN

SAGE

MORNING CAME SLOWLY, CRAWLING over the edge of the horizon in hues of orange and gold. The first faint threads of sunlight slipped through the cracks in the bunker's old walls, stretching thin, golden lines across the dull concrete floor. The warmth of it barely reached me, but I could feel its presence—soft, tentative—like the world was holding its breath, unsure of whether it was safe to let the light in just yet.

Reich was still asleep beside me.

His body was pressed close, his arm draped heavy over my waist, anchoring me there. His breath was warm against my bare shoulder, slow and steady, stirring faint shivers along my skin in contrast from the cool, new morning air. His hand rested just beneath my ribs and his fingers curved like they were molded to me.

Like he was afraid to let go, even while he slept.

I should have moved.

We should have been getting ready to leave. We should have been making sure we were ready, tightening straps, checking our packs and sharpening knives.

But I didn't move. Not yet.

Instead, I stayed where I was, and just watched him.

His face was different when he slept this time. Something about it was softer and vulnerable. A side of him that he rarely showed.

The lines that cut deep into his brow, the tension that always knotted in his jaw, was all smoothed out, like he had let something go. Like—for this moment at least—he had found a way to rest.

Almost peaceful.

But I knew better.

Even in sleep, his fingers twitched against my skin. Small, involuntary movements, like he was reaching for something just beyond his grasp.

The more I watched, the worse it seemed to get.

And then—*just for a second*—his face shifted. His brow was pulled tight, with a faint crease that appeared between his eyes. His mouth started to harden.

Fear.

It flickered across his expression, fast, but it was there.

And it wasn't the kind that was lost in his nightmares. Not the kind that fades when you wake up.

It was the kind that lingered. The kind you carried like a second skin. The one that never goes away, even when you try to escape it through sleep.

I knew that fear.

I had lived in it. I sometimes still was living in it.

I watched Reich begin to twitch more.

What was bothering him? I wanted so badly to know.

But I didn't wake him to ask. Not yet.

He wouldn't have answered me if I did anyway.

So instead, I shifted slightly, slow enough not to disturb him and reached up with my fingers to lightly brush through his hair. He kept it longer now, and I let the strands slide through my fingers before curling them around one.

My other hand trailed down, following the slope of his temple, tracing the sharp line of his jaw. His skin was warm beneath my fingertips. Rough with stubble.

His breathing started to change. Just a hitch.

A faint catch before he exhaled again, slower this time. His grip tightened around my waist, fingers pressing into my skin like he was reminding himself I was here. His eyes fluttered open, lashes lifting slowly.

For a moment, there was that flicker in his eyes. But it was something different this time.

Something dark. Something haunted.

And it scared me.

I saw it before it was gone, before he forced it back down into whatever place he kept things he didn't divulge.

I'd never seen anything like it before.

His eyes … they were pitch black…

Then it was gone, and he smirked at me with that same familiar curve of his mouth that made me melt.

Maybe it was nothing.

His voice was still rough, thick with sleep when he spoke. "Couldn't resist watching me, huh?"

My whole body seemed to soften, as the tension lifted.

I rolled my eyes, shoving half-heartedly at his chest. "Don't flatter yourself."

The sound of the chuckle that left his lips was low and warm. He stretched, muscles shifting under my hand, lean and solid, before he rolled onto his side and pulled me against him.

Like he needed to. Like he couldn't resist.

"I think you like watching," he murmured.

I arched a brow, trying for casual even as my heart pounded too hard in my chest. "I think you like giving me reasons to watch."

He grinned, but it didn't reach his eyes.

There was something behind them.

Something that made my throat tighten.

I almost said something. Almost told him about the shift in his eyes I had seen and about the fear that I also saw hidden there. But before I could, he leaned in, brushing his lips along the curve of my neck, slow and deliberate.

"We have a long trip ahead of us and…," he murmured trailing his mouth against my throat, his breath hot where his lips grazed the curve of my neck.

"And?" I whispered, already breathless from the anticipation curling low in my stomach.

His fingers slipped beneath the sheets, slow and deliberate, tracing the sensitive line of my thigh with the kind of reverence that made my pulse stutter before he replied, "…And I think we have time to make it even longer."

I barely had time to respond before his mouth claimed mine—urgent, commanding, a collision of want and need that drowned out every thought that wasn't him. His tongue slid past my lips, coaxing mine into a rhythm that left me trembling beneath him.

His hand slid higher as his fingers brushed over the heat between my legs, teasing me through the thin barrier of my clothing until I was arching into him with a soft gasp. "Ready for me already," he murmured against my mouth, voice thick with heat. "You really did miss this, didn't you?"

"Yes," I breathed, shameless and aching as he pushed the fabric aside and sunk two fingers inside of me—slow, deep, curling just right.

My back arched as I clutched at his shoulders, desperate for more, but he wasn't in a rush.

No.

He was savoring every reaction, every tremble and every shaky breath I gave him.

"You feel immaculate," he growled, his mouth trailing down my throat, teeth grazing the skin just above my collarbone as his fingers moved faster. "I could stay buried in you forever, wildflower."

The words alone nearly undid me.

He pulled back just enough to tear the sheets away from our bodies, eyes drinking me in like he had been starving. His mouth trailed lower, licking a slow path down my stomach, and I could feel the moment his tongue replaced his fingers.

I cried out, thighs trembling around his shoulders as he devoured me with a hunger that bordered on worship. He didn't stop until I was coming apart against his mouth, gasping his name like a prayer.

And when he finally rose over me, I reached down and guided him to where I needed him most.

"Please," I whispered, already wrecked and needing to be ruined all over again.

He pushed in slow—*inch by inch*—until he was fully one with me and there was no space left between us. He held still, forehead pressed to mine, letting me feel every piece of him, every heartbeat.

Then he moved.

Hard, deep, deliberate—each thrust claiming, each breath shared as the world outside disappeared.

We stayed there for a while before we finally got up and finished what we were supposed to be doing.

I was on my knees by the nightstand, grabbing everything I needed and stuffing it into the worn canvas bag at my feet.

I double-checked the straps.

I did it again.

Anything to stay focused and to keep my mind from spiraling.

Reich moved quietly behind me, as I slid his knives into sheaths and started to grab more supplies, tucking them into my bag. He was too silent. Too still. And when his voice finally cut through the quiet, it was deceptively light.

"You know," he drawled, dragging the edge of his blade along the leather strop in slow, practiced motions, "I'm starting to think you're just using me for my resources."

I glanced at him over my shoulder, smirking as I tossed a folded shirt into my pack. "Oh? Is that what you think?"

Reich nodded, leaning against the table with a lazy sort of grace that didn't quite disguise the tension in his shoulders.

"Mmhmm. First, my knives. Then my supplies. What's next? My clothes?"

I pretend to think it over, tapping my chin. "Well, now that you mention it..."

He scoffed and tossed a shirt at my face.

I laughed, swatting it away.

But when I looked back at him, his amusement was already slipping. He turned his head down, hands lifting to his neck, rubbing hard beneath the edge of his hairline.

Over the *mark*.

I frowned, standing slowly. "Reich?"

He didn't look at me. His fingers tightened over the scarred skin at his nape, pressing down like he was trying to hold something in.

Or keep something out.

His jaw locked as I saw his shoulders tense nearly bringing him to his knees.

I dropped my bag, stepping closer. "You're not telling me something." I said pointblank.

He didn't answer.

His head lifted slightly but his eyes stay locked on the fireplace, watching the flames curl and snap like they're speaking to him. Like they hold answers I couldn't hear.

But I saw it in his eyes. That same look from before.

That same strange flicker.

They were black.

I took another step, ignoring the ache in my ribs at the fact that he wouldn't respond. "Reich."

Nothing. Not at first.

Then his jaw tightened. His breathing turned sharp, more controlled than it was, like he was working through whatever just happened.

He immediately composed himself and said, "Sorry about that."

I stood dumbfounded.

"What was that? ... Your eyes," I said quietly. "You looked different, Reich."

That got him.

His shoulders went rigid, his chest stilled for half a breath before he forced it out, "I don't know what you're talking about."

"Liar." I retorted.

And he knew it.

He turned slowly, those hazel eyes finding mine.

But they weren't quite the right color.

For the briefest moment, they flickered again.

Like something else was looking back at me.

Something not him.

And he quickly looked away again.

I gripped the edge of the table, grounding myself before demanding, "Tell me what's happening to you."

A long silence stretched between us.

Long enough for my pulse to thunder in my ears. Long enough to feel like I was already losing him.

"You don't want to know, Sage." His voice was quieter now. Rough. "Trust me."

I should have stopped pushing.

I should have.

But I never had.

And I wouldn't start then.

"I do trust you." My throat felt tight, but I forced the words through anyway. "That's the problem."

Before he could answer, I watched his whole body lock up.

His breath shuddered out.

And then he winced. His hand flew to his neck, gripping the mark hard enough to turn his knuckles white. His breathing sharpened again with each exhale forced.

And then his eyes shifted—toward the door. Past me.

Panic. A small fragment of what looked like terror seeped into his eyes.

"What is it?" I whispered cautiously.

He didn't answer right away, but he was focused, like he was listening for something I couldn't hear and when he spoke, his voice was low. Controlled.

"They're coming."

Every part of me went still as I froze in place. "Who?"

Reich's expression hardened. Like iron hammered flat. "The ENA."

My stomach flipped. "What?"

He grabbed my wrist. Tight. Urgent. "Listen to me." His voice was sharper now. "Crouch down. Get in the closet. Do not watch. Do not make a sound. No matter what you hear."

I stared at him. Searching his face.

The set of his jaw. The fear in his eyes. The panic I never see.

But it was there now.

"Reich, what—"

"I'm not asking, Sage."

His grip tightened.

He needed me to move.

Now.

I nodded once.

No more arguing. Not this time.

I crossed the room quickly, dropping low as I reached the closet, slipping inside. The cool metal pressed against my back as I crouched down, pulling the door almost closed.

I left it cracked, just enough to see through the sliver.

Reich stood in the center of the room.

His stance was loose.

But wrong.

Like he was holding himself still only because he didn't know what else to do yet. Like something was coming and he was bracing for it.

The front door creaked open. The sound was slow. Painfully slow. Metal scraping over concrete.

And my blood ran cold.

Chapter Eleven

REICH

THE FEAR SAT HEAVY in my chest.

It was a hard, brutal weight that pressed up under my ribs, coiling tight behind my sternum. I could feel it in my throat, cold and sharp, cutting deeper with every breath I took. But I didn't let it show.

I couldn't.

Not here. Not now.

Not when Sage was already picking up on the fact that something was wrong with me.

Not when I knew she saw something in my eyes that shouldn't be there.

And certainly, not when I was standing in front of Cresil and Berith, calculating exactly how long I had before they noticed the girl hiding in my closet.

I could feel them watching me. The two of them were made for this—hunting wolves sent by the ENA, their presence a message without having to say a damn thing.

They arrived at my bunker with some victim in tow, like they owned the place.

No hesitation. No fear.

Because why would they be afraid?

They carried the weight of the ENA behind them like it was an inheritance.

A fucking birthright.

The leadership's right-hand lackeys.

Their hammer and nail.

Cresil stood by the fireplace, her fingers trailed along the mantle in slow, lazy lines, like she was testing the wood for cracks. Her long, shiny pitch black hair gleamed in the low light, and her clothes were as pristinely white as the first day I met her.

But it was her posture that unsettled me.

Relaxed. At ease. Like she had already made her decision about how this was going to end.

And she was just waiting for me to realize it.

There was a small smile on her lips. Just a curve. Nothing more.

But her gaze? Sharper than any blade I'd ever held.

She was always the one they sent to make sure orders were followed and to make sure none of us forgot who they belonged to.

And Berith...he was never far from her side. A step behind. Silent. Watching. A statue with eyes.

He kept his arms crossed over his chest, his expression blank, but I could feel the weight of his stare pressing down on me like an headsman's axe.

Like he was waiting for me to flinch.

Like he wanted me to.

At their feet, kneeling on cold concrete, was a boy. Presumably a traitor they wanted me to take care of. But he was young. Too young. In his early teens, maybe. His wrists were bound behind his back, a rough cord biting into skin that was already rubbed raw. His chin was lifted just enough to show a defiance that hadn't been beaten out of him yet.

But I saw the way his throat bobbed when he swallowed.

He was scared. He didn't really know what was coming but he had an idea that he probably wouldn't survive it.

Cresil exhaled, like this was all taking too long. Like she was already bored.

Her gaze cut toward me. "You know why we're here, Reich."

I didn't answer. Not yet.

Because without them saying it, I did know why they were here.

They wanted me to do what they taught me to do. They wanted me to strip the skin from this traitor's body in clean, precise pieces. So, they could take those pieces back to the ENA—their twisted church—for whatever hollow rituals or "spiritual atonement" bullshit they needed them for.

For their gods. For their power.

My fingers twitched at my side, curling slightly before I forced them still.

I couldn't hesitate.

Not in front of them. Not if I wanted to keep Sage safe.

But this time—this time, I wanted to.

I looked at the boy again.

I didn't know what he did. I didn't ask.

It didn't matter at this point.

The ENA had declared him a traitor, which meant his body no longer belonged to him.

It belonged to their favorite executioner.

Me.

I took a slow breath, swallowing the bile rising thick and sour in the back of my throat.

Then I met Cresil's flat, cold gaze.

And said, "Leave him with me. I'll handle it."

Her smile widened as she said, "Oh, we're not leaving, Reich." She stepped away from the mantle. Her heels clicked once against the concrete, and the sound made the hair on the back of my neck rise, as she continued, "This is an educational visit."

My pulse kicked hard against my ribs.

I kept my face neutral even as my stomach turned.

Berith took a slow step forward. His boots scuffed faintly on the floor, and it felt like the sound stretched forever. He stopped just to the side of Cresil. Close enough that I felt him there even when I wasn't looking.

"You're hesitating," Cresil murmured, circling me now. Her movements were lazy. Almost graceful. But the gleam in her eyes was anything but. "Why are you hesitating?"

I grit my teeth hard enough that my jaw ached. "I'm not."

"Then do it." Her voice was sinister.

I stepped toward the boy. One foot in front of the other. Deliberate and controlled. I felt Berith's stare on my back like a knife poised to strike. One wrong move and he would gut me.

And worse, they would find Sage.

The boy that was knelt before me couldn't stop shaking now. I saw it in his shoulders. The slight tremor of his bound hands behind his back. He was braver than most. But bravery didn't matter. Not here.

I told Sage not to watch. Not to listen. But I knew she was doing both right then.

I could feel her through the wall.

The press of her fear. The weight of her breath. And I couldn't stop her. But maybe I could make it easier.

I pulled my phone from my pocket, scrolling with numb fingers until I found a certain track.

One that she would know.

One from the playlist I made for her years ago.

I tapped play.

IN REICH AND RUIN

The bass hit first. Heavy. Raw. A wall of sound filling the room and pounding in my chest like another heartbeat. I turned it up louder. Until it drowned out almost everything.

Cresil raised a brow, amused, as she yelled over the noise, "A soundtrack?!"

"I have a process!" I yelled back evenly.

Her smile stretched wider. "By all means then...don't let us stop you!"

Berith chuckled. Low. Cold. "We wouldn't dare!"

I crouched in front of the boy.

The music pulsed, thick and heavy.

I hoped it was enough. For Sage. For *me*.

I drew my knife from my belt. The blade gleamed under the flickering light, wicked and sharp, like it was taunting me. I pressed the tip against the boy's jaw, just below his ear.

His breath stuttered. His pulse fluttered wildly under the thin skin of his throat. But he didn't pull away. Because he knew deep down it was useless.

"Hold still," I murmured.

I wasn't sure he could hear me, but he flinched and then obeyed.

The first cut was always the hardest. But I made it anyway.

I had to.

The blade slid through skin with the kind of practiced ease that still sickened me, especially with the knowledge that Sage was watching. Warm blood spilled over my fingers, running down my wrist in slow, thick rivulets. The boy gasped. Sharp. Ragged.

But he didn't scream.

He was certainly stronger than most.

Cresil watched like she was admiring art. Berith watched like he was waiting for me to fail.

But I didn't fail because I never do.

I had been doing this since I was barely older than the boy that knelt in front of me.

This was who I was.

What I was made to be.

What I had been forced to perfect.

Even now, when bile burned at the back of my throat.

Even now, when I knew Sage was behind the closet door, her breath likely shallow and her heart breaking.

I didn't stop.

I peeled the skin back in careful strips. Neat. Clean. Blood pooled at my knees.

The only sound was the scrape of my blade and the music thundering through the speakers.

I forced my hands to stay steady. Forced my mind to go blank. Focused on the ritual. On the routine.

I had done this more times than I could count. Granted it was never anyone this young but still.

This was who I was and had always been.

I kept repeating it like a mantra.

But I still felt her eyes on me the whole time.

Even through the wall. I felt her watching. And I knew.

I knew she would never look at me the same after this.

And I wouldn't blame her because I wouldn't either.

When it was over, I sat back on my heels. The knife still slick in my hand. Blood still warm on my skin. I breathed in slow and controlled as I turned the music off.

Cresil hummed in approval. "Still got it, I see."

I said nothing. *Because what was there to say?*

She stepped closer. And I resisted the urge to move away or trip her so she would fall on her smug face.

"You were born for this," she whispered.

Like it was a secret.

Like it was a promise.

"Get out," I said.

My voice was quiet, but I let it cut like a blade.

She smiled. "We'll see you soon, Reich."

And then she turned as Berith followed, dragging the pieces of a now lifeless corpse behind them.

The door opened. Closed. And the bunker fell silent again.

I stayed where I was. The knife in my hand. The blood on my skin.

I didn't look towards the closet door.

I couldn't.

Because if I did, I might have broken when I saw her face.

All I said, with my back turned was, "You can come out now."

And I didn't move until I heard her step out. Quiet. Careful.

She didn't say anything and I watched her out of the corner of my eye as she curled up in the farthest corner of the room, wrapping her arms around her legs.

Watching.

I slowly walked to grab my supplies to clean up the mess.

I cleaned the knife. Cleaned the floor.

Silent. Mechanical.

Like nothing had just happened at all.

Chapter Twelve

SAGE

I KNEW I SHOULDN'T have looked.

I knew I should've squeezed my eyes shut and pressed my hands over my ears.

I knew I should have curled tighter into myself and shrunk so small that I vanished into the darkness that was already swallowing this room.

I should have done anything to block it out.

Anything to make myself forget that it was happening—there, then and with *him*.

But I couldn't.

Because it was Reich out there. And I had to know.

I had to see him.

Even if it ruined the image, I painted of him in my mind.

My breathing was shallow, each inhale burning sharp at the top of my throat like I was breathing smoke instead of air. I could feel my heart hammering behind my ribs.

Still, I stayed quiet. I stayed small. Curled against the back wall of the closet, knees hugged to my chest so tightly my muscles were starting to cramp. But I didn't move. I couldn't.

I pressed harder against the cold wall, willing myself to disappear into it. Wishing this wasn't real.

But I wasn't that naive anymore.

Through the narrow sliver of space left between the door and its warped frame, I could see them.

Four of them.

The woman stood closest to the fireplace, her fingers gliding over the mantle like it belonged to her. Like everything in the room belonged to her. She trailed her hands along the wood in idle circles, polished nails catching faint glints of light.

There was something lazy about the way she moved.

But it was wrong. Like a predator stretching because it's already fed and knows it'll hunt again before long.

She smiled to herself. A slow, thin curve. And I felt my stomach twist.

A broad, heavy-set shadow of a man stood in her orbit like she was a planet, and he was one of her moons. His face was empty—blank in a way that made my skin crawl.

His eyes didn't move. He didn't even seem to blink. He just waited.

There was a boy kneeling before them.

And then there was Reich.

Standing stiff and sharp, like a line drawn too tight. His shoulders were squared, his spine straight, but there was a tension there.

I saw it. I felt it.

The way his fingers twitched at his side, flexing once, twice, like they didn't know whether to close into fists or reach for something to hold on to. Then there was the faint clench of his jaw. The smallest shift in his breathing.

I could tell that he was holding it all in by the thinnest thread.

And I think they knew it too.

The boy that knelt at his feet was young. Like a highschooler. His wrists were bound tight behind his back, rope cutting into skin rubbed raw. His body was too still, his chin tipped toward his chest in quiet, hopeless defeat. But the way his shoulders hunched told me what his face didn't.

He was terrified.

I swallowed hard, my throat sticking from the dryness.

"You know why we're here, Reich." The woman's voice broke the quiet. Smooth. Controlled. Almost pleasant.

The way she watched him made my stomach crawl.

Reich didn't answer.

I couldn't see his face from here, not fully. But I knew him well enough to read the angle of his head, the weight in his silence.

He was choosing his words carefully. Or he was choosing not to speak at all.

The woman's fingers drummed against the mantle once, then twice.

She smiled again. Sharper this time.

"Leave him with me," Reich said, his voice a controlled cut through the air. But there was something behind it. Something desperate he was trying to bury. "I'll handle it."

My breath stuttered.

Please just leave scary people. Please.

But I knew better and something told me they weren't leaving without some form of bloodshed.

The woman turned toward Reich, her expression softened in a way that made my skin crawl all over again. "Oh, we're not leaving, Reich." She took a step closer. And my stomach dropped. "This is an educational visit."

I didn't realize I'd clenched my fists until the sharp bite of my nails cut through skin, digging crescent moon patterns into my palms.

They were watching him. They didn't trust him.

And that meant something terrible was coming.

I should have closed my eyes. I should have squeezed them shut, blocked this out and bit down on the sound of my own fear. But I didn't.

So, I just watched.

Reich didn't move at first. And Reich always moves first. He never holds back.

But now he was.

The woman noticed. Like she had been waiting for it. "You're hesitating," she said, sweet as syrup, sharp as glass. "Why are you hesitating?"

His shoulders stiffened again. His fingers twitched.

"I'm not," he replied.

But it was a lie and I'm pretty sure they could tell.

Her smile widened. "Then do it."

I bit down hard on my lip. So, hard I tasted blood.

The low thrum of music vibrated faintly through the walls of the closet. I didn't notice it at first. It was loud. Out of place.

But then I recognized the sound.

A song.

One of mine. *Ours.*

One that Reich added to a playlist he made for me years ago.

Hearing it in this moment—*here*—felt wrong.

I pressed my palm flat to the cold floor, grounding myself in the pulsing beat.

Reich was playing it for me.

I knew he was.

He was trying to drown out the sounds he didn't want me to hear. Or maybe trying to drown himself in something that reminded him who he was before they barged in.

Either way, the song filled the space between us. And I listened.

I didn't cover my ears. I just lost myself for a moment as I listened to the music.

Because it was the only thing left that connected us.

They didn't like it though. I watched as it looked like they were mocking him about playing a soundtrack.

But before long Reich moved.

His fingers tightened around the knife at his side, the gleam of the blade catching in the dim light. His breathing was slow. Even. Terrifyingly controlled.

He stepped toward the boy and gripped his jaw, forcing his chin up and tilting his head back.

He murmured something to the boy that I couldn't quite catch.

The boy flinched but he didn't fight. He just shut his eyes and waited.

The blade flashed.

And then—blood. So much blood.

I didn't breathe. I couldn't.

It was not fast. It was not merciful. It was a show for the calculating eyes watching him.

The knife slid through skin slow, but precise and clean. Reich's hand was steady as a stone.

The boy shuddered under the touch, his jaw clenched so tight I thought it might crack, but he didn't make a sound. His body trembled. His fingers curled behind his back, desperate for something to hold on to, but there was nothing there.

The woman watched with something close to admiration. The man behind her didn't move at all.

And me?

I sat there.

Watching. Frozen. Sick.

But mostly—*mostly*, afraid.

Not of Reich. Not of what he was doing.

But of the fact that he was doing it like it was some kind of job.

Because he had to. Because he had done it before. And because this wasn't new.

It was not a breaking point. It was a routine. A ritual.

One he had practiced and perfected for them.

And somehow, I never really knew.

Not until now. Not until I actually saw it with my own eyes.

The seconds stretched into an eternity that didn't end. Not until Reich stepped back. The knife still dripped in crimson rivers from his hand.

His breath was still slow. Still even.

He didn't look at what was left of the boy. Didn't look at the others. Didn't look at anything really.

The music faded out at that point.

A hollow feeling seemed to fill the room. I could see it in everyone's eyes. Not just the young boy who laid in pieces on the ground.

The woman hummed low in her throat, approving. "Still got it, I see."

Reich said nothing. Did nothing. He just stood there.

She stepped closer. Close enough I could feel the shift in the air even from where I hid. "You were born for this," she said, her voice slipping soft.

My stomach twisted.

But Reich's reply was colder than steel. "Get out."

The woman smiled. "We'll see you soon, Reich."

Then she turned, with the other man she came with dragging the body behind and left.

The front door swung shut behind them and the bunker fell silent.

I didn't move. Neither did he.

He stood there for a long time. Knife still in hand. Blood still dripping. Breath still controlled. Like he had been carved from stone.

He didn't look towards the closet, towards me. Didn't move in my direction.

And I—I didn't know what to do.

So, I didn't do anything. I just waited.

Then I heard him say, "You can come out now."

I slowly and carefully, pushed the closet door open. My body felt disconnected, cold and shaking as I stepped out, barefoot against the frigid floor.

I said nothing. I didn't ask. I didn't push. I just moved to the farthest corner of the room and curled up, wrapping my arms around my legs.

And I watched as he finally moved.

He didn't speak. Didn't explain.

He just went and grabbed a few things, knelt down and began to clean.

Silent. Mechanical.

Like nothing happened.

Chapter Thirteen

REICH

The scent of blood was immediate and overwhelming, thick enough to cling to everything—my skin, my clothes, the concrete floor beneath my feet. Yet despite this, every movement felt precise and habitual. Blood coated my fingers, seeping beneath my nails, embedding itself deep into every crevice with grim familiarity.

I'd stopped counting how many times I'd cleaned up after moments like this.

There was no hesitation, no discomfort—only a numb detachment forged by repetition. Another job, another mess erased. It didn't matter how young the boy was. At least that's what I told myself.

I moved automatically, without thought and without feeling.

It shouldn't have mattered.

But it did.

Because *she* did.

All I saw was Sage.

She was curled against the wall, knees tight against her chest, shrinking herself away from everything—including me. Her arms wrapped around her legs, fingernails dug sharply into her thighs.

She wouldn't look at me.

Not at first.

And I didn't blame her.

I should have said something. I knew I should have—words to mend the tear between us.

But I also knew words couldn't fix this.

They never did.

So, I waited because it was all that I could do.

Wait for her to come back to me if she would at all.

The room was dim, illuminated by a single, warm bulb that buzzed faintly, casting long shadows across cracked walls. I stayed in the darkness, beyond the reach of light, yet I felt the weight of her stare the moment she finally lifted her head to meet my gaze.

Her expression was wounded, vulnerable in a way that unsettled something deep within me.

She always had a way of doing that with a single look.

I held her gaze steady anyway, even as I felt the sharp edge of what felt like her scrutiny cut through me.

She was searching for something in me.

Remorse, maybe.

Horror.

But I had neither to offer her.

So, instead, I offered patience—the only thing left for me to give, even if it felt like its own cruelty.

Her lips began to part, pale and dry, and her voice emerged barely more than a whisper. "What was that?"

Her words settled into the void between us, fragile but powerful enough to pierce my practiced detachment.

I didn't answer.

There was no easy explanation, no words to define what I was.

Instead, I focused on my hands, dragged a nearby cloth over them, slow and methodical.

The fabric was damp, stained with red. But it didn't matter. The blood remained on my hands. No matter how hard I scrubbed.

It always would.

Sage watched my movements, observing carefully, as if understanding my actions might somehow change what she witnessed.

But it wouldn't.

"I told you not to watch," I murmured.

Her response was sharp, bitter. "And you think that changes anything?"

Her small, scoffing laugh cut deep, unsettling me in a way I never anticipated. But I didn't let her see the sting—not entirely.

"It changes everything, Sage," I responded quietly.

Something flickered across her face—uncertainty, accusation, maybe both.

She hesitated, voice softer now, cautious. "There was something in your eyes... You looked different—" Her breath caught, reluctant, afraid of my response. "—when you were doing it. Something changed in you. You were almost robotic."

I clenched the cloth tighter, grounding myself. Folding it deliberately, as though the weight of her words didn't matter.

But they did.

I knew exactly what she meant.

"There's a part of myself that I can't bury... someone I became a long time ago... who keeps making me who I am now." I admitted, the words scraping harshly in my throat.

Her expression softened slightly, yet there was no relief, only the quiet hurt of recognizing a truth that can't be changed.

"But you're still trying?" she asked gently. "To bury it or get rid of it? Killing people this way because some organization drops them off at your doorstep?"

For the first time, I hesitated. The truth was heavy, complicated, and I didn't want to give her another reason to hate me or have to explain how I got here.

Yet, I couldn't lie. Not to her.

After a long silence, I finally said, "Yeah I am... for you. Always."

She exhaled shakily—something real, something alive—and her gaze fell to the floor, searching for answers in the cracks and stains.

I watched as she slowly got up and began to walk towards me, but I continued cleaning up my work.

Slowly and painfully while she shifted—just enough for her fingertips to brush against mine.

My throat tightened and I turned my hand palm-up, offering her the choice. After a fleeting moment of hesitation, she slid her fingers into mine.

The simplicity of the gesture nearly undid me.

She was still here.

She still chose me.

When I moved closer, she didn't withdraw. When I reached for her, she let me. My lips brushed gently against her temple, cautious as if she might vanish at any moment. Her breath shuddered, real and unsteady.

"I'm not afraid of you," she whispered, soft yet certain.

I laughed, "Yet."

The word landed heavier than it should have.

And I believed her. That she wasn't afraid of me... now.

But I also sensed what she left unsaid.

She feared what she saw, feared who I became—who I might become again.

Yet, somehow, right then, she remained.

Her fingers curled into my shirt, grounding herself in me as her body leaned into mine, fitting against me like it was exactly where she belonged.

My forehead rested against hers, our breaths blending in the thin space between us.

"My wildflower," I whispered.

I felt it all—the rapid beat of her heart, the grip of her hands, the fragile sounds she made when breathing became difficult.

Nothing lasts forever. But right now, we had this.

And that was enough.

After a moment, without a word, she gently took the cleaning cloth from my grasp. Slowly, silently, she began to wipe what was left of the blood from my hands.

Her touch was careful and tentative, but also deliberate.

It meant everything.

Because it was more than just cleaning—it was acceptance.

She saw all of me, even now, and still chose to help.

To stay.

And that truth alone broke me.

CHAPTER FOURTEEN

SAGE

THE BLOOD WAS HARDER to clean than I anticipated, though I'm not exactly sure what I expected. I'd never cleaned that much blood off any surface before.

It seeped deep into the cracks of the floor, staining the old concrete as if it was always meant to be there. As it dried, the edges darkened and stiffened, clinging stubbornly to every abrasion. I pressed the wet cloth down and dragged it in slow, forceful circles, grinding my palm through the thin fabric until my arm ached with the effort. It didn't seem to matter—the red remained embedded, persistent and unyielding.

Like a ghost refusing to fade.

Beside me, a bucket of water sloshed, already murky and tinged a deep rust-brown, whenever I shifted my weight. The smell was nearly unbearable, sharp and metallic enough to slice through my senses, but I kept going. Every rinse of the cloth swirled pink at first, quickly darkening, thickening and settling heavily at the bucket's bottom. It felt as though the water itself was consuming something unseen.

Something Reich wouldn't acknowledge.

Something I witnessed but haven't dared to question and maybe never will.

Reich didn't speak as we worked, caught in a distant headspace I'd never seen before. A stark stillness emanated from him—not calm but controlled. As if any sudden movement might fracture whatever tenuous hold he had on himself. His movements were efficient, methodical strokes scrubbing blood from the floor. Each pass of the cloth tightened his shoulders, sharpening the tension etched into his muscles. His jaw clenched rhythmically, the muscle in his cheek twitching every time the rough fibers snagged on the uneven surface.

His hands were stained red to the wrists, dried blood caught in every crease and painting his calluses dark. These were the same hands that held me close last night, the same fingers that steadied my trembling body. Now, stripped down to their darkest truth, they reminded me that he was truly capable of anything, even acts I'd never imagined him performing.

I felt the weight of it all pressing down on me. The heaviness of Reich himself—not just the chilling aftermath of what unfolded here, not just the stark brutality staining his skin. But the gravity of witnessing him within it.

He crouched near me just a few feet away, but an unbridgeable gulf appeared to stretch between us. He seemed slowed, distant and locked away in some unreachable place behind walls I feared I'd never be able to scale.

I wrung out the cloth again, twisting until water seeped through my fingers in slow, reluctant streams—warm despite the chill that permeated every corner of this bunker.

I still couldn't get over how big this underground mansion was.

Maybe that's why it was always cold.

Reich exhaled softly, a carefully measured breath that hardly moved his frame.

When he spoke, his voice was rough, low, as though dragged across broken glass before reaching me. "You should be resting."

I glanced at him from beneath lowered lashes, arching one brow slightly. "And leave you to clean this mess alone?"

His hand paused for just a heartbeat, a fleeting ripple beneath his carefully maintained composure. Then he resumed, scrubbing harder, determinedly avoiding my gaze. "Wouldn't be the first time I've done this alone."

His words fell heavily into the space between us, landing with a silent thud against the floor, echoing against the stark walls and pressing against the tightness in my chest. I felt them sink, weighty and cold, like stones plunged into depths too dark to measure. They sliced deeper than I was ready to admit.

I didn't know how to respond—so I remained silent.

I inched closer, ignoring the dull ache in my knees from the unforgiving concrete. My fingers brushed his hand as I reached for another cloth from the pile. His skin was colder than I anticipated, the chill stark against the warmth of my skin. He didn't pull away, didn't flinch, but he didn't acknowledge the connection either.

We scrubbed quietly, our silence expanding until it filled every crevice of the room, heavy and expectant. It pressed inward, thick enough to feel tangible. Like the world itself was holding its breath, waiting for one of us to speak—to break the fragile calm and to risk shattering everything we had carefully left unsaid.

It was Reich who spoke first.

"Cresil and Berith..."

I glanced up. His gaze remained fixed on the blood-stained spot he was scrubbing, his expression sharpened into tense lines along his cheekbones while his jaw locked.

He was contemplating how to explain what just happened.

I decided to speak for him when I felt the trepidation in his speech.

"The two that brought the boy," I said softly, carefully piecing together the fragments of what I had seen and heard over the last few years. "They're part of the organization you work for—the ENA."

He nodded once, short and firm. A nod that said he had been waiting for this conversation, knowing it would come eventually.

Knowing that sooner or later, I'd see exactly what I'd seen today.

He started, "Cresil is... *'theirs'*. She belongs to the leaders." He didn't say the leaders' names, and I didn't ask as he continued, "She is their wife. Or consort. Or something close to that."

I pressed harder on the cloth, scrubbing until my wrist stung. "So, she runs things?"

His snort was hollow, sharp enough to make me flinch. "Not officially." His jaw tightened, a visible ripple traveling down his throat. "But she's the one they fear. She doesn't need to run things for show. She simply is it."

My mind returned to the woman standing by the fireplace earlier. Her arms crossed as though she needed them for nothing but to emphasize her authority. Her expression carved from something cold and translucent, like clear ice. The way she looked at Reich—like she owned him.

And me?

I was nothing. Just some girl hidden away in a closet, hoping desperately to go unnoticed.

"And the other one? Berith, you said?" I asked even quieter now.

Reich exhaled sharply through his nose. "Nothing but a loyal dog. That's all he is." His fingers clenched the cloth until red-tinged water seeped through the fabric, dripping and staining the freshly cleaned floor. "He follows her everywhere, does whatever she commands without hesitation. Like he's spent his entire life waiting for someone to give him orders."

A faint smirk touched my lips. "So... literally her dog?"

The silence quivered, and he released a breath—not quite laughter, but close enough. His shoulders loosened slightly, just enough for me to feel the tension easing as he responded, "Yeah... something like that."

I watched him for a long moment, the way his eyes remained downcast, the bitter twist of his mouth hinting at thoughts I couldn't fully grasp.

"You hate them," I murmured.

He didn't reply. He didn't need to. The silence spoke clearly enough.

"They make sure no one ever forgets who owns them." His voice was raw, a quiet confession heavy with the price of speaking it aloud. I heard it and I felt it sink into my bones, pressing painfully against my lungs.

I sat the cloth down slowly, my fingers leaving faint streaks on the floor as I withdrew them to my lap.

"And what you did tonight?" My throat felt tight, constricted. I'm not sure I wanted to hear the answer.

But I asked anyway.

Reich dragged a hand through his hair, pushing it away from his face. His skin gleamed with sweat and something else I couldn't quite place. In the low light, the sharp angles of his face appeared even harsher.

"It wasn't the first time," he murmured. "And it won't be the last."

His words settled heavily in my stomach, sinking like lead. I swallowed hard, but the heaviness remained.

He wouldn't look at me. Instead, he scrubbed harder at a spot that was already clean, as if stopping meant confronting something he feared even more.

But then after a moment of silence, he spoke, "You shouldn't have had to see that."

I didn't argue. I didn't tell him that I needed to witness it—that deep down, a part of me wanted to. I didn't think he'd understand that. To grasp the fact that I craved knowing him, and I had ever since the beginning. I had longed to know every hidden piece, not just the polished exterior he showed the world. I'd always wanted the truth of him and what made him who he was, raw and exposed.

Just like he wanted of me all those years ago.

But I couldn't make myself believe that he would understand that.

Or worse, push me away for digging too deep.

So, I picked up the cloth again and dipped it back into the murky water.

"You shouldn't have to do this alone," I said quietly, steadily, and started wiping away another smear.

Something flickered across his face as he glanced at me—something unreadable yet softer, somehow.

I forced a weary smirk. "This is a lot of work. I don't know how you manage to clean up this much…" I felt myself trail off before he finished the sentence for me.

"Blood." He answered. "You can say it."

I looked at him, as I asked, "You really have to do this all by yourself? Nobody helps you?"

His lips twitched, nearly forming a smile as he murmured, "Not even Cas."

His words tightened something inside me, but I buried it deep, ignoring the pull of emotion. But the realization still hit me harder than I expected.

I was the *only* one who'd seen this, seen Reich at his most vulnerable, wounded, and taken advantage of. Witnessing him in ruin was something I'd never imagined, let alone thought I'd be here for.

"Well," I whispered, dipping my cloth back into the water, "Let me be the first to stick around and help you clean up your inconvenient murder messes."

I forced a smile, "I feel like I am setting a new precedence."

His expression shifted, subtle yet profound—a softness around the edges, a crack in the carefully maintained mask. "Yeah," he breathed, voice quieter than before, "—I guess you are... Thank you."

The silence that settled afterward wasn't heavy anymore. It was changed—softer, warmer.

We finished cleaning the blood side by side in that newfound quiet. When we were finally done, I sat back on my heels, my body aching. Knees stiff, arms trembling from exertion.

But the blood was gone, as if it never stained this place.

I glanced at Reich, as I wiped the sweat from my temple with the back of my wrist.

"You know," I said slowly, a playful edge slipping back into my voice, "this place is clean enough to have your way with me on every surface now."

Reich blinked caught off guard. Then—a sound escaped him. A low, breathy laugh that forced a smile. It sounded like it had been trapped inside him for years, or maybe he was simply astonished by my humor at a moment like this.

But that quiet laughter and that smile did something to me.

Something shattering. Something dangerous.

It sparked hope, and hope was always where I unraveled.

He shook his head slowly, but a smirk began to lift from one corner of his mouth. "You're something else."

I shrugged lightly. "I prefer irresistible."

Then he moved. Fast. One second, I was kneeling beside him, and the next, I was on my back, breath punched from my lungs as his weight pressed above me. His rough hands skimmed my body, lifting my shirt, exposing my skin to the chill in the air. His palms remained cool, but his breath was hot as it brushed against my ear, and he spoke.

"You want to test that theory, wildflower?"

I did. God, I always did.

So, I pulled him closer.

I shouldn't have been touching him.

Not after what I'd witnessed. Not after everything he'd done or while his hands were still stained from the blood. But I couldn't stop myself.

I didn't know how to exist anywhere else.

Because nowhere else had ever felt like home.

Even covered in blood. Even with hands marked by sins I couldn't begin to understand, Reich remained the only thing in this world that felt truly mine.

He pulled back slightly, murmuring, "We should clean ourselves up, too." He rose, turning his back to me. I followed him, quietly coming up from behind.

My fingers found the edge of his shirt, sticky and stiff with dried blood. I peeled it away slowly, carefully, feeling the muscles beneath tense under my touch.

He didn't stop me. He didn't speak.

He didn't turn around.

My fingertips traced the scars etched across his back. Some old, some fresh, some so deep I couldn't fathom how he still breathed. The brand at the nape of his neck was dark and swollen, angry as if freshly torn open.

It looked unhealed, as if time had refused to touch it.

I lifted up on my toes to press my lips gently against where it branded him.

He shuddered.

"You really shouldn't be here, Sage," he said, voice ragged, broken.

I closed my eyes, breathing him in. "I'm exactly where I'm supposed to be."

When he finally turned to face me, it was cautious, gentle, like he was afraid I might vanish.

His eyes weren't cold anymore.

They were raw. Bare. Almost bleeding.

"Don't look at me like that," he whispered.

"Like what?"

"Like there's something left worth redeeming. Like I could ever still deserve a delicate wildflower like you."

I stepped closer, my palm cradling his face. My thumb stroked his cheekbone, softly. Reverently.

"You do," I whispered. "You always have."

I gave him a light kiss as we stripped ourselves bare in the process, dropping our clothes piece by piece onto the floor, not caring about the mess it made underneath our feet. We entered the shower, as the hot water cascaded over us, steam enveloping our bodies, blurring the edges of our shared pain and regret. Reich's lips were desperate, hungry and consuming every breath as if it was the last he would ever take. His hands roamed my body, memorizing every curve, every scar, every wound that had ever been inflicted upon me or marks he believed that he failed to protect me from.

"Sage," he breathed my name like a plea, his forehead pressing against mine. Water dripped from his dark lashes, mingling with what looked like tears from his eyes. "This is a mistake. I don't want to break you any more than I already have."

I threaded my fingers through his wet hair, forcing him to meet my gaze. "You're not breaking me, Reich. You're the one putting me back together. You always have. Let me do the same for you."

He exhaled sharply, eyes haunted by shadows of his own making. "How can you say that after everything I've done? After all the blood on my hands? This incident is a fleck of sand on the shore in comparison to all of the things I've done."

I guided his hand over my chest, letting him feel the fierce rhythm of my heartbeat beneath his palm. "Because I see you, Reich. Not the monster they tried to create, not the sins you've been forced to carry—*I see you*. And that man deserves to offer himself forgiveness."

His chest heaved, heavy with disbelief, longing, and something deeper that was aching and raw. "I want to believe you," he whispered, voice fractured with emotion.

"Then trust me. Trust this, just like you asked me all those years ago." I murmured, pulling him closer until every inch of our skin was pressed together, hearts beating in tandem, aching for connection. He groaned softly, surrendering to the warmth, to the truth between us that no darkness could extinguish.

We lost ourselves in each other, in a gentle, almost sacred act of redemption, a mutual healing. Every kiss, every caress whispered promises neither of us dared to voice aloud. The world outside this embrace faded until it was just the two of us, raw and vulnerable, stripped down to the essence of who we truly were beneath the masks of pain and guilt.

When we finally parted, breathless and spent, Reich held me tight against his chest, the steady drumbeat of his heart anchoring me.

"Promise me something," he murmured against my hair.

I tilted my face up, meeting his gaze. "Anything."

"Don't ever let me become someone you fear."

My fingers traced the contours of his jaw, imprinting every detail into memory. "I won't. I'll always find you, Reich. Even in the darkness."

He exhaled, relief softening his hardened features. "Then maybe there's still hope for me."

I pressed a lingering kiss to his chest, feeling him shiver beneath my touch. "There always was."

Later, breathless and tangled in the sheets, I watched Reich reach for his phone. I wasn't sure who he was calling at first, but when I saw the concerned look on his face when he opened his phone. I knew it had to be Castor.

The call rang once, then abruptly clicked to voicemail.

His body tensed—jaw clenched, fingers trembling slightly. The tension radiating from him told me he was getting more worried, afraid something might have happened.

Slowly, I sat up, breaking the silence gently. "Still nothing?"

He didn't respond immediately. Instead, he exhaled slowly, forcibly controlled, his hand coming up to rub at the back of his neck.

That's when I noticed it.

He was gripping the mark again.

Digging his fingers into it as if he could rip it away.

"Reich—"

"It's nothing."

But his voice was sharp, edged with strain. Frayed.

He didn't say much else that night, but those words lingered as I drifted off to sleep.

I knew something was off.

And more than that, I knew better than to believe him when he says, "*It's nothing.*"

CHAPTER FIFTEEN

REICH

THE CANDLE ON THE table flickered, its flame wavering as though caught between life and extinction. Wax pooled slowly at its base, molten drops creating gentle patterns as they fell causing a faint blend of smoke and vanilla that lingered in the stillness. Shadows danced quietly across the walls, appearing and disappearing without rhythm, fleeting shapes that reminded me of everything I couldn't hold on to.

Beside me, Sage slept calmly, her breathing steady, her body relaxed. She had accepted me—seen glimpses of the truth and embraced them anyway. Yet, even now, as she dreamed quietly beside me, fear whispered through my veins.

I should have rested. Closed my eyes. Silenced my mind. Pretended—if only until dawn—that nothing was changing inside me, that I was still human, still worthy of redemption. Still something close to whole.

But that would have been a lie.

Because I felt it now more than ever. Something burned within my mark, burrowing deeper beneath my skin, shifting restlessly and unsettling the very core of who I was. I couldn't name it or comprehend its meaning, but I sensed its darkness growing, claiming more of me with each passing moment.

My gaze settled again on the shadows dancing quietly around us, and I wondered how long I could keep her from seeing the full truth—the truth I wasn't even sure I could bear to face.

Hell, I didn't even know what the truth looked like.

All I knew was I could sense that something was wrong.

Deeply wrong.

I watched her as she laid on the cot next to the chair where I was perched, her breathing was soft and steady—rhythmic in a way that almost made me forget the world around us seemed to be collapsing. She was curled into the blankets I wrapped around her before she drifted off, her body tucked tightly into itself, small and perfectly still. For a moment—maybe longer—she looked peaceful. Like we could remain here indefinitely, hidden away in this secluded bunker, untouched by the chaos outside.

But I knew better. It wasn't safe. And we couldn't stay.

Not with the ENA dropping by unexpectedly.

And not when I had already made a promise to her that we would leave for the Bloodwine.

My gaze fell to the cracked screen of my phone, the jagged surface catching the candlelight in sharp, fractured lines. My fingers hovered over the screen hesitation heavy in my chest. Heat seeped gently from the device, a subtle pulse beneath my fingertips, waiting for me to seek answers I wasn't prepared to face. I flexed my hand once, twice, before finally pressing the call through.

The connection hummed, a low, grinding sound that set my teeth on edge. Static crackled sharply in the quiet space, gnawing at my nerves as I waited for the line to stabilize, hoping the sound wasn't enough to disturb Sage's sleep.

Nael's line wasn't always easiest to access, especially at night—he made certain of that. Layers of encryption, coded fail-safes, and intricate verification protocols I had memorized and loathed having to use.

But right now, I needed to know if what I was thinking was correct.

If the legends and things that I had read about with the ENA and the brand were true.

At last, his voice came through—"You don't call unless something's wrong." His tone sliced through the static, flat and unnervingly calm.

"Something's wrong," I admitted, the words tasting bitter in my mouth.

Silence filled the line.

Not casual silence—the dangerous kind.

I could hear him breathing, the faint rustle of papers shifting beneath his fingertips. Nael was always working, always clawing at the edges of the world as if determined to make it bleed out its secrets. He knew things long before anyone else did, relentlessly pursuing the truth, no matter what part of himself he had to sacrifice to uncover it. It was something I had always admired—and sometimes even feared—about him.

He had no limits. *Ever.*

"I need information," I said. "On the ENA. The brand and ... their bloodlines."

There was a long exhale, like something old and weary being dragged up from deep within him. When Nael spoke again, I noticed how his tone has shifted.

Never a good sign.

"Why?"

I hesitated. I shouldn't—*not now*—but Sage's voice echoed stubbornly from earlier.

Your eyes... You looked different, Reich.

She said it more than once, and she was right.

I was *different.*

Something was wrong, and I didn't know what it was.

"I read once that the brand would activate under certain conditions. I thought it was some old lore but maybe not... Have you ever heard anything unusual about them?" I asked instead, keeping my voice even. "Something beyond the usual power struggles and petty politics? Like the reason we need to eradicate the families in order to dismantle them?"

Another pause, this one deeper and longer. I imagined him setting his papers aside, narrowing his focus. He was always ten steps ahead, always ready—but this? This was different. I had thrown him a curveball, and we both knew it.

"Where are you getting this from?" he asked cautiously.

"You tell me first." My fingertips drummed once against the table. My pulse was too rapid, too loud.

Each second of silence sharpened my nerves.

Then came a mutter—low, sharp, likely meant only for himself.

"When I first started digging into them," Nael began tightly, "I figured half of what people whispered was bullshit. Superstitions, prophecies. Bloodlines claimed to be chosen, legacies older than the cities, older than even the fall. It sounded exactly like the kind of lies designed to keep people afraid. And now..." His voice trailed.

"And now?" I asked.

I already knew what he would say, but I needed to hear it from his lips.

When he spoke again, his voice was quieter. Heavier. "Now, Reich, I'm not so sure."

His words landed like stones in my chest, sinking heavily into my gut.

"What else do you know?" I pressed.

Static crackled again. Dead air filled my ears. Nael never hesitated—not with me—but he was hesitating now, and it chilled the room, making the air thick and hard to breathe.

"No," he finally said, almost reluctant. "Not over this. Some things are better explained face-to-face."

Tension coiled in my stomach, sharp and insistent.

"Nael—"

"I mean it, Reich." His voice was firm, edged with something close to fear—and Nael didn't get scared. "Get here soon. So, we can figure this out together."

The line clicked off abruptly, plunging me into a heavy, suffocating silence.

I sat frozen with my eyes fixed on the blackened screen. The silence swelled around me, an oppressive hum, louder and more insistent than before. My hand moved instinctively, fingertips pressing against the back of my neck, against the mark. The scarred ridges seared beneath my touch, so hot I flinched away. This wasn't a simple ache anymore.

It burned like it was alive.

I dropped my hand, balling it into a fist as urgency coiled in my gut.

The Bloodwine could wait. Any leads I thought we had there—*none matter right now.*

And Nael's bunker was safer. Secure. Remote. And if he had answers… if he knew what was happening to me… I had to know.

I rose slowly, my body protesting every movement. Rolling my shoulders until they popped as I stretched out the stiffness in my muscles. The trek ahead would be grueling. We'd have to hike in alone, stick to back trails, erase our tracks as we go.

This changed everything.

But there was no other choice.

Cas wasn't answering, and the thought of leaving him behind gnawed at my gut. But something happened to him—something tied to the brand. Probably just like what was happening to me.

Nael would know what to do. Because Cas wouldn't meet us at the Bloodwine. I knew it. Deep down I knew it, even though I didn't want to admit to it.

And I needed to get Sage somewhere safe.

Because whatever was silencing Castor… I could feel that it was coming for us next.

I turned toward the cot, and for a moment, I just looked at her.

My wildflower.

Sage lied tangled in the sheets, her hair spilling like dark ribbons across the pillow. Her face was soft as she slept, but still there was a faint crease between her brows—as if real peace remained just beyond her reach, even in her dreams. Her breathing was slow and steady.

I didn't deserve it. I didn't deserve her.

But she was still here. Still mine. Even after everything she'd witnessed, after everything I had done.

And I was going to keep her safe, no matter the cost.

Moving toward the cot, I sat carefully on the edge, my hand rising again to drag heavily over my face. I needed sleep—just a few hours—enough to stay sharp when we left.

I eased back into the pillows, muscles protesting with every movement. My eyes drifted closed.

And for the first time in what felt like days, I let myself surrender to the darkness completely.

I kept having this dream since she came back into my life.

I'm standing in a room encased by stone walls, slick with condensation, pressing in from every side. Candles form a perimeter, their wavering flames low, boxing me in with flickering shadows.

Reminding me of the old ENA rituals I was part of during their initiation.

Wax spilled down in twisting rivulets, pooling in molten puddles across the uneven floor. The air was dense with something unfamiliar. Something that shouldn't be here.

There was a figure across from me.

IN REICH AND RUIN

Tall. Unmoving. Its face hidden in shadow, features blurred beyond recognition, yet its gaze felt tangible giving off a heavy pressure that built behind my eyes.

"You are not ready," it would say.

The voice would slice deep, sinister, carrying an almost ancient weight.

I stepped forward, but the ground beneath me shifted uneasily. Too soft, unstable. Like wading through quicksand that pulled me down with agonizing slowness.

"Ready for what?" I demanded.

The figure tilted its head, examining me like something damaged, before finally responding, "To become what you were meant to be."

I tried to speak, but my voice was lost.

All at once, the candles fanned out. The walls vanished, leaving me suspended in emptiness.

A vast, endless abyss that swallowed me whole. Silence thick, suffocating in its depth. And then—a whisper.

That same voice reaching out, lingering in the darkness, saying, "Come home, Reich."

I had that dream that night and woke violently.

A sharp breath tore from my lungs as I jolted upright, my body rigid from the lingering echo of it. My fists were clenched, nails biting deep enough into my palms to carve crescent-shaped imprints.

The mark burned.

Heat seared into me, stealing my breath.

I pressed a trembling palm against the back of my neck, jaw locked tight as pain pulsed through me like a second heartbeat.

I was beginning to notice that it always seemed to burn when I considered leaving—or when I considered anything at all.

Beside me, Sage shifted restlessly, her brow furrowing. She murmured softly, words I couldn't quite make out, her breath hitching before she began to wake. Her eyes fluttered open, clouded and heavy with sleep.

"Reich?" Her voice was quiet, but it sliced through the silence.

I didn't respond immediately. I just breathed—in, then out, slow and controlled.

Finally, I turned to face her.

"We're leaving."

Confusion clouded her eyes as she blinked awake, trying to catch up. "What?"

I sat up straighter, my muscles still taut but moving with purpose now as my hesitation was replaced by resolve. I raked a hand through my hair, forcing my composure back into place.

"Change of plans," I said firmly. "We're going to Nael's."

Sage pushed herself onto one elbow, her gaze sharpening, quickly alert despite lingering sleep.

"When?" Her voice was steady, calm, and unafraid.

I saw the questions she held back, hidden behind her eyes, but she didn't ask them.

She simply nodded like the good girl she had always been for me.

Willing. Submissive. *Trusting*.

I swung my legs off the cot, reaching instinctively for my boots.

"Now."

Chapter Sixteen

SAGE

THE SILENCE BETWEEN US hung heavy, not like absence but like a presence all its own. Almost suffocating, as it pressed into every inch of space, thick and immovable. It settled deep within my chest like smoke, making each breath a quiet struggle. Every passing second seemed to stretch painfully, like an empty echo filling the void where conversation should be. But there were no words—from either of us.

Reich moved through the room with ruthless efficiency, each motion sharp and mechanical, like it was guided by some internal checklist visible only to him. There was a purpose in his movements now, hard-edged and cold, though I couldn't tell if it was intended as protection or merely distraction from whatever was tearing at him beneath the surface.

But he moved as if he was outrunning something.

And I couldn't help but think that perhaps he was.

Perhaps he always had been.

I didn't interrupt as I tried to piece it together. We had already packed the things we needed for our trek to the Bloodwine earlier but I watched as he gathered more supplies, methodically inspecting each item twice before stashing it away in the same spot it came from. More weapons vanished into hidden seams and concealed pockets with practiced precision—knives, ammunition, tools whose names I didn't know but whose lethal potential was clearly visible. I watched quietly as he slipped all of this additional gear into our packs, adjusting the weight effortlessly, as though we were not about to walk headfirst into something neither of us was truly prepared for.

He didn't look my way. Not even briefly. And perhaps that was what unsettled me most of all.

I stood near the bed, arms crossed tightly over my chest, fingers gripping the fabric of my sleeves as if I was the only one holding myself together in the space that he was too preoccupied to fill. My gaze traced the sharp lines of his shoulders, the rigid tension etched into his back—the subtle shift of his jaw as I watched him try and fail to push something from his mind. He was unraveling in slow motion, and I could feel every fragment as it slipped away.

"Reich." I finally said.

His name was soft, but it cut through the heavy silence.

He didn't stop moving—didn't even slow down.

I watched his hands tighten around a roll of gauze before he stuffed it roughly into the side pocket of his pack. His breath escaped in a thin, controlled line through his nose. He gathered a few more items before finally—*finally*—casting a fleeting glance over his shoulder, as he spoke.

"The trip to Nael's will be a bit of a walk."

I arched an eyebrow, unwilling to let him off that easily. "How much of a walk?"

There was a beat of hesitation, subtle but unmistakable. He didn't answer, just turned away, shoulders rigid, mouth pressed flat with words left unsaid.

That silence told me everything.

I already knew it wouldn't be easy—nothing with him ever was—but the way he avoided my eyes then…it was worse than I'd imagined. Worse than he was willing to voice aloud.

Yet I didn't push him. *Not yet.* Not when I could sense how dangerously close he was to breaking.

I stepped forward, bridging the distance between us, each movement deliberate until I was close enough to touch him—close enough to feel the restless heat radiating off his skin. My fingers gently encircled his wrist, brushing the spot where his pulse was beating rapidly. My thumb moved in slow, soothing circles, drawing out the moment until I felt the slightest hitch in his breath, a tiny fracture in the armor he kept clinging to so desperately.

And he didn't pull away.

I let myself count that as a victory.

"Whatever it is you're carrying," I whispered, voice low and steady, "you don't have to shoulder it alone."

His jaw tightened, throat bobbing as he swallowed something down.

He flicked his eyes to mine, and for an instant—a fleeting, fragile moment—I glimpsed it.

Something raw. Something hollowed out but still bleeding. Then it vanished, drowned beneath the merciless control he always retreated behind.

A defense that felt more like penance.

He leaned in suddenly, forehead pressed against mine with an urgency so sharp it stole my breath. His eyes closed, and his exhale brushed my lips—warm, uneven, weighted with truths he had never spoken and probably never would.

"The only thing I am shouldering is protecting you because whatever's coming doesn't stop once it starts. And I don't intend to let it reach you."

My stomach twisted violently.

I forced words past the burning lump lodged in my throat. "Then tell me what to do."

He didn't.

Instead, his hand slipped behind my neck, fingers rough, calloused, trembling faintly. Then his lips found mine—slowly at first, then deeply—like he was trying to memorize every part of me. Like he was counting down to something he knew he wouldn't escape.

It wasn't the kiss that frightened me.

It was that something about it felt too much like a form of goodbye.

The night air hit cold and sharp as we stepped outside ready to leave. It smelled of damp earth and pine—clean, but in a way that only heightened the unease. Everything felt too quiet, too still.

The bunker vanished quickly behind us, swallowed by darkness and towering trees. Our footsteps were muffled by soft ground, barely audible against the whispering hush of the forest. Stars scattered across an endless, ink-black sky, but somewhere in the distance, beyond the pitch-black horizon, dawn crept closer.

Reich set a consistent pace, every movement efficient, controlled, wound tight like a precision-made machine. His shoulders were rigid, his spine a taut line of tension I couldn't soften, no matter how closely I followed. I fought against the spiral of anxious thoughts circling tighter the deeper we moved along the dark path and into the depths of the woods.

Branches clawed at one another overhead, casting jagged shadows across our path. In the corner of my eye, they stirred something painfully familiar.

The last time I was here, in woods just like these, I was running.

My breath burned sharply in my throat as I remembered the footsteps crashing behind me as I tried to outrun the horrors lurking in the shadows.

I exhaled slowly, forcing that memory back into the darkness where it belonged.

This time was different. This time, I wasn't *alone*.

I stayed close to Reich, fingers twitching restlessly at my sides, desperate for something to hold onto. He noticed—he always noticed the smallest things.

After a few minutes, without looking, he reached back, his fingers lightly brushing mine. Quick. Brief.

But just enough.

Enough to ground me.

I curled my hand around the echo of his touch, holding tight before it left.

The silence that stretched between us then was steady, matching Reich's unwavering presence.

He continued glancing back, checking my pace, never letting me drift more than a few feet behind before subtly easing his stride, ensuring I could keep up. It was careful and deliberate, soothing something tense and knotted inside my chest.

And somehow, it was all I needed to steady my pace and my mind with his too.

We walked through dawn, midday, and dusk.

Time blurred.

Paths twisted and narrowed, unfolding into quiet clearings. We crossed streams and felt the icy rush of rapids numbing our feet as we pressed forward. Navigated around fallen trees that blocked our path, and we scrambled over slick bark, grasping desperately for footing. My legs burned as we hiked steep inclines, each breath tearing from my lungs, as I kept up.

My body ached deeply. The wound from a few days ago still burning. My shoulders screamed beneath the weight of my pack. More than once, my legs threatened to give out—but I didn't let them, and I didn't complain.

Neither did he.

Though the trek seemed effortless for him.

We pushed forward silently, bound by our shared stubbornness, neither willing to quit. Only when the sun dipped behind the tree line, streaking the sky with indigos and bruised purples, did Reich slow with his gaze sharp and assessing towards me.

After a moment, he nodded towards a small clearing. "We'll stop here."

I wanted to argue—to push further, to reach Nael's sooner and find true rest—but exhaustion clung heavily to me, threatening to pull me under. So, I nodded silently and sunk myself onto a fallen log as he cleared space for a fire.

Reich moved with practiced ease, efficiently setting up a small fire that caught immediately. I watched him quietly, noting the rigid set of his shoulders, the subtle tremor in his hands when he thought I wasn't looking.

"How close are we?" I finally asked, my voice louder than intended.

Reich glanced at me briefly, then nodded toward the darkening forest ahead. "Close."

Relief loosened a tight knot in my chest.

Almost there. *Almost.*

He rose, approaching me slowly, his shadow stretching over me as the fire's glow flickered across his unreadable face.

"Get some rest," he murmured.

I blinked up at him, exhaustion flooding my bones now that I had stopped moving. "Are you going to sleep?"

He let out a quiet, hollow laugh. "No."

"Reich—"

"Sage..." He shook his head slightly, kneeling beside me. His hand settled gently on my knee—a faint, grounding touch. "I'll rest when we get to Nael's."

I searched his face for signs he was lying.

He must have noticed my doubt because his mouth tilted into a faint smile as he commented, "I find rest when I get to watch you sleep knowing that you're somewhere far away from all of this."

I rolled my eyes, but warmth bloomed slowly in my chest, chasing away some of the exhaustion. "That was probably the cheesiest and sweetest line I have ever heard you say." I gave a small laugh.

"Maybe." His smirk softened. "But you're smiling."

I shook my head lightly, as I laughed, breathing out and leaning back onto my hands. The fire crackled softly between us, warm yet fragile.

"Promise you won't leave while I'm sleeping," I whispered.

For a heartbeat, his expression faltered, revealing something raw and aching beneath his composed exterior. Then, slowly, he nodded.

"You should know by now — walking away isn't an option I have left."

I held his gaze a moment longer before finally allowing myself to trust his words.

I moved towards the ground and curled onto my side. I watched as the firelight danced across his features, painting them gold and orange. He remained close, his presence anchoring me to reality.

I started to drift in and out, feigning sleep as I held on to alertness only to look up at him and whisper, "You're still here."

That earned a smile from him before I decided to give in.

As sleep pulled me under, I clung tightly to that one truth: *He was still there.*

CHAPTER SEVENTEEN

REICH

THE FIRE CRACKLED FAINTLY, spitting embers that flared briefly before vanishing into the darkness. The flames struggled, fragile ribbons of warmth barely holding back the creeping cold pressing in from every direction. I leaned closer, fingers outstretched, desperate to coax more heat from the dying blaze. It wasn't much—it was barely enough—but right now, it was all I could give her.

It was everything I had left it seemed.

Beneath the frayed edge of my coat she wore, her chest rose and fell, unevenly at first, as if her body still clung to the waking world, hesitant to let go. I watched her for a long while, not because duty compelled me, but because I needed the certainty. Proof she was still here, that I hadn't lost her yet.

When she was finally asleep, I could tell. I'd memorized her enough... watched her enough.

I knew from the gentle rhythm of her breathing—soft and steady, each exhale slower and deeper than the last.

I knew from the calm that would instantly veil her face.

I shifted my weight on the log, elbows resting on my knees, hands hanging loosely in the space between. A sharp ache pulsed behind my eyes, the kind that had been building for hours and wouldn't fade until I surrendered. But sleep wasn't an option. Maybe it never would be again. It felt like I had forgotten how, a lifetime ago, and when I tried, it was replaced by nightmares too vivid to escape.

And maybe that was my fate.

Or at least it was beginning to feel that way.

The forest was unnaturally silent, a dangerous stillness that hummed beneath my skin like static, seeping deep into unreachable places. It was the kind of quiet that signaled something out there, hidden in the shadows.

Waiting. Watching.

I scanned the tree line once more, my vision sliced through the darkness even though I already knew deep down that there was nothing truly to find. Not yet. If they were coming, they wouldn't attack now. They never did. They would wait until daylight broke, until exhaustion had already robbed us of resistance, leaving us with nothing but brittle bones to shatter.

I glanced up at her. She laid curled beneath the heavy coat, drawn tight around herself as though trying to become invisible. Her face was ghostly pale in the dim glow, shadows cascading deeper hollows beneath the sharp edges of her cheeks and jaw. She looked cold. She must have been cold. Probably had been for hours. Yet she hadn't awoken or complained—not once. About anything. Not about the punishing pace, not about the relentless chill that seeped through every layer we owned, and certainly not about me or the choices I had made to drag her into this nightmare.

She was stronger than she should have been. Stronger than anyone should have to become after enduring what she had. After everything I inadvertently put her through since I first met her.

And I knew that it would kill her eventually.

I would be the reason it did.

It was just a matter of time.

I scrubbed a hand roughly across my face, the scrape of stubble reminding me vividly that I was still there. Still breathing. Still alive when I shouldn't be.

"You're still here."

It was something she whispered just before drifting off—words so quiet, I wasn't sure she even realized she'd spoken them.

"For now," I thought.

But forever? I knew better.

But even so, I was going to make damn sure that I avoided it at all cost.

This time I was going to fight harder. Protect her.

A sharp crack split the silence, echoing through the trees like a whip. Like a branch had broken under a heavy weight, maybe—or something worse. My body reacted instantly, adrenaline surging through my veins. Before my mind fully processed it, I was already on my feet, knife tight in my grip, eyes scanning the darkness for shapes that didn't belong. My pulse hammered in my ears, drowning out everything but rapid breathing and the whisper of cold steel against my palm.

But the forest settled again. Still. No movement. No sound. Just shadows. Ghosts, as always.

I exhaled slowly, deliberately calming my racing heart. I forced my body to obey, even though every instinct screamed at me to stay alert—to stay standing, knife ready, prepared for the inevitable. But I made myself sit again. I made myself return to the fire.

Return to *her*.

She shifted slightly in her sleep, her hand twitching as though reaching for something unseen.

This time, I sat closer. Close enough to feel the faint warmth radiating from her skin. My fingers hovered above her hand, mere inches separating us, so close I could almost sense the tremor of her pulse beneath her skin.

I stopped myself before I touched her.

Because I knew if I did, I wouldn't be able to stop.

And if I couldn't stop, I wouldn't be able to do what needed to be done and stay on guard.

"Just a little bit longer, wildflower," I murmured, the words barely more than a breath.

I kept watch until the sky began to lighten, until the cold started to lift, until the shadows crept back to wherever they go when the sun rises. And until I was staring at the line between night and day, wondering which side I belonged to.

By the time the sun broke over the horizon, the fire was nothing but dying coals and lingering smoke. Shadows stretched long and cold between the trees, reaching out like specters with unfinished business. We hadn't said much since dawn broke—both trapped in our own thoughts, silently counting down the hours and the minutes. But I felt her gaze fixed on me. I always did. She looked at me like I was something she wasn't sure whether to hold onto or to let slip away. Like I was both the lifeline and the blade.

She was close. Too close. Her shoulder brushed mine with each subtle movement. I could sense her through the scent of smoke and earth—something purely her, something unchangeable despite everything. She was wrapped in my jacket, too big, sleeves hanging past her fingers, swallowing her whole in something undeniably mine while her eyes were fixed on me.

We found a place to sit for a moment before making the rest of the trek.

"You're staring," I murmured, voice rough from the hours of silence.

Her lips curved faintly, knowingly. "You're hard to look away from."

I turned to face her then, truly seeing her.

And whatever restraint I had been clinging to, whatever thin thread of control I had managed to keep all night—it snapped. Cleanly. Completely.

I seized her wrists and pulled her toward me, rougher than intended, but she came willingly, effortlessly settling over my lap like she had done it countless times before—as if this was the only place she belonged. A soft sound escaped her lips, part protest, part invitation, but she didn't push me away, even as she said, "Shouldn't we be going?"

"You want me to stop?" I asked, voice a dangerous whisper, already knowing her answer.

She pulled her hands from my grip and fisted her fingers in my shirt, defiant and daring. "No and you won't."

"No," I confirmed, slipping my hands beneath the jacket. "I won't."

I slid the sleeves off from her shoulders, exposing her skin to the crisp bite of morning air. She shivered yet remained steady, tilting her chin upward in quiet challenge. I accepted it, pressing my mouth to the soft curve of her throat, teeth grazing sharply enough to leave a mark. Her body responded instantly, pressing into me, needing more, needing everything. My hands clamped down on her hips, holding her still, making her feel every deliberate, punishing movement beneath her.

"Reich," she breathed, voice raw and vulnerable.

I lifted my gaze to meet her eyes. "Say it again."

She did—and it wrecked me. Tore through me, slow and merciless, just like it always did.

I lowered her to the hard, unforgiving ground, covering her body with mine—*my protection*. My hands worked in frantic motions, stripping away every barrier between us until there was nothing left but skin and the desperate ache that never seemed to dull.

For a single, breathless moment, I hovered above her—just looking. Memorizing her. Reminding myself she was real and that she was *mine*.

Her cry shattered the quiet, her hands flying up, grasping for something solid in a world that kept slipping. I caught them, pinning her wrists high above her head, my fingers digging in as I moved. The only language we seemed to speak when words weren't enough.

"Quiet, wildflower" I whispered harshly against her ear, teeth grazing her skin. "We may not be alone out here."

She bit her lip, trembling with the effort to obey. But she broke instead—*beautifully*. And God, I loved her for it. For trying. For giving in. For the way she ruined me every damn time.

I lost myself in her until there was nothing else. Just heat and hunger and the sacred chaos between us. Until even the silence forgot how to be quiet.

When she finally gave in completely, shuddering beneath me, I followed instantly, burying my face in her neck, breathing her in like she was salvation and I was still worth saving.

Afterward, neither of us moved for a while. It was only skin against skin, hearts aligned, even as the chill slowly returned.

"We're not going to survive this, are we?" she whispered, her voice fragile, barely audible.

I pressed a gentle kiss to her shoulder, tasting salt and inevitability. "Who said anything about surviving?"

Chapter Eighteen

SAGE

THE FIRE SLOWLY DIED, and it felt as though we were fading with it.

I sensed it in the way the cold returned to my skin, slow and enveloping, seeping through layers of tiredness. I felt it in the quiet rhythm of Reich's breathing, with each exhale that gently stirred strands of my hair, hesitant and careful—as if he was desperately holding onto something he could sense slipping away.

I laid next to him, feeling every second stretch into eternity, letting his weight press into me, anchoring me to that fleeting moment. His heartbeat pulsed against my chest, rapid and uneasy—not because of us or what we had just done, but because fear rushed through him.

He wouldn't admit it—*he never would*—but it hummed through his bones like distant thunder signaling a storm neither of us was ready to face.

Slowly, carefully, I untangled my fingers from his grip. He released me without protest, yet his touch lingered, haunting the space it once occupied. My hand found his face instead, gently tracing the harsh stubble along his jaw, following the defined curve of his cheekbone. Reich didn't flinch, but his eyes watched me from beneath heavy, dark lashes, cautious and waiting.

Perhaps he waited for reassurance, an empty promise that everything would be okay.

Perhaps he waited for me to finally say I was leaving and never coming back.

I couldn't decide which lie would be more painful.

Instead, I whispered, "We should go," the words scraped raw from my throat, carrying exhaustion and words left unspoken.

His gaze shifted downward, lingering briefly on my lips as if searching for words I refused to speak. For a moment, the world stood still.

Then he moved—*slowly, deliberately*—drawing away from me as if leaving fragments of himself behind, scattered and lost in the dirt.

I dressed silently, fighting the tremors that threatened to overwhelm my hands. Reich watched me, his expression carefully masked, revealing nothing but the intense depth behind his eyes.

When I slipped his jacket onto my shoulders, his scent enveloped me. It shouldn't have comforted me.

But it did.

As he straightened, his face was carved from stone, unreadable in the muted light of dawn.

I hated it. And yet, I loved it.

"We're not far," he said, voice low and devoid of promise.

"You said that yesterday," I stated, sharper than intended. Frustration seeped through, despite my attempt to match his detachment.

His jaw tensed, a subtle muscle flexing beneath his skin. "Yesterday, it was true."

"And today?"

His gaze met mine, darker now, heavy with unspoken truths that neither of us dared to acknowledge.

"Today, we're closer."

It was no real answer, yet I accepted it.

I shouldered my pack, the straps biting into muscles already battered and aching from the grueling journey. I felt raw, exposed in ways that couldn't be seen but pulsed painfully beneath my skin throughout my body.

He stepped toward me, fingers brushing lightly over my wrist. The brief contact nearly shattered me just like it did before.

But I didn't pull away.

"Ready?" His voice was quiet, cautious.

No.

But I nodded anyway.

We moved through the trees, swallowed whole by the silent, oppressive weight of the forest. It was too quiet—not peaceful, but heavy with tension—the kind of unnatural stillness that preceded inevitable chaos.

Reich's hand stayed close, hovering near the small of my back or briefly grazing my wrist, always maintaining some point of contact, as though he feared I would dissolve into the nearby shadows the instant he stopped.

We walked without speaking, our footsteps muffled by damp earth, my heartbeat louder than the oppressive quiet around us. Time stretched, losing its meaning as minutes bled into hours, reality blurring at the edges, fluid and merciless in the dense, unyielding wilderness.

When we finally paused to drink, I watched Reich carefully over the rim of my canteen. His features were hard, the lines sharpened by unspoken anxiety, eyes vigilant as they swept over our surroundings. His posture coiled, ready to strike, or defend.

He always seemed to anticipate confrontation. It was almost like he craved it and yet, dreaded it in equal measure. And there was no use or need to ask him why because he probably wouldn't have told anyone anyway.

We both knew that something dark must be waiting for us ahead, even if neither of us spoke it aloud.

And something told me that we weren't about to survive whatever lied ahead. Yet, we would both fight furiously and desperately to protect one another until there was nothing left.

That was the most painful truth.

That was the most *beautiful* truth.

That was our definition of love.

We continued forward, side by side—no one leading, no one following, just together. Our hands brushed once, then again, hesitation mingled with yearning, sparking in the small space between us.

On the third touch, I reached out deliberately, entwining my fingers with his, gripping tight.

He didn't pull away.

Neither did I.

Chapter Nineteen

REICH

Nael's bunker was buried deep in the woods, hidden beneath the wreckage of what once was a small city—now little more than a graveyard, or what the leaders liked to call their "military base." It was the kind of place you had to want to find. And even then, it wasn't enough.

You had to know how to survive once you did.

Layers of stone and rusted steel rose like barricades, more fortress than shelter—thick, impenetrable, and absolute. They didn't just keep the world out or the ENA from visiting often. They kept Nael in. Not that he seemed to mind. If anything, I think he preferred it that way.

This was no place for the careless or the curious. There was no space for either here. Only the sharpened edge of calculated paranoia—honed over years of watching the people he loved turn into bodies.

Nael didn't trust easily. Maybe he never did. And if he ever could, that part of him was long dead, buried beneath the concrete and iron bones of this place.

The path to his door wound through collapsed buildings and twisted scaffolding. Only a handful of us knew the route by memory—winding corridors, sensor traps masked as rubble, and coded steel doors that only responded to hands that knew exactly where to press.

And Sage... I could tell she had stepped into the space like she was waiting for it to bite.

She shifted beside me, arms crossed tightly over her chest, fingers digging into opposite elbows like she was barely holding herself together.

When we finally entered, her eyes swept the room—slow and calculating. I watched her closely as she took in the low ceiling, the concrete walls, the steel beams ribbing the structure like a cage. The air was thick with something like a metallic bite—burned wiring, old steel, and beneath it, something unexpectedly sweet. Nael's incense, probably. But just a whisper of it, tangled with the dry, papery scent of books I imagined were stacked in uneven towers against the walls.

Sage didn't like it here. That much was obvious. She hadn't relaxed since we walked in. Her shoulders were locked, her weight balanced on the balls of her feet like she was ready to bolt—or maybe, fight. It was subtle, but I knew Sage. This place scratched at something buried in her. Something that didn't do well boxed in.

Nael watched her from where he was propped against the edge of his desk. His arms were crossed, posture easy, but it was a mask.

He was measuring her—every movement, every breath, every flick of her eyes. We both did it, but he was better. More exact and clinical. His face gave away nothing.

It was a hell of a talent, and I still couldn't decide whether I envied him for it... or pitied him.

"Still breathing, I see," Nael said at last, his voice slicing through the silence like the slow drag of a blade over stone.

I lifted a brow. "Not for lack of trying," I answered, dryly.

His mouth twitched—*almost a smirk, almost a smile*—but it didn't touch his eyes. Those stayed cold.

"And her?" His gaze slid to Sage. "Still in one piece?"

Sage's chin lifted, spine snapping straight like he had flipped some invisible switch. "You could ask me directly you know," she said, giving him a skeptical glare.

Nael exhaled through his nose—a sound more dismissive than amused. "I could," he said. "But I didn't."

Her jaw locked. Hands flexed where they were crossed, nails pressing into the coat. She was holding back. I could feel it—that sharp edge of restraint. She wanted to say something back.

But she didn't.

Nael watched her the entire time, gaze unblinking, dissecting her reactions like he was tallying them in some private, silent ledger.

She didn't like him.

And I could tell the feeling was mutual.

Nael never trusted anyone who hadn't bled for him—or stood beside him. And Sage... she was a variable. A wild card. Unpredictable in all the ways that made him uneasy.

"Go," Nael said to her, quieter now but no less commanding, waving a hand toward the hallway. "We have things to discuss. I don't need you here interfering."

She didn't move right away. I felt her hesitation in the breath she held, in the way her weight shifted subtly toward me—like she was asking without asking whether she should listen to him or stay. Her eyes flicked to mine, searching for something. Assurance. A reason not to leave.

But I didn't have it. Not when I didn't even know what Nael was about to say. Not when I was already bracing for something I wasn't sure I was even prepared to hear.

"It's better if you do." I finally spoke.

"Down the hall and to the left." Nael chimed in.

A little bit of hurt crossed her features but she didn't let that dictate her actions.

Her glare lingered—burning in Nael's direction a second longer, in a way that was sharp and defiant.

After a beat, she turned on her heel and disappeared down the hall. Silent. Controlled.

And even after she was gone, I could still feel her tension in the air. Like static clinging to the walls. Almost unshakable.

When the door to the next room clicked shut behind her, Nael finally pushed off the desk. His steel toed boots were soundless on the worn concrete as he crossed the room, a master at keeping his presence unknown, arms folded across his chest. He moved like he had already had this conversation with himself a dozen times already.

"She shouldn't be here," he said, flat and final.

"You don't trust her," I replied. Not a question.

He snorted quietly. "You know I don't trust anyone."

Fair enough.

I leaned back against the nearest wall, keeping my stance loose. There was no point posturing with Nael. He didn't care who looked tougher—only who was still standing when it was over.

"You said you'd heard things about the ENA." I finally said, shifting the focus from Sage's presence.

His expression shifted, darkening, as his mouth flattened into a thin, hard line.

"More than hearing," he said. "I've seen the movement myself. They're digging deeper into the bloodlines of the families—pulling up old names, old debts, even the ones they buried."

His gaze locked onto mine. Cold. Focused.

"They're looking for something. Or someone. That's why I was surprised when you called and brought them up."

His words landed like a stone in my gut. So, I told him everything. Or at least, everything I knew. Hoping he could make more sense of it than I could.

"They came by with this young boy. It wasn't routine—none of it felt normal. They wanted something from me. I didn't know what, but I could feel it." I paused, the memory still tight in my chest. "Cresil and Berith were there. I had to hide Sage in the closet just to keep her out of sight."

My voice dropped. "Nael... what could they possibly want from me? Do you think this is because we've been digging into the families? Do you think they're starting to realize we're the ones responsible for their disappearances?"

His silence was louder than anything else in the room. He watched me, jaw tight—until I saw it. The moment the decision clicked into place behind his eyes.

"I'm not sure," he said finally. "But it doesn't change the plan. We still need to find the remaining families. Even if they're starting to poke around, it's the only way to dismantle them completely. I don't know why it's the only way but that's what the letter from the previous rebellion said. And I trust it."

It came from his lineage. Nael's family had fought against the ENA undercover for decades. He had found it in a fireproof box hidden in his family's home under a staircase. A letter stating that the only way to dismantle the ENA was to eradicate the lines of seventy-two different families. They were apparently the silent puppeteer strings that held the whole thing together.

My train of thought was interrupted when Nael spoke again.

He continued, "But...I've been known to be wrong, so I'll still look into it."

And I believed him. Because Nael didn't make promises he didn't intend to keep. He didn't say it unless he meant to follow through.

For a long moment, neither of us spoke. The candle on his desk flickered in a phantom breeze, the flame bowing and steadying again.

Shadows stretched long and thin across the room, like they were listening.

I exhaled slowly. Then forced the words out before I could second guess them.

"Sage said something to me."

Nael lifted a brow. "She seems to say a lot of things."

I shot him a look, but he didn't flinch. Didn't care in the slightest.

"This was different," I said.

Now he was watching. Really watching. Something shifted behind his gaze—quiet and focused as he waited expectantly.

I ran my hand down my face, as I heard my pulse pounding behind my ears. "She said I looked different... before the ENA came and then after."

Nael didn't blink. "What do you mean?"

"They turned black." The words tasted bitter in my mouth. "She said my eyes..." I trailed off, shaking my head. "I don't know what she saw. But it wasn't normal. And it wasn't the first time she has mentioned it. I've had this burning sensation by my brand and it seems to happen during the times it burns."

Nael went still in the way he does when his thoughts are racing ahead of his body. When he was calculating. Stacking a thousand possibilities behind his eyes.

When he finally moved, it was slow and measured.

"That's not something you should ignore," he said. No fear. No surprise. Just quiet certainty.

"Have you ever had that happen to yours? Do you think it means something?" I asked, even though I already knew the answer.

"No, Reich. My brand hasn't burned since the day I got it, but I think I'll look into how that's possible." His voice was lower now, heavier—each word deliberate. "And I think you should hope I don't find anything."

I nodded once. It was all I could do.

IN REICH AND RUIN

Because we both knew—whatever he found, it wouldn't be good.

Chapter Twenty

SAGE

THE DOOR SLAMMED SHUT behind me with a sharp, echoing finality that made my teeth clench. The sound reverberated through my skull—a hard, hollow percussion that underscored Nael's dismissal that still rung in my ears.

The room was dim. Shadows sprawled across rough stone walls, stretching long in the soft amber glow of a bedside lamp, its bulb flickered weakly from its perch on a warped nightstand. The light did nothing to soften the weight pressing down on my chest. If anything, it made it worse—like I was being watched, judged, by the dying pulse of that tired little bulb.

I stood frozen, the silence on this side of the bunker thick and suffocating. Only my breathing seemed to break it, though it came out rough and uneven.

I exhaled, trying to steady the tightness in my chest. My hands came up to my temples, as if that could quiet the irritation still crawling under my skin. But Nael's words lingered, heavier than I wanted to admit. They replayed in my mind, each repetition cutting a little deeper.

I'd expected some hesitation. I thought I'd prepared myself for it. But the look in his eyes—cold, certain, like I didn't belong—hit harder than I was ready for.

He didn't know me, but his dismissal still hurt. It made me feel smaller, like my voice didn't matter.

A faint sound rustled behind me and drew a flinch I couldn't hide. My body snapped tight, instincts screaming to brace for the worst as the door clicked shut. Even though I knew who it was the moment his scent came trailing in.

"You handled that well," Reich's voice broke through the silence—dark, smooth, and soaked in amusement that leaned more toward sarcasm than comfort.

He was mocking me. I could tell.

I turned slowly, finding him already making his way toward the battered bed. He sprawled across it like he had nowhere else to be, settling in with one arm tucked behind his head and the other draped loosely over his stomach.

When his gaze met mine, it held. Hazel-green eyes with flecks of gold, catching the light like molten metal. And that smirk—just a hint of it—curled at the corner of his mouth. The kind that made it impossible to tell if he was amused by me... or by the dilapidated space we were now occupying.

Probably both.

He leaned back and started to undress. Completely relaxed, as if he hadn't just dismissed me a few minutes ago.

I crossed my arms, more out of habit than need, and frowned. "Don't start."

Reich sat up slowly, stretching his arms over his head before dragging both hands through his dark hair. The ink along his ribs shifted with the motion, drawing my gaze even when I didn't want to look.

"I'm just saying," he drawled, voice laced with that lazy, infuriating calm. "Storming off like that? Not fighting back? Wasn't your best moment, wildflower."

Heat flared behind my eyes, but I forced it down. "Yeah? Well, it wasn't Nael's either when he sat there treating me like I was some kind of enemy."

Reich sighed and pushed off the bed with slow, predatory ease. He moved toward me in unhurried steps, bare feet silent on the cold stone.

"Sorry about Nael," he said finally, voice lower now. Softer. But not gentle.

His lips twitched. "He can be—"

"Rude?" I cut in, arms folding tighter across my chest.

"Protective," he corrected smoothly, like he'd already made peace with Nael's sharp edges long ago. Like he understood him in ways I never would.

And he probably did.

I shook my head, frustration bubbling under my skin—at Nael, at Reich, at myself.

I thought back to the first time I met Nael.

He was the first face I saw after I'd been taken, hovering over that ice box Klay and his brother stuffed me in. I remember how I warned Nael, how I signaled that Hugh was about to strike from behind.

He thanked me then.

You'd think that would've meant something.

That maybe I'd earned a fraction of his trust.

Apparently not.

I paused before speaking again, reminding Reich, "You'd think after what I did for him with Hugh—back when I was kidnapped—he'd have a little more faith. He was a stranger, and I could've just let Hugh gut him from behind. So why doesn't he trust me now?"

Reich was close now. *Too close.* I could feel the heat radiating off his skin, see the faint sheen of sweat on his collarbone. His gaze softened—just a little. Barely enough to notice, but enough to feel.

"He will," Reich said. "Eventually."

"Eventually," I echoed softly.

His jaw flexed. Something unreadable flickered in his eyes before he exhaled slowly through his nose.

"He's just—" Reich stopped, like the words cost him. I watched the effort. "He's had a rough past. Worse than mine and Castor's. Worse than Keenan's. What he's been through... it changes people."

I swallowed hard, the familiar press of guilt tightening beneath my ribs. It wasn't new, that feeling—it always showed up when I started to forget that pain doesn't look the same on everyone.

It made me realize something.

I didn't have the right to judge how someone else carried their scars when mine still woke me in the dark.

So why was I doing that with Nael?

"You're right," I said softly. "We all carry things. And it's not fair for me to decide how someone else copes."

He studied me for a moment, eyes tracing my face like he was searching for something just out of reach. Then his mouth curved—slow, deliberate. Not smug this time. Warmer. It wasn't a smile meant to end the conversation; it was one that pulled me in deeper.

The air between us shifted, thick with everything we didn't say. Understanding. Unspoken guilt. The kind of quiet that hummed like static, familiar and electric all at once.

I sighed, the last of the fight seeping out of me. "Thank you."

"For?" he asked, though the shift in his expression said he already knew. His smirk deepened, expectant—waiting for me to feed his ego.

I rolled my eyes but gave in anyway. "For reminding me to see things differently... You always do that."

His smirk softened, the sharp edge of it fading. Then, with a surprising gentleness, he reached up and tucked a loose strand of hair behind my ear. His touch lingered on me, warm and unhurried, before he pressed a slow, lingering kiss to my forehead.

His lips were warm. Steady. Almost anchoring.

"Someone has to keep you from being an insufferable know-it-all, wildflower" he murmured against my skin.

I let out a soft, breathy laugh, but my chest tightened strangely, like his touch was stitching something closed that had been bleeding too long.

Then his hand slid to my waist, fingers curling lightly as he guided me toward the bed. He lowered us both with quiet purpose.

And when his mouth found mine, the kiss was slow. Intentional. Not demanding this time but claiming, like he was tasting me and had all the time in the world to savor it.

When I opened my eyes again, I caught a glimpse of our reflection in a mirror hanging directly overhead, something Nael had clearly placed there. Probably another way he 'coped', I thought to myself.

A flush of heat rushed to my cheeks, and before I could stop it, laughter bubbled up in my throat and slipped free, shattering the moment in the softest way.

Reich pulled back slightly, one brow arched. "What's so funny?"

I pointed upward, watching his expression shift as his gaze followed mine to the mirror. The sharpness in his eyes softened, touched with amusement.

"I've never seen myself like that before," I said, grinning. "In a mirror, I mean—while being in this position. It's kind of… fun."

Reich chuckled, low and deep, the sound rumbling through his chest. "Nael has some… interesting design choices for his guest room."

"That's one way to put it," I said, biting back a smile. "Can't tell if it's a creative decision or a warning—like he's watching his guests at all times."

His smirk darkened, a slow curl that hinted at something wicked. "Oh, Nael has an imagination. You'd be surprised how many mirrors he's got in this place. No clue what the fuck they're all for, and every time I ask, he just says, 'testing boundaries.'"

"So he clearly likes to look at himself," I said. "It's a little cocky, but kind of inspiring too. At least he's not afraid of his own reflection."

His fingers drifted down my arm—slow, deliberate—leaving goosebumps in their wake. I stilled, my breath catching as his voice dropped lower, velvety and dangerous.

"Tell me..." he murmured, his thumb tracing the flutter of my pulse. "Do you feel *inspired* to *test boundaries*?"

My pulse jumped. I drew in a sharp breath, anticipation curling tight in my stomach.

"I think so," I whispered.

His fingers tilted my chin until our eyes had no choice but to meet and stay there locked and steady.

"Good... girl."

I barely registered his reply and movement before his hand was at the back of my neck, pulling me into a kiss that left no room for hesitation. It stole my breath, dizzying and hot, as heat bloomed low in my stomach.

Then—out of the corner of my eye—I saw the door.

Still open.

I pulled back, gasping. "You should probably close that," I managed, my voice shaking.

Reich turned his head, following my gaze. His smirk sharpened—slow, wicked. "You giving the orders now?" he asked, amusement curling at the edges of every word.

I lifted a brow. "Just a suggestion."

He chuckled, low and dangerous, then pushed off the bed in that smooth, predatory way he moved when he wanted me to watch. He crossed the room and clicked the door shut—slow, deliberate, like sealing a deal.

I started to follow, sneaking up behind him—but never made it.

His hands were on me as soon as the latch barely clicked.

My back hit the wall, breath knocked from my lungs as he pressed against me—solid heat, burning through skin. His lips brushed the side of my throat, feather-light, yet loaded with threat.

Or promise. I wasn't sure which.

Maybe both.

"Sneaky wildflower," he murmured, voice smooth—too smooth. The air between us thickened, heavy with want, as his fingers toyed with the hem of my shirt.

"You know…" Reich's head tilted toward the adjoining wall, his tone dark and amused. "Nael's right on the other side of this wall." His voice dipped, almost a whisper. "And he's a light sleeper."

A shiver danced down my spine, shame and excitement tangling in a rush low in my belly. I knew what he was doing.

Worse—*I liked it.*

"Please, Reich," I whispered.

His hand stilled against my side. His eyes flickered—something unreadable passing through them—then his grip tightened. Just for a second. Enough to make me ache.

Then he laughed, soft and dark.

"Please what?" he asked, dragging his fingers up my ribs, slow and torturous. "Please stop?" His mouth brushed my ear. "Or please *don't*?"

I bit the inside of my cheek, refusing to give him the satisfaction of an answer. But it didn't matter.

Because even then, a soft whimper slipped past my lips—barely audible.

And his grip only tightened.

Reich hummed. "You always beg so pretty," he murmured, his voice slipping into something softer, something more dangerous. "Even when you don't know what you're begging for."

"Reich—"

His mouth claimed mine before I could finish.

I should have stopped him. I should have reminded him that Nael was just on the other side of this wall and that made this reckless and desperate.

But I didn't and I wouldn't.

His fingers dug into my hips, pulling me against him, and I could feel the restraint in the way his muscles tensed beneath my touch—like he was holding himself back and waiting for me to push him over the edge.

Like he knew I would.

And God, I wanted to.

I lifted onto my toes, pressing my lips to his ear, my voice barely more than a breath.

"We shouldn't—"

Reich's breath stuttered, his hold on me only growing tighter.

"Stay quiet," He warned, his hand over my mouth, his voice a rough whisper against my throat. "You understand how to be quiet for me... right, wildflower?"

I nodded, already breathless.

We were in Nael's bunker, tucked away in one of the back rooms. The thin walls did nothing to muffle sound, and Nael was in the next room, no doubt listening for any hint of betrayal. But that wasn't why Reich's hand was over my mouth.

It was control.

His control.

And I gave it to him willingly.

His free hand slid beneath my shirt, slow and deliberate, fingertips gliding over ribs that still ached from old wounds. His touch was softer than I expected—deceptively tender, given the sharpness in his gaze. A moan slipped free before I could stop it.

"Quiet," he playfully said as he sank to his knees in front of me.

I pressed my mouth to his palm as he dragged my pants down my legs, his lips following the motion—hot breath skimming over sensitive

skin. His tongue found me with unerring precision, with slow, taunting strokes across my body, as his grip sat firm on my thigh—holding me open and still.

I whimpered into his hand as he chuckled darkly against me.

Then I felt his mouth and thoughts ceased to exist. My hips jerked, instinctive, but his hands pinned me in place, his mouth relentless until I was trembling, knees going weak and shaking beneath me.

The release came hard with the cry of his name swallowed into the palm covering my mouth.

I was broken and breathless.

He rose slowly, licking his lips like he'd tasted something sinful—*something he wasn't done with*. His hand finally left my mouth, but before I could speak, he spun me around, pressing me into the wall with a gentleness that betrayed the hard, unyielding line of his body behind me.

His lips brushed my ear. "No sounds," he breathed. "Or I'll stop."

A quiet moan escaped me—soft, pleading—but it was swallowed by the harshness of my own breathing.

He turned me, guiding my back to him, fingers twisting into my hair and pulling my head back as he pushed into me from behind—slow, deep and unforgiving.

I gasped. He didn't stop.

His hand found my mouth again, silencing the broken sounds I couldn't control. Without it, I knew I'd fail.

"I can feel you trying," he whispered, voice molten at my ear. "I can feel how badly you want to scream."

The pressure built fast, sharp and unbearable. I clenched around him, unraveling with each relentless stroke. His teeth found the curve of my neck, biting just hard enough to shatter me.

I cried out—in broken bits of muffled silence, against his hand—as I came completely undone and trembling.

For a moment, we didn't move.

His breath was harsh in my ear, lips brushing my skin in something that was almost... tender.

Almost a *kiss*.

"You're mine," he said. "Even here. Even now."

And I believed him.

Chapter Twenty-One

REICH

The room was dark. Darker than it should be.

Shadows collected in the corners like they were watching. Pressing in around the edges, heavy and silent. The candle on the nightstand burned low, its flame swaying with every faint draft that slipped through the cracked mortar of the stone walls. Each flicker casted golden light across the sheets in slow, fractured waves.

It was dim and *dying*.

And yet it held the space between us like a fragile barrier against something I couldn't quite seem to name.

The only real warmth came from Sage.

She was pressed against me, soft and steady, her skin warm where it touched mine. I felt her breath on my chest—light, even—ghosting over me like a promise. Like a prayer I had no right to make but kept whispering anyway.

For now—*for this moment*—we were safe.

But I knew better than to trust it.

Because something was *wrong* with me.

It started as a whisper.

A shiver that crawled up the back of my neck, raising goosebumps like a warning I was already too late to catch. It slithered down my spine, a cold, thin coil winding tight at the base of my skull before settling like a knot in my gut.

I went still.

Listening.

Feeling.

The wrongness bloomed slowly. A familiar pull beneath the surface of my skin—deeper than muscle, deeper than the bone.

My mark.

My *damn* mark.

It was always there. Always humming beneath the surface like a second heartbeat I learned to live with. Learned to ignore. Learned to forget.

But not now.

Now, it was hurting again and again.

And getting worse and worse.

I held my breath, every muscle drawn tight. Willing myself not to move too fast. Not to wake her.

But my heart pounded—fast and heavy—each beat crashing against my ribs. I exhaled through my nose and shifted carefully onto my side, easing my arm out from where it rested across Sage's waist. She made a faint sound in her sleep—soft and instinctive—but didn't wake.

The pain sharpened as I moved. Not agony. Not yet. Just a slow, deliberate burn—like an ember buried under the skin waiting to expand and overtake everything.

And I knew better than to ignore it.

This wasn't pain that stayed quiet.

This was a warning.

A promise of something worse.

My fingers rose almost without thought, reaching for the back of my neck. I traced the jagged edges of the mark branded there. The skin was hot. Too hot.

Like something was simmering beneath it.

I pressed in, testing—

And that's when I felt it.

A faint pulse. Rhythmic. Alive.

And then, as I pulled my hand away, I saw it.

A drop of blood.

It slid down my wrist in a slow, deliberate path from where my fingers touched the mark. Crimson against my skin, gleaming in the faint, broken light.

It shouldn't be there.

My stomach knotted hard, a coil of instinct and dread that twisted until I felt sick. This wasn't normal. This wasn't right. Nothing about this was *right*.

I carefully pushed myself up completely, moving slowly to keep silent, the sheets slipping away from my legs like silk. Sage shifted in her sleep, murmuring something too soft to catch, her body turning toward the space I had left behind. My breath caught. I wanted to stay there. To anchor myself to her warmth, to that quiet steadiness she offered without even trying.

But I couldn't.

Not right now.

I stood, cold air biting against my skin, as I crossed the room on bare feet, attempting to stay as silent as a shadow. The mirror waited on the far wall, tall and cracked along one side, its silvered surface dull in the flicker of candlelight. My reflection met me there, ghost-like in the gloom. The same face. The same hollow and haunted eyes. The same faint scar cutting across my jaw. I didn't recognize myself most days, but tonight... tonight it was worse.

And then as I turned, I glanced back and saw the mark.

Something inside me knew.

This was a warning.

A call.

And I already knew who was calling.

The ENA. Their leash. Their chains. Even after everything, they still knew how to tighten them. It was getting worse. The blood was thick on my wrist now, smeared across my fingers from where I tried to wipe it away. I closed my hand into a fist. I pressed my palm over the mark, pressing it in, breathing through the burn, the pull, the fucking summons.

It didn't matter.

Didn't make any bit of difference.

I turned, eyes dragging back to the bed, to see her.

Sage.

Tangled in the sheets looking like temptation itself with her golden skin that caught the faint glow of the candlelight. She looked untouched by the things gnawing at the edges of my sanity. Untouched by the rot that followed me everywhere I went.

Safe. *For now.*

And I couldn't lose that.

I wouldn't.

The darkness at the edges of my mind could wait.

The ENA could wait.

Hell could wait.

An idea came to mind, a hidden room under the bunker that I knew about in Nael's place and I realized that tonight, I needed and craved something else.

Anything to quell this fire in my mind.

And Sage had always been that.

Even when I didn't deserve her.

Especially then.

I wiped the blood away with the back of my hand, my skin streaked red, but I didn't care. I moved back to the bed, each step measured. Quiet. My shadow falling over her before I could stop it. She stirred, her brow creasing faintly, lashes fluttering as her awareness pulled her up out of sleep. Her head turned, just a little, and then her eyes opened.

"Reich?" Her voice was soft, thick with sleep, husky in a way that made me ache at the pressure increasing inside me. She blinked at me, pupils dilated, trying to focus. She knew something was wrong. She always did. She could read me too easily. But I fought myself to not give anything away.

I reached out, brushing my fingers over her cheek, and felt her lean into the touch. I knew she could see it in my eyes. The fear. The burn of whatever was clawing at me. But she didn't pull away.

"Come with me," I said, my voice low. Rough.

Her brows knit, worry flickering in her gaze. "What's wrong?" she asked, her hand lifting to cover mine on her cheek.

"Nothing that matters right now." I lowered my head and pressed my lips to her temple, holding there for a second longer than I should. "I need you... *Again.*"

That was all I gave her. It was all I had.

But it was enough.

It always was.

Because she never hesitated. She never made me ask twice.

My wildflower obeyed.

She sat up slowly, the sheet falling from her body, baring skin that should distract me, but it didn't. Not yet. She didn't ask more questions. Didn't try to pull answers out of me I wasn't ready to give.

She just took my hand.

And followed.

Chapter Twenty-Two

SAGE

I'D NEVER SEEN HIM like this. Not even close.

He woke me with barely any words, fingers brushing my shoulder with a kind of urgency that didn't match the softness of the gesture. We'd just been together—his skin still warm, breath still lingering against mine—and yet, he said he needed me again.

And I'd be lying if I said I didn't need him whenever he wanted me.

I didn't ask what was wrong. I didn't need to.

There was fear in his eyes.

Real, quiet fear.

The kind I knew sat behind his mind, hollowing him out from the inside.

So, I followed and stayed quiet too as he brought me to another room.

A dimly lit space... with not much in there, except a circle of candles... it reminded me of an emptied-out version of Reich's old basement back in Providence, but smaller and more closed in.

Memories came back of when I was last there... years ago when he and Castor took me from the House of Music.

I'd be lying if I said that fear also didn't creep up every once and awhile.

But the difference was that I trusted him now. Completely.

I watched as he lit the candles, each movement deliberate, almost sacred. The match rasped against the box, sharp in the stillness, and the sound clawed through the silence like it was scraping something buried. The flame caught fast, casting golden flickers across his face—his jaw, his cheeks, the crease between his brows that hadn't eased once since he touched me.

It should've felt foreign.

Because it was.

I'd never seen him do anything like this before.

The candles—the way he carefully adjusted them in a perfect circle surrounding him, like each one carried a weight only he understood. Like the spacing mattered. Like the order mattered.

He didn't explain and I didn't ask.

But something about it pulled tight across my ribs, a tension I couldn't name.

I didn't know what this was. Not really.

But watching him—silent, focused, holding himself like he might come apart if he moved too fast—I couldn't shake the feeling that I wasn't meant to see this. That it was private. Sacred. Or maybe even dangerous.

I didn't have the words for it.

Just a feeling.

It felt like a ritual.

Like it belonged to something ancient. Heavy. Buried deeper inside of him than words could reach—woven into the silence he never let me touch.

Maybe it was the ENA.

Maybe it was just Reich, trying to hold himself together with fire and intention.

Whatever it was, it wasn't about power.

It didn't feel like penance.

It felt like *survival*.

Like he was lighting those candles just to keep from unraveling. Like if he didn't, something inside him would break wide open—and I'd see every jagged piece he was trying to keep hidden.

He didn't speak. Just moved with sharp precision, every breath measured like he was afraid of what would come out if he let them slip. One, two, three. Inhale. Hold. Exhale. But nothing settled in him—not really. His hands were steady until they weren't, trembling when they retreated from the flames. His shoulders were drawn too high.

And still, I didn't ask.

I just watched. Stayed.

Gave him whatever silence he needed.

Even if every part of me longed for him to let me in.

When the flames caught, I caught something else in him.

A flicker.

More Fear? Anger this time?

I wasn't sure.

The light bled over him as he knelt there, bare from the waist up, the long lines of his body carved with old scars that the candlelight found and traced. His skin gleamed with a thin sheen of sweat, and the rise and fall of his chest wasn't nearly as calm as he probably thought it was. The shadows slid over him, pooling in the hollows of his body, making him look ancient. Feral. Untouched by mercy.

It made me forget how to breathe.

For a moment, I couldn't move. Couldn't think.

And then I saw it—the way his hands curled into fists at his sides, his knuckles white, shaking like he wanted to hit something or someone, like he needed to let go.

It all made sense to me then.

He wasn't just setting up a scene. He wasn't indulging in ritual for pleasure or control.

He was trying to forget. Trying not to feel something that was clawing at him from the inside out.

Or maybe... trying to keep it from feeling him.

When he turned toward me, I froze.

The look he gave me was hooded, guarded, the kind of look that hid too much and revealed everything all at once. His gaze raked over me, slow and heavy, dragging shivers across my skin. And there was hunger there, yes—but not the kind that could be sated with simple desire.

It was darker and *deeper*.

It was need sharpened into something *dangerous*.

"I know I brought you here, but you don't have to do this," he said, his voice low, rough, like it was being dragged out of him against his will. His throat worked around the words like they hurt to say. "I need to feel something... feel something I can control."

I didn't hesitate. I didn't need to. I stepped toward him, as if closing the distance between us was the only thing anchoring me to this moment. I slid my top from my shoulders, letting it fall in a whisper of silk to the hard stone beneath my feet.

"I want to feel something too," I said, my voice steady despite the shaking in my legs. "With you."

The air was cold, but his stare was colder.

And yet, it burned.

A muscle ticked in his jaw, and for a long moment, I thought he might change his mind. Might shove me back and dismiss me. Putting distance between us. He was good at that.

But he didn't.

He nodded once, short and sharp, swallowing hard like the word stuck in his throat.

"Safe word," he said.

"*Wildflower*," I whispered, knowing the significance wouldn't be lost on him.

Something changed in his expression. Not softness. Nothing so simple. It was satisfaction. His smile was sharp, almost cruel, a twist of his lips that cut something inside me wide open.

"Good girl," he murmured.

The words curled down my spine, heat coiling low in my stomach. I shivered, not just from anticipation. From something else. Something I didn't have a name for yet.

He guided me to the center of the circle he'd made with the candles, his hands careful, but not gentle. Like he was handling something volatile and dangerous all at once. The stone was cold beneath me, grounding and unyielding. But it wasn't enough to dull the weight of the moment—or the sound of my heartbeat pounding in my ears as he positioned me where he wanted me, knees spread, hands behind my back.

"You tell me if it's too much," he said, but his voice was distant. Like he wasn't fully here.

"It won't be," I promised.

But deep down, I wasn't sure this was about me at all.

And that terrified me.

And *thrilled* me.

He picked up the first candle, the wax already melted at the edges, thick and glistening, threatening to fall. His eyes found mine before he tilted it.

That look was a question.

And an *answer*.

"Breathe," he told me.

I did. Inhale. Exhale. Slow. Just like him as he intimately guided me.

Then he let the wax fall.

The first drop landed just below my collarbone. White-hot. A warm sting that hit through me, making me jolt. My breath caught, and pain bloomed, but then it dulled, seeping into something that made my stomach twist in ways I was starting to crave.

"That's it," he murmured, his voice smoothing out as if he was breathing easier now. Like this... this was what pulled him back from the edge.

Kept him distracted.

He worked methodically. Tilting the candle to let the wax drip in deliberate patterns across my skin. Lines and drops that stung, burned, marked. He painted me with pain and precision, and I could feel it—him shifting with every drop. Every gasp that left my lips seemed to soothe something wild and thrashing inside him.

This wasn't a game.

It wasn't even play.

This was prayer.

Or ritual.

I wasn't sure which.

I just lifted my chin and gave him what he needed.

My surrender.

"More," I said, voice thick with something close to begging. "Please."

That word did something to him.

And I watched as his mouth curved, but there was no amusement in it. Only reverence. Like I'd just handed him a blade and asked him to cut me open.

"Always begging so pretty," he murmured. "Even for pain."

And he gave me *everything*.

The wax trailed over my stomach, pooling in my navel, sliding in slow, molten rivers down my thighs. I was throbbing, my body vibrating with the rhythm of his breathing, his hands, his control. And when he tilted the candle again, letting the wax fall between my legs, the sting was a punch that left me moaning, raw and desperate.

He set the candle down, hands finding my legs, spreading me wider as if he needed to see the ruin he'd made. His fingers were gentle, tracing the cooling wax, peeling it away with slow precision.

"You're shaking," he said quietly.

When he leaned in, his mouth was soft where the wax had been cruel. His tongue flicked over tender skin, soothing and tasting, then biting. And when I felt myself between his lips, I nearly screamed.

I was trembling under him as his hands held me steady, stripping me bare.

He pulled me into his lap, holding me close, his heart pounding so hard I felt it through his ribs.

Like he was running or maybe *hiding*.

"More?" he asked once again, his voice hoarse, frayed around the edges.

I nodded. "Yes."

He laid me down gently, covering me with his body like a shield. Lining himself up and sliding inside me slow with an unforgiving depth. His forehead pressed to mine as he held still, just breathing. In. Out. Again.

"You're everything," he said after a long moment. "Everything I shouldn't have and everything I won't give up."

And then he moved.

Slow. Deep. Measured.

Like it was the only thing keeping him alive.

I let him have me.

Because maybe a part of me needed to forget something too.

And maybe, just for now, we could lose ourselves together.

Chapter Twenty-Three

REICH

I took Sage back to our room later that night—completely spent after everything we'd just let ourselves indulge in. There was an intensity between us that felt new, even for us. Even though it felt like we were indulging every chance we got.

We stayed there lying next to each other, closer than ever.

She understood what I needed.

Understood what I craved.

And I loved her for that.

When I slipped out that morning, easing the door shut behind me, Nael was already waiting.

He was leaned against the far wall of the hall, one shoulder pressed to the concrete, arms crossed in that deliberate way that said he'd been here a while—long enough to get bored. One brow arched, the faintest smirk playing at his mouth like he'd been stockpiling sarcastic commentary just for this moment.

From the glint in his eye, he was ready to let it fly.

"You know..." he started, voice pitched low, that familiar thread of dry humor slicing clean through, "...this bunker isn't soundproof."

I sighed, dragging a hand down my face like I could tear off the secondhand shame. "Nael... don't."

But mercy wasn't in his wiring.

"And here I thought I kept the guest room mirror for my own entertainment," he went on, tone still flat but his grin cutting in sharp as glass. "Didn't realize it'd be the backdrop for a Davidian brother and his girlfriend acting out ... *all night*.... while I'm trying to *sleep*."

I shot him a flat look meant to warn him off. But there was a traitorous twitch at the corner of my mouth I couldn't quite kill.

Nael chuckled under his breath, quiet and low, peeling off the wall with the slow ease of someone who was rarely surprised.

"You done?" I asked—more out of routine than hope.

He shrugged, loose and lazy, like the weight of the world hadn't been riding his shoulders for weeks. "For now... Not like I don't have more important things to think about."

And just like that, the humor drained from his face like it was never there. What was left in its place was brittle and sharp. The air between us tightened, drawn taut by something unspoken.

My gut knotted. Instinct already bracing for the thing he hadn't said yet, but I chose to ask something more pressing.

"Have you heard anything from Cas?" My voice came out quieter than I meant it to, but I didn't bother repeating myself.

Nael's mouth pulled into something that wasn't quite a grimace but there was confusion sparked there, wondering why I was asking. "No... Not a word. Why do you ask?" He finally said.

"I spoke with Keenan a couple of days ago and he hadn't heard from him... neither have I. Cas and I were supposed to meet before I changed course here and I haven't been able to reach him."

The knot in my spine coiled tighter. The silence was heavy—*too heavy*—and in my gut I knew Cas wasn't the type to go dark without a reason.

Nael seemed to catch where my mind was already spiraling, cutting in he said, "I'll have Keenan head to Castor's bunker, if he hasn't already. He'll check in when he gets there."

His voice sharpened, the kind of razor-edge tone that silences arguments before they're made. "Until we hear something, you and Sage should stay here."

I nodded, but the agreement tasted like ash in my mouth. Staying put had never been my strong suit—especially not when someone I cared about might be bleeding out in places I couldn't reach.

Nael watched me like he was already expecting the fight and was bracing for the inevitable pushback.

But before I could speak, the door behind me creaked open.

My head turned on instinct.

Sage stepped out, rubbing sleep from her eyes, one hand braced against the frame as she blinked into the low hallway light. Her hair was a mess of dark waves around her face, her expression soft with that lingering haze of sleep. She was still half in dreams, but her gaze was steady when it landed on Nael.

And Nael... his expression shifted—subtle and fast, but I caught it.

The slight narrowing of his eyes. The twitch in his jaw. The flicker of calculation.

He was guarded. Always is around people he doesn't fully trust. But I knew it wasn't suspicion.

It was *survival*.

He would never say as much, but I could read it in the tight set of his shoulders.

Sage was the unknown. The variable he still didn't like in his orbit but was tolerating on behalf of me.

She stepped forward anyway, calm and unbothered by the weight of his presence. Her spine straightened. Her eyes, now clear, met Nael's with something that looked like a mix between respect and quiet defiance.

"Morning," she said softly. There was a faint curve to her mouth—not naïve, not sweet. Measured. She knew exactly who she was addressing.

Nael nodded back, slow and stiff. Arms still crossed over his chest like armor he wouldn't lay down, as he remarked, "You sleep all right, noisy houseguest?"

The words landed flat—not cold, not warm. Just... cautious and I braced myself for Sage's response.

She leaned into the doorframe; one shoulder propped there like she belonged. "Better than you, apparently."

Nael didn't answer. Instead, his gaze narrowed slightly, reassessing her like she was a riddle he hadn't decided how to solve.

Sage noticed—but she didn't press. Instead, she turned to me. A glance. Silent, quick.

I nodded once.

Without a word, she slipped back inside, the door clicking shut behind her.

Nael exhaled slow through his nose—a deliberate release, like he was letting go of more than just air. "I can see she's trying...not very well...but I appreciate the effort," he said after a long pause, voice quieter now, like he was not entirely sure he wanted me to hear it.

I studied him for a beat. "So, why don't you try with her?"

His scowl was faint, but familiar. "You trust people too easily."

I raised a brow. "I trust you."

He huffed—somewhere between a laugh and a curse—shaking his head. "Exactly," he muttered. No bite behind it. Just worn-out resignation.

He ran a hand along the back of his neck, before tracing his face and dragging his fingers through the stubble at his jaw. "I'll try," he added, softer this time.

It wasn't much. But it was *something*.

So, I decided to press. "You know…she reminded me about Hugh. Back when we pulled her out of that hellhole. Three years ago. You were in bad shape, Nael—but she saw Hugh first. And she didn't hesitate. She made sure you knew he was there."

Nael's jaw tightened. I saw the memory hit him like a body blow—Klay bleeding out on the floor, Keenan's hands slick with blood from the brutal blow, all of us hanging by a thread.

And Sage? She could've stayed quiet. Let Hugh take him out from behind.

But she didn't.

She warned him even though he was nothing but a stranger in a mask.

"I know," he said finally, voice low.

The silence stretched longer this time, heavy and settled between us like dust in a room no one had breathed in for too long.

Nael shifted, eyes flicking towards the guest room door like he was expecting Sage to step out again. Or maybe hoping she wouldn't. "Lyla used to make me promise I wouldn't write people off before they had a chance to show me who they really were," he said at last, voice rough—like something worn down by time and memory. "And she turned out to be a liar."

I nodded. I already knew, not the full story, but enough. Lyla turned on him in a way that left scars deeper than most of us had names for. Nael didn't talk about her anymore. Not really.

And I didn't ask. None of us did.

So instead, I offered him something else, "You've had my back since day one. I never doubted you. Sage won't either."

He stared at me for a long moment before he nodded. Just once. "We'll see."

He said it like a challenge—like he was daring her to prove him wrong. And knowing Sage… *she would.*

Nael ran a hand through his hair, slow and tired, then pushed off the wall. "I'll check in with Keenan. If he finds anything out about Castor or if I do, you'll be the first to know."

"Thanks," I murmured, voice quieter now, the weight of everything catching up to me.

Nael turned and gave me one last look—something heavy in his eyes that I couldn't quite name—and then he was gone. Moving down the hall without a sound.

And I was left standing in the stillness, staring at the closed door of the guest room.

As I thought about Cas and what he might be doing right now. I wondered how much longer I could keep the people I cared about from slipping through my fingers.

Wondering if I ever really could.

Chapter Twenty-Four

SAGE

I SAT ON THE edge of the bed, fingers drifting over the stitching in the blanket beneath me. The fabric was uneven—worn thin in places, the threads pulled tight in others. Like it had been used too long and washed too little. There was a faint scent of smoke clinging to it. Subtle, but enough to make me wonder how much blood it probably had soaked up over the years.

The room was quiet. Too quiet. Just the low hum of the generator somewhere in the walls, and the occasional groan of Nael's bunker settling deeper into the foundation.

It should have felt peaceful. It should have felt safe.

But it didn't. Not for me. Not *here*.

I could still feel the weight of Nael's stare from earlier—the way his eyes held me like a blade balanced in his palm, judging whether I was worth the risk of drawing blood. Measuring me. And finding something inadequate.

I exhaled slowly through my nose and closed my eyes, pressing a thumb into the spot between my brows to dull the tension gathering there.

I told myself it didn't matter. That I didn't need Nael's approval. That this wasn't about being liked.

But I was lying. And I wasn't even good at it.

Because I loved Reich.

And if we had a future, then Nael was a guaranteed part of it. Just like Castor and just like Keenan.

They were Reich's family.

Which meant, in some way, they would hopefully be mine too.

Because despite the dangers, I wanted to belong in this world.

In *his* world.

Not just the parts that are easy, but the ones that were rough, jagged ... and dark. *Especially those.*

But Nael's walls were high. Built from years of damage and distrust.

And I didn't know if I'd ever be able to climb them.

Or if he'd ever let me try.

However, that really wasn't the only thing that was bothering me... it was this dream I had, after last night.

I couldn't make sense of it.

I just remembered that I didn't know where I was. I was surrounded by stone walls, a flickering torchlight in the distance, voices murmuring in a language I didn't recognize. The air was thick with the scent of incense and something old—almost ancient.

A small hand pressed against mine.

The warmth was familiar, but I didn't know who they were. I tried to turn, to look, but the moment I did—*crimson streaks of blood came pouring.*

Dripping from my palm. Pooling at my feet.

Then there was this voice, low and eerie, murmuring in my ear: "Blood recognizes blood."

What did it even mean?

I shrugged off the memory as the door clicked open, and I looked up as I was pulled from the tangled mess of my thoughts.

Reich stepped inside, closing it behind him with that deliberate kind of quiet he always carries—like he was bracing for something. Or someone.

The air shifted the moment he entered. It didn't fix anything. But it made it easier to breathe. Even if just a little.

He crossed the room in a few long strides, boots silent on the concrete, and dropped into the chair across from me. His elbows rested on his knees, fingers loosely laced like he was trying to look relaxed.

But his eyes were sharp and steady. Already reading me.

"You alright?" he asked, voice low—rough around the edges, smoke-drenched and steady in that way that always makes me feel like he's dragging the truth out of me before I'm ready to give it.

I lifted a shoulder. "I'm fine."

It was a weak avoidance.

We both knew it.

Reich tilted his head, that familiar look cutting into me like a scalpel—not to find what was broken, but to figure out how to fix it.

I sighed, dragging my fingers through my hair until my scalp ached. "I'm trying with Nael. But it's like slamming into a wall that punches back."

The frustration crept into my voice before I could rein it in.

I hated that I cared this much, and I hated more that it felt like I was failing.

Reich smirked faintly. Not mocking—just... knowing. There was an understanding in it, maybe even a flicker of something like sympathy.

"That's his default setting," he commented.

Like that was supposed to make me feel better.

"Yeah, well," I muttered, shaking my head, "...maybe he could tone it down a little. Not everything has to be war."

Reich's expression softened as he leaned forward, his elbows perched up on his thighs as if he was demonstrating how intently he was listening to me.

"He'll come around...eventually," he said.

I glanced at him, arching a brow. "Is that supposed to make me feel better?"

His smile flickered. Barely there. But it was.

"It should," he said.

And something about the way he said it made my chest ache.

Because he believed it.

"He doesn't not like you..." Reich added after a beat.

I gave him a flat look.

"Okay... let me rephrase..." he amended with a ghost of a laugh, "...he just doesn't trust easily... like most of us to be honest... but you already knew that."

I breathed out through my nose and leaned back, letting my head hit the wall with a quiet thunk.

"I want *this* to work," I said.

The words hung there between us, heavier than they should have been.

Reich tilted his head slightly. "What's '*this*'?"

Like he wasn't sure what I could possibly be talking about. Like he wanted me to draw the answer out for him.

I looked at him. Really looked.

"What's *this*?" I reiterated before I gave in. Just like I always do. "You... Me... *Us*..."

I kept my voice steady. Because if it cracked now, I wouldn't be able to hold it together.

For a long moment, he was silent.

That Reich silence.

Measured and careful. Like he was weighing the truth before he spoke it out loud.

Then he reached for me, his fingers curling around my wrist. Warm and steady. The kind of touch that felt like an anchor.

"It already does work," he said. Soft. Sure. Like it was the simplest thing in the world.

And maybe for him, it was.

But for me... For me, it was acceptance. So, it wasn't simple.

The silence between us shifted again.

And then he tugged me forward, guiding me until I was standing between his legs and his hands settled on my hips like they were molded to them.

"You need to get out of your head, wildflower..." he murmured, tilting my chin up to look at him, "...besides we've got other things to worry about."

I huffed a breath that was almost a laugh. "Like the fact that there's still a mirror above this bed?"

I jerked my pointer finger towards the ceiling.

Reich's grin flashed. Lazy. Wicked. "It's for his fantasies."

I wrinkled my nose. "Don't ruin it."

He laughed. Low and rough. It slid through me in a way it shouldn't. In a way I let it.

"You didn't seem to mind last night," he murmured.

I smiled but before I could fire something back at him—

He stiffened. All at once.

His breath caught and his hand flew up to the back of his neck like it was a reflex. Like he was trying to stop something from ripping out of him.

My pulse skipped hard. "Reich?"

He grimaced. His fingers pressing into the skin beneath his hairline, rubbing hard.

For a second—

Just a second—

His eyes flickered just like they did before.

Like they kept doing.

And then it was gone. Buried. Like it was never there.

But I saw it. And he knew I did.

"I know what you're thinking, Sage... it's nothing," he said, too quickly. Too smooth.

"Reich..." I leaned in closer. Firm and certain before continuing, "Don't tell me it's nothing."

He blew out a slow breath, jaw tight. "Nael and I are figuring it out."

"You're deflecting," I said flatly.

"I'm redirecting," he shot back.

But there was no heat in it. No tease.

"Reich." I tried to reach him again.

He stood slowly, towering over me in that way that's always made my chest twist.

His hands settled back on my hips. Casual. Possessive. Like he was trying to make it normal again.

"Whatever's happening to me," he said, voice lower now, "...it's not important right now."

"It's very important," I snapped.

"It's handled," he said and then he leaned in, and I couldn't help but cave.

Because when his mouth brushes mine, I forget how to be angry. And I forget how to be afraid.

Because it was always like this with him.

He gets close and I fall closer.

He kissed me like he was trying to steal something from my chest. And maybe he was. Maybe he has always been good at that. Stealing something from me.

My breath. My reason. The parts of me I swore I wouldn't give away again.

And I let him.

Because I wanted him to take it.

He walked us backward until the bed hit the back of my knees, and when I fell, he followed, his weight grounding me.

Pressing me into the moment like it was the only thing holding either of us together.

"You always give in too easy," he murmured against my skin and I huffed a shaky laugh responding, "You're lucky I do."

His teeth scraped my bottom lip before he bit down.

Just enough to make me gasp.

And just enough to make me *want*.

"I know," he breathed.

And for now, I got pulled under again.

Even though I knew something was coming.

Even though I could feel it in my bones.

Something not right with his eyes.

Something unknown. Something *dangerous*.

But somehow it didn't seem to matter, because right now all I felt was him.

Chapter Twenty-Five

REICH

The pain woke me first.

At first, I told myself it was a dream—another fragment of memory bleeding into my reality like smoke through broken glass. But then I felt it.

Sharp. Wrong.

A searing heat exploded at the base of my neck, flaring out in jagged streaks that ran like a wildfire through my veins. My breath jerked out of me as I rolled onto my side with teeth gritted. I pressed the heel of my hand to the mark as if I could force it back down.

It didn't help.

If anything, it got *worse*.

I pushed up from the bed, my pulse ragged in my ears, the weight of it building heavier in my skull. My hand fumbled behind my neck, fingers brushing the raw heat of the brand. The skin there was fever-hot, pulsing like it had its own heartbeat.

No.

This wasn't right.

It had never been like this before. Never made my vision blur at the edges.

I pressed my hand harder against it, jaw clenched so tight I could hear something almost crack. My whole body felt like it was twisting, like something inside me was beginning to shift or rise.

Something I didn't recognize.

Something I didn't *want* to recognize.

Then—*movement*.

Sage stirred beside me, her hand finding my arm first. She was warm and steady.

"Reich?" she murmured, sleep roughening her voice. She blinked slowly, and then all at once. She was awake, sitting up, tension bleeding out from her body.

Her eyes found me. She saw *everything*.

"What's wrong?" she asked, panic laced in her speech.

I tried to answer. I couldn't. My throat was tight, my chest aching. I shook my head, trying to pull in a breath that didn't burn on the way down.

She reached out, her fingers brushing lightly over the mark.

Pain spiked so fast, so violent, I jolted back with a strangled noise, a sound I didn't even know I was capable of making.

Her hand snapped back like she'd been burned, yet her voice stayed calm and concerned. "Reich—"

I forced myself to breathe, dragging my mind into place, stacking the panic into boxes I could deal with later.

Right now, there was only one thing I knew for sure.

I couldn't stay put. *We* couldn't stay put.

"We need to leave." I said.

Sage didn't move for half a second, like she was debating pushing back. She had always been like that—on edge when being told what without the why.

But this time, she just nodded. Quiet. Steady.

Because she trusted me.

IN REICH AND RUIN

And it felt like a sharp cut to my chest, knowing I didn't deserve it.

I moved through the room quickly, grabbing only what we needed. Extra rounds, rations, the map Nael marked for me three years ago that still had all the best exits out of his maze.

Sage followed without question, packing up her things without a word.

That silence was almost worse. *Almost.*

Because I knew her.

I knew how much she hated not asking questions. How much it killed her to stay quiet when I gave her nothing.

But she was doing it. *For me.*

I shoved the last of the gear into my pack, tightening the straps. My hands wouldn't stop shaking. Not from fear but from the instinct that something was wrong.

As if to prove me right, Nael appeared in the doorway.

Hair wet like he just showered, dressed in the same dark clothes he always wore, but his expression was different. Grim. Eyes sharp. Focused.

"You're up early," he said as he looked me over. "Or maybe you didn't sleep at all."

I glanced at him, my hand still gripping the pack strap. "We're leaving."

Nael's brows lowered. "What happened to staying here while we figure things out?"

I gave him a look, one that said I was doing this, regardless.

He didn't argue and maybe it was because he knew that we needed to or that he wouldn't be able to talk me out of it.

He spoke instead, "I was just about to wake you. Keenan called."

I stopped. "And?"

Nael stepped further inside, gaze flicking to Sage for a beat before returning to me.

"Castor's bunker was overturned. Completely."

I felt Sage stiffen next to me.

Nael kept going. "Keenan is finishing up his search but he said it looked deliberate. Like whoever did it wasn't looking for him but for *something*."

My chest tightened. "Does he know what?"

Nael's mouth flattened into a thin line. "Files. Notes. Castor was digging into something. Keenan found pages scattered across his bunker. He was onto something. Something to do with bloodlines and the Ovitts."

My jaw clenched. "He didn't tell me."

Nael's eyes narrowed. "He didn't tell any of us."

I exhaled slowly, dragging a hand down my face, but it didn't do much to ease the pressure behind my eyes.

"He must have been digging for me," I said.

Nael tilted his head, watching me.

"The Ovitts," I told him.

I saw Sage flinch from the corner of my eye as I mentioned that name.

Nael's expression shifted, cold calculation running behind his gaze. "I thought that was settled," he said. "We took care of the rest of them after—"

I let out a low, bitter breath. "We did... but I also thought I killed them before that."

Nael said nothing. He just waited.

"And I was wrong," I continued, voice flat. "Not just once... Five times."

The weight of it never left me.

Five men. Five *wrong* men. I wiped them from existence without question. Without hesitation because I was so sure.

"Cas was helping me track what went wrong," I said, jaw tight. "I couldn't get anywhere on my own. He said he'd keep looking."

Nael exhaled sharply through his nose. "And Castor never found anything?"

I shook my head once. "He told me he was coming up empty. That someone had erased every trace of them. I thought..." I trailed off, my hands curling into fists. "I thought he let it go after we went dry."

Nael's expression darkened. "Clearly, he didn't."

His tone sharpened. "I'll look into it when Keenan gets here. I didn't realize Castor was still chasing that thread."

"He was," I murmured. "And now he might be paying for it."

The burn at the back of my neck throbbed again like it knew something I didn't.

Sage stepped closer, resting her hand lightly on my arm. "Do you think... he found out something he wasn't supposed to?"

Nael answered for me. "We're not just dealing with a cult. We're dealing with a dynasty. Bloodlines that stretch back further than any of us can track. If Castor got close to something..."

"They took him," I finished, my voice cold.

Nael nodded once. "Or worse."

I gritted my teeth, shoving down the sudden, hot rush of anger that threatened to break through.

Castor wouldn't be sloppy.

He wouldn't disappear without a fight.

Unless someone had the power to erase him.

And if that was true...we needed to be ready.

We needed to get somewhere safe and neutral.

Keenan's.

Even though he was closest to the ENA compound, he had less monitoring around his premise because of it.

They didn't care about what happened near there because that's what the soldiers who patrolled that area were there for.

But I could manage them.

Better than I could here.

Because if they came here, there was no escape. We would be trapped in. So we had to go, it only made sense.

I shifted my attention to Sage.

"We leave now and stay at Keenan's until he gets back," I said.

She nodded.

No questions. Just trust. Again. And I wasn't not sure how to carry the weight of that.

But I knew one thing. I'm not losing anyone.

Not Castor. Not Sage. Not this time.

Chapter Twenty-Six

SAGE

THE URGENCY IN REICH'S voice unsettled me as we prepared to leave Nael's.

Not because I didn't trust him.

But because I'd heard that tone in his speech before—

And it never seemed to end without blood.

Still, I didn't question him. Not yet.

I just moved.

Because whatever had him on edge—whatever had made his voice tight and his body coil—wasn't something he was ready to explain.

And that terrified me more than anything he could say.

My fingers fumbled at my boot laces, clumsy in the rush. I wrenched them tighter, anyway, barely registering the sting where bruises still bloomed around my ankles from our last trek.

But pain didn't matter right now.

Survival did.

Finding out what happened to Castor and Sam did.

I shoved my foot into the other boot and snatched my jacket from the rusted chair.

"Where are we going?" I asked, trying to sound steady. To sound like I didn't notice the silence stretching between his breaths.

I didn't expect an answer.

But I needed something to fill the void he left me with.

The silence in his voice. The silence in his eyes.

Reich didn't go quiet like this unless something inside him was breaking.

And I knew he was about to snap.

He was strapping on his belt now, his fingers unsteady. The metallic clink of the buckles sounded too loud in the stillness.

I watched his hands as he continued to gather the knives he hadn't packed from the table—sliding them into place with practiced precision.

It should have comforted me, but it didn't.

His movements were fluid, sure— but there was something wrong.

Off in the rhythm of him.

Like he was falling into muscle memory just to keep from unraveling.

"Are you going to answer?" I asked.

His hands trembled again. He paused, flexing his fingers as if he could shake the tremor loose—then tightened the last strap with too much force. The leather creaked in protest.

I swallowed hard.

Still no answer.

But when he finally lifted his head, his gaze hit me—sharp and hollow like he was already halfway gone.

"Somewhere safe," he said at last, voice low.

"Safe?" I echoed, the word tasting foreign in my mouth.

I hesitated. I wanted more. I wanted answers.

But I already knew he wouldn't give me any.

But I wasn't going to let that stop me from trying.

"Reich—" My voice softened; a plea wrapped in his name. Hoping it might reach him.

Pull him back.

But he flinched. Just barely.

I saw it.

I *felt* it.

"We don't have time, Sage."

He said my name like a lifeline he was scared to break.

He grabbed my face in his hands as he spoke, "Just trust me, wildflower."

As if calling me by my nickname would quell the storm of questions inside of me.

I bit back my reply so hard it begged for release behind my teeth.

I wanted to scream. Demand to know what was going on.

But instead, I nodded.

Because I did trust him.

Even when I shouldn't. Even when his hand drifted to the base of his neck, fingers curling tight as a quick pass of pain crossed his face.

Telling me that whatever that was, it was getting worse and changing.

But not in ways he could control.

I shoved my arms into my jacket, ignoring the pull in my shoulder and the ache in my ribs. My body begged me to stop, to rest—but I didn't.

Because this was Reich.

And when he moved like this, I moved too.

The door creaked open as he stepped through first, knife hand low, body tense like he was already bracing for impact. His head tilted every few steps, listening for something I couldn't hear.

Something he expected.

I followed, close enough for the back of his jacket to brush my fingers every time he paused.

Outside, the cold hit sharper than it should. The wind carried something with it—something *different*.

The day was heavy. It swallowed sound. Even our footsteps felt muffled—like the earth didn't want to betray us or maybe like it had already been warned.

Reich's stride was long and focused. Every step looked deliberate, but his hand never left his blade.

And every few paces, he glanced back at me.

Not like he was checking pace.

But like he was making sure I was still there. Like he was afraid if he blinked, I wouldn't be.

I wanted to ask why.

Why now?

Why does he look like he's seen something he can't unsee?

Why does it feel like we're not running toward anything at all—just away?

But I didn't ask. Because I knew better.

Reich didn't run. He didn't walk away from a fight.

Not unless what was coming was the kind of thing even, he couldn't face head-on.

And if that's what this was—then maybe I should have been just as afraid too.

We kept moving. The path narrowed to cracked stone and twisted roots. The forest pressed closer, trees leaning in like they were listening. Like they were *waiting*.

Our breathing was too loud and beneath it, I could hear what seemed like the faint hum of Reich's mark. Somehow it felt like it was in my ears.

Pulsing. Slow. Steady. Like a warning bell buried in his skin.

And for the first time, I wondered— are we running toward something worse or are we already too late?

CHAPTER TWENTY-SEVEN

REICH

THE WIND RUSHED THROUGH the trees in a sharp and unforgiving way. The kind that hurts when debris catches your face.

It stirred the dust along the path in thin ribbons that twisted and scattered in the overcast light. They danced for a breath, then disappeared — devoured by the weight of the forest that swallowed everything whole.

We had been walking for hours by then. Maybe longer.

And Sage had barely said a word since we left.

She was waiting for me.

I should have said something.

I know I should have; but I didn't.

Because if I opened my mouth then, I wasn't sure what was going to come out and part of me was afraid she'd hear exactly how close I was to breaking.

Instead, I kept moving. Step after step. Every muscle in my body was coiled tight, like something waiting to be unleashed. Every nerve screamed for me to do something.

But there was nothing I could do.

Not when Nael's words were still tearing through my head like a storm I couldn't outrun.

They were looking for something. Or *someone*.

And somehow, I seemed to know exactly who Nael meant.

And if he was right—then the ENA wouldn't stop.

I'd be the one stripped down to the bone and rebuilt into whatever it is they think I was meant to be.

A legacy. A weapon. A monster.

It seemed they'd already altered those parts of me.

What more could they take from me?

Bu that wasn't the worst part. It was that I wasn't sure I could stop them.

Because some days, I could already feel it.

I didn't want to admit it to myself but something clicked.

There was this part of me that was triggered to wake up. Waiting for permission to take over.

Maybe it already had. Maybe that was why Sage was so quiet. Because she felt it too.

I glanced at her out of the corner of my eye.

She was steady but there was something in the way she walked. Tense. Guarded. Like she was waiting for me to snap.

Or run. Or worse.

And I couldn't blame her.

Because I didn't know which of those things I was going to do either. Not right now at least.

All I knew was that I was starting to lose control.

Somewhere in the distance—faint. Barely there.

I heard it.

Music.

Soft. Haunting. A melody that didn't belong in this place.

Maybe I was imagining it... I couldn't tell anymore.

The song drifted on the wind like it was finding its way to me. Like it was a memory clawing its way to the surface, demanding to be felt.

It was too clear to be imagined but too intact to be real.

But it was there.

Wrapping around me. Pulling tight.

The words hit harder than they should. They dragged something out of me I thought I buried years ago. When things felt too heavy. When I needed something—*anything*—to remind me I was still human.

Back before this. Back before the mark. Before the ENA.

And whatever this was.

I wasn't sure I even recognized myself anymore.

Maybe I was already gone.

I didn't realize I'd stopped walking until Sage's fingers brushed against mine.

Just a graze. Soft and grounding but it made me jolt. Her gaze flicked to me. Sharp and measuring. Waiting for me to give her an answer I wasn't sure I had. I pulled in a breath that didn't do a damn thing to steady me.

My voice was rough. Too rough as it disturbed the silence between us.

"We need to keep moving," I said.

Even though I was the one that stopped moving in the first place.

Sage narrowed her eyes. "Reich."

I didn't look at her, just spoke, "Not now."

Not when I can still feel the burn under my skin.

Something was coming and we weren't ready for it. Hell, I wasn't sure we could ever be ready for it.

The song faded as we moved, swallowed by the forest.

But the weight of it lingered heavily. Like chains I didn't realize I was still wearing.

Sage stepped closer. Her fingers brushing mine again. Not an accident this time.

A choice. A quiet reassurance.

I didn't pull away. But I should have.

But then I saw it. We both did.

In the distance, a figure. A body with shifting eyes.

And somewhere deep inside me I heard it—a voice that didn't belong to me.

"You were born for this...just let go and come home."

The familiarity cut through everything else.

I knew that voice. I didn't know how but I did and it sent a chill down my spine.

My hand tightened around the handle of my knife.

But I didn't draw it.

Because whatever was coming, it was already here and we were surrounded.

I could feel it in the air. I could feel it in the ground. And then—the figure stepped forward.

Pale skin stretched too thin over bones that don't fit right. Hollowed eyes that looked like they were watching and had seen too much.

My stomach twisted as my jaw tightened.

I didn't look at Sage, but I could feel her tense beside me.

"Who sent you?" I attempted to keep my voice steady.

Even though I wasn't able to.

The figure smiled. A thin and crooked line. *"You already know."*

And I did. Even if I didn't want to.

I clenched my jaw. "Get out of our way."

The figure didn't move. *"You cannot run from what you are,"* it said. Its head tilted slightly, curious. *"It is already inside you."*

Sage shifted beside me. I felt her move. The twitch of her fingers toward the blade at her hip.

I exhaled through my teeth.

Then I moved. My knife was out in a breath, cutting through the space where the figure stood but it was gone before I made contact.

Like it was never there at all.

I felt her shaking beside me, but we already knew what to do.

So, I grabbed her hand tightly and we didn't stop moving.

We couldn't.

The forest and nearby ruins closed in around us. Stone and vine swallowing the world behind us.

Sage stayed as close as she could. Her breath steady. But I could feel the weight of her thoughts pressing against mine.

She saw what I saw. She didn't ask what it was.

I didn't know either. But I knew it had to be the ENA. And that should terrify me more than it does.

But it almost felt *expected*.

Not that strange figure appearing out of nowhere but the call that it made to me.

... Come home.

That same music played again in my head. Looping back to the chorus like an echo from a life I would never have.

But I didn't want to believe that.

I wanted to believe that I could make it out with everybody still in one piece.

I wanted to believe that the ENA didn't have a hold on me.

But after seeing that thing, after what it said... that small fragment of hope I had left died.

"Sooner or later," Sage said, "you're going to have to tell me what the hell is going on." Her voice was steady but there was a strain behind it, and I hated that I was the reason for it.

I clenched my jaw. "Not now."

She scoffed under her breath, but she didn't push.

Not yet. But I knew she would. Eventually.

And when she did—I didn't know what I was going to say.

I wasn't sure there was anything left to say.

Not when this was what I was now.

Not when they were *calling me home*.

Chapter Twenty-Eight

SAGE

M Y HEART WAS STILL pounding violently in my chest like it was trying to crack itself out of my rib cage as we moved quickly through the trees.

Reich's hand stayed tight around mine, his grip unrelenting, as if letting go would cost him something he couldn't afford to lose.

Neither of us spoke after our brief exchange.

Not because there was nothing to say—but because neither of us had the words for what we just saw. What was following us now like a second shadow neither of us could outrun.

But I knew one thing, clearer than anything else as we moved through these ruins and our boots thudded too loudly on the beaten path:

Whatever Reich was running from—

Whatever was alive under his skin, breathing in the space between his mind and underneath the pulse at his brand—

It wasn't just a mark.

It was *something else*.

And I was terrified neither of us was going to survive it.

And if we did, we wouldn't ever be the same again.

The silence between us stretched tight. Almost painful as I glanced at him out of the corner of my eye.

He hadn't looked at me once since we started running from that thing.

His jaw was locked and breath just a little too sharp. His body was wound tight enough that it felt like he could splinter apart if I touched him wrong.

And his grip on his weapon—

On *me*—

It was like he was holding back something worse than anything waiting for us in these woods.

Something he was afraid might slip free.

And that's when I felt it—more than just tension.

He was afraid.

Not of the thing that was hunting us. Not of the ENA or their chains, or whatever horrors we've already survived. He was afraid of *himself*.

And that unsettled me more than anything else.

He was unraveling and he was trying to hide it from me.

And I knew that if I had any chance of saving him, I couldn't let him hide any longer.

He didn't let me hide all those years ago. And I wouldn't let him now.

Especially not when whatever was inside him seemed to be slowly taking over and *winning*.

I yanked on his wrist, harder than I meant to, forcing him to stop.

He did. But it wasn't relief I felt.

It was dread.

Because when he looked down at me, I saw it, that look in his eyes that wasn't just a fleeting glance—his eyes were blank.

Empty in a way I didn't recognize. Not cold. Not angry. Just— gone.

Then... that flicker of *black*.

"Reich," I said softly trying not to panic. His name felt fragile in my mouth like if I said it wrong, he would shatter. "Whatever this is—whatever's happening to you—we face it together."

For a second, he didn't move. Didn't even seem to breathe.

And then his throat worked. A slow swallow. Like he was forcing himself to stay here *with me*.

"You don't understand," he said.

His voice was rough. It was Reich, but it wasn't.

And I hated it. I hated how much I wanted to flinch from him.

"Then make me understand." I yelled, gripping his wrist tighter, feeling the heat radiating from his skin. It was too hot. Like something was burning him alive from the inside out.

He opened his mouth, but nothing escaped.

And then— the ground shifted, and he turned to where I was met with his back.

It was subtle until the air started to thicken all at once, congealing into something that coated the inside of my lungs, making my pulse spike hard enough that I felt dizzy. A shadow flickered at the edge of my vision.

Too fast to be human. Too smooth. Too deliberate.

I felt a chill run down my spine, cold like ice water being dumped down the back of my neck, making me jump.

"Reich," I whispered.

He heard it, as he turned toward me for a moment and then turned back forward, slow and cold, like he was looking for something in the distance. I couldn't tell what was going through his mind but I felt it— the way his whole body went still.

A low and hollow voice cut through the silence.

"Reich Davidian."

My blood turned to ice because the voice didn't sound human, just like the last figure that approached us in these woods and it knew his name.

It didn't speak it like a person would in greeting. It spoke like having already made its decision. Like whatever this thing was already owned him. Like it always had.

Reich ushered me to follow as we moved deeper into the woods, but I felt it closing in behind us.

The air got heavier with every step even though the night around us got quieter.

And then I saw and felt the movement. Not from behind like would be expected but ahead.

A similar figure, rising out of the darkness like the air around it had been given bones. I couldn't make out its shape... but it wasn't just a shadow of dust. It looked like a disfigured man or what was left of one.

Pale skin stretched too tight over the sharp protruding bones that shot out at odd, broken angles. Eyes like bottomless pits, so dark they swallowed any light around. Its mouth opened too wide. Too wrong.

We stood paralyzed as its jaw unhinged, splitting the seams of his face until it was just an endless void.

And then a voice— sickeningly powerful and devoid of emotion.

"The time has come for you to be step into the light."

I couldn't scream.

My throat locked up before I could, but my body knew fear. It flooded through me, stealing the air from my lungs and replacing it with fire. I was shaking before I realized it.

Reich moved.

Fast. Faster than I'd ever seen him.

One second, I'm standing next to him.

The next, he's in front of me, shoving me behind him, with his hand gripping mine. His body shields mine, his stance defensive, lethal but he doesn't move toward it.

He didn't attack. He *waited.*

Like he was hoping for something I didn't understand.

Then he spoke, his voice sharp but low, leaving no room for argument, "Sage... run."

But his hand was still tight around mine like he didn't want to let go.

Even now. Even if he knew I needed to move.

"What is that?" I choked out.

"Not something we can kill," he said.

Fear overtook me completely knowing Reich wouldn't say something like that.

He didn't believe in impossible fights.

He *was* the impossible fight.

But this? This was different. This was worse.

The figure didn't move toward us.

It just watched. Its eyes—shifted.

They changed.

One moment, black void. The next—hazel-green.

Exactly like Reich's.

I felt his body lock up in front of me.

His breathing stuttered once and then he tightened his grip on me. Hard enough to bruise.

And I realized— The ENA wasn't hunting Reich anymore.

They had already found him. They had always had him and now they were calling him back to them.

Chapter Twenty-Nine

REICH

As soon as I saw it shift again, I didn't wait for her to argue. I didn't give her the time.

I shoved Sage behind me—harder than I meant to, but I couldn't risk hesitation. My hand caught the curve of her shoulder, fingers digging in tight before I let her go, sending her with the force of it.

"Go," I snapped, sharper this time, the word burning my throat on the way out.

For a second, I thought she would look back. That she would freeze.

But she didn't.

She moved.

Her boots struck the ground in a dead sprint, fast and sure.

I followed. Keeping pace behind her.

Close enough that I could reach out and grab her if I needed to. Close enough that if it took one of us, it was going to be me.

My lungs burned. Each breath felt like knives under my ribs, but I didn't slow. Not even for a second.

It was still behind us.

That thing.

I could feel it pressing up against my back, cold and faint. Not quite touching. Not yet.

But I knew that it would.

If we slowed down, even for a second, it would catch us.

The ruins next to the woods we fell into twisted around us like broken teeth. A maze of shattered stone and iron bars, crumbling in on itself but still standing tall enough to make me feel trapped.

Sage ducked suddenly and I reacted without thinking.

She slipped low between two overgrown trees that merged on both sides, leaving only a narrow gap just wide enough to squeeze through.

I twisted sideways to follow, my shoulder scraping against the rough branches.

And then a noise hit.

A screech—high and warped. Wrong in every way something can be wrong. It tore through the air, through me. My teeth clenched hard enough I was surprised they didn't crack under the pressure. The sound drilled in deep, vibrating through my core.

Sage stumbled. Her boot caught on a jagged edge of broken rock. I saw her about to go down and I lunged forward, grabbing her arm just below the elbow. My fingers dug in tight, and I yanked her back to her feet before gravity had the chance to drag her down.

"Don't stop," I yelled. My voice was more growl than words now.

And she didn't.

She kept running, her breath ragged, but steady. Always steady and ready for a fight. Even when I wasn't.

We broke into a wider clearing, just for a second.

I pointed, jabbing a finger toward a half-hidden cave on the far side.

"Sage, there!"

Her gaze snapped to where I was pointing, and without hesitation, she bolted for it. I was right behind her, boots slamming against cracked earth as I closed the distance.

The entry was narrow, carved into the side of an old mountainside, half-choked with vines thick as ropes. We entered, following the depths of the inside deeper and deeper, turning on our flashlights, as the darkness swallowed us.

Then came the whispers. Soft at first. A low hum, just at the edge of hearing. Then louder. Familiar voices—too familiar.

Castor. Keenan. My mother. Even Sage, though she ran ahead of me. They all started to say the same thing in my mind. Over and over, like a chant I couldn't drown out.

"Let go."

I gritted my teeth, shaking my head hard enough to make my vision blur.

"*No*," I softly hissed to no one under my breath.

Sage cleared the upward little hill inside the cave and disappeared into a narrow passage. I ducked my head and followed a breath later, shoulders tearing against the hard earth on both sides as I squeezed through.

No time to stop. No time to breathe.

We spilled out into what looked like a hidden courtyard but this one was broken, strangled by roots thicker than my arm. They twisted through the cracked stone, wrapping around shattered statues, some carved with faces I almost recognized.

But I wasn't looking at them or trying to identify them.

I was looking for a place to hide. To catch our breath. To think.

I grabbed Sage's wrist and pulled her behind a crumbling wall, pressing her flat against the cold stone. My back to her. My knife in hand. Listening and waiting.

Our breaths came hard. Shallow. But it was all we had.

I risked a real glance at her.

Her eyes were wide, wild with fear and fury in equal measure, but she kept that same alertness.

"Are you ok?" I asked.

It was a stupid question but it was something.

She nodded. Barely.

Her voice was shaky, but she found it. "What the hell are these things?"

I shook my head. "Something we can't fight," I reiterated.

Her jaw tightened. I could see that she wanted to argue and to demand answers I still didn't have but she didn't.

She gripped my hand tighter instead.

And we listened.

For a long minute, there was nothing but our breathing and the faint crackle of the forest.

Then— the screech again.

Fainter now. Further away. Hunting. But I thought it had lost us for now.

I took a breath, trying to focus.

We're not out of this.

Not even close.

"We need to move," I murmured.

She nodded and we do.

Hours passed, maybe more as we maneuvered in silence through more ruins and wreckage deeper inside that partially enclosed area.

We kept searching for its outlet. Trying to find a way back to our path. But there was *nothing*.

Sage stayed close keeping her steps measured.

I could feel her watching me when she thought I wasn't looking. Questions she wasn't asking. Because she knew me. Knew I wasn't ready to answer and that maybe I never would be.

I felt my pocket vibrate. Sharp. Sudden.

I froze.

Sage stopped, eyes on me as I pulled it free.

Nael's name flashed on the screen and I answered without thinking. "Nael."

I didn't even have time to react and tell him about what we just saw without him immediately interjecting.

And I wasn't sure if I even wanted to.

"Keenan made it back," he said.

For a second, relief but I heard his hesitation. "And?"

Nael's voice sharpened. "The papers he found at Castor's bunker."

My pulse spiked. "What?"

"He came in person to tell me," Nael said.

And that's when I knew it was bad. That whatever Nael was about to tell me was going to change everything, just like what Sage and I had witnessed. Because Keenan wouldn't come in person unless it was worse than bad.

"Nael," I said, low and dangerous. "What did he find?"

A pause. Then— "You remember what you told me? About the Ovitts? That you and Castor never found out why others ended up killed in their place?"

"Yeah." I swallowed hard.

Nael exhaled slowly. "Castor knew."

The words hit like a punch to the chest.

"Knew what exactly?" I grinded out.

"He knew that the people you had killed were pawns. They were sent by the ENA," Nael said quietly. "He found out a while ago."

I was shaking...

"How long did he know?" I asked, voice raw.

Silence. Long enough.

"The files were dated when you both left Providence." He responded.

I felt the world narrow.

Three years.

Three years I'd spent clawing for the truth— letting it eat me alive every single day since the moment I learned something went wrong.

And this whole time... Castor already *knew*.

"I trusted him," I said quietly.

Nael was silent for a moment.

Then— "There's more."

I already felt sick but I still listened because I had to.

I had to know.

"Keenan found something else that Castor had been looking into...about your bloodline." Nael said.

The world tilted.

Why would Castor even be looking into that?

And since when the fuck did he start keeping all of these secrets?

Sage stiffened beside me because she knew something was wrong. She saw it on my face, even though she couldn't hear what Nael was saying.

I heard Nael clear his throat as he said these next words carefully, "Reich...your bloodline traces back to the Ovitts."

"What are you saying?" I asked carefully, not wanting to connect the dots aloud.

His voice lowered. "Ezra Davidian was never your father... Harry Ovitt was."

For a long time, I didn't move.

I didn't know how I managed to breathe because it felt like an impossible task. All I heard in my head was that name.

Harry Ovitt.

The man who helped build the ENA into what it was.

The man whose sons broke Sage into pieces.

And now—*me.*

I was a part of them.

Sage's hand brushed my arm. "Reich?" she whispered.

I couldn't look at her.

I stepped back but I was already sinking.

The mark at my neck burned hot. *Alive.*

"Reich," Sage said again. More urgent.

My pulse hammered. My skin felt too tight. My hands shook profusely.

Nael was still on the line and asked, "Reich."

"Yeah." I managed.

"You never should have left here. Get back right now... so we can sort this out."

"Ok, we're on our way." I responded as I ended the call and finally looked at Sage. Her eyes were wide like she was searching. Like she already knew the answer.

But that? That might break us.

I reached for her hand because it was all I had for now.

The path stretched out before us as we finally found our way out of the enclosed area and by a nearby road. It was all cracked stone and silence as we moved in the dark. The weight of what was coming pressed down on me like a dark cloud.

Sage stayed close as I focused on the road.

The next step. The next breath.

Because if I stopped—

If I spiraled and thought too much— I might fall apart and never come back together again.

Chapter Thirty

SAGE

REICH HAD BARELY SPOKEN a word to me since the figure disappeared and we escaped.

He spoke with Nael. I didn't even know what the conversation involved.

All I knew was that we were heading back to his bunker and Reich was as unsettled as ever.

His shoulders were wound, coiled like a thread pulled too tight, waiting to break. His jaw was set hard enough that I could almost hear the faint grind of his teeth whenever he exhaled.

And his hand— still gripped the knife, white-knuckled, like he had forgotten how to let go. Or maybe he didn't want to. Maybe it was the only thing grounding him right now.

I should have pushed him. Should have demanded answers.

Forced him to speak, to say something.

But I didn't.

Because I had already tried and I knew what this was.

I'd seen this before. I knew this version of Reich.

The man who built walls faster than I could tear them down. Brick by brick. Sealing himself behind them. Closing himself off until there was nothing left but the soldier. The weapon. The survivor who thinks he has to bleed alone because that's the only way he knows how to stay alive.

I hate it. I hate it because I knew better. Because he knew better. But knowing didn't mean he could stop it and I knew not to fight him when he was like this.

So, I just stayed beside him. Quiet. Close enough that our arms brushed every now and then. Close enough that he knew I was still there. And I hoped he would let me in before it was too late.

Later we made camp, agreeing to rest as nightfall hit.

Though I wasn't sure resting was really an option after everything that happened.

I watched him from across the fire.

But he didn't meet my gaze.

The flames cast long shadows over his face, making the hollows under his eyes deeper, sharper. He stared into the fire like he was looking for something or waiting for it to burn him.

His expression didn't change.

Not when the wood cracked. Not when an ember spit out close to his boots.

He didn't blink. He didn't move. Something was different about him now.

Not just in the way he carried himself.

It was deeper than that. Something fundamental was shifting or fracturing within him.

And for the first time since I found him— since I dragged him back from whatever edge he was standing on— I wondered if I made a mistake.

Maybe— *just maybe*— Reich Davidian wasn't someone I could save.

Maybe he was already too far gone. Maybe the man I fell in love with… maybe he had already been hollowed out.

And this—*this* was just what was left.

But I wouldn't let myself believe that. Not yet. Not until all hope was lost. And even then... I think I would still keep trying to pull him back.

I woke to the sound of his breathing. Uneven and gasping like he was drowning on the air that he took in.

My pulse spiked instantly. I sat up, the cold bite of the night's air rustling over my skin as I twisted toward him. He was sitting against the tree, his body hunched, head bowed, arms braced on his knees.

"Reich?" It came out soft. I already knew he wouldn't answer but I had to try.

The firelight flickered over him in broken pieces. It made his face unreadable like he was a stranger's face carved in shadow and flame, but I could see it.

The tension in his shoulders. The tremor in his fingers. He was not asleep against that tree. He was fighting.

And whatever he was fighting— he was losing.

I carefully crawled toward him slowly like he was something wild that might bolt if I moved too fast.

"Talk to me," I whispered.

For a moment, he didn't move.

And then—he lifted his head and my stomach drops as he opened his eyes.

They were black again like before. But not a flicker. They were staying that way for much longer.

But I didn't flinch. I looked directly at him.

And then... gone.

I should have been afraid. I should have run. I should have screamed.

But I wouldn't.

Because this was Reich and I had to believe that it was still him inside somewhere.

He was the man who pulled me out of darkness all those years ago.

The man who kissed me like I was worth something.

The man that I loved with every part of me.

And I wouldn't lose him. Not to them. Not to this.

And especially not without a fight.

I knelt in front of him. Close enough to feel the heat rolling off his skin.

His breathing was ragged now, his jaw tight, his body trembling like he was trying to hold something back and failing.

My hands rose slowly as I reached to cup his face. My cool palms in contrast against his fevered skin. My thumbs brushed over his cheekbones, wiping away the sweat beading there.

"Look at me," I whispered.

He already was but I said it anyway because I needed him to really see me. I needed him to find himself in my reflection.

"We fight this," I told him. "Together."

His breath shuddered out of him. His hands flexed against his knees.

And I saw it— the flicker of fear behind his burning eyes. Not for himself.

For *me*.

I leaned in until our foreheads touched. His skin burned against mine, but I didn't pull away.

Instead, I anchored him. Or maybe really, I anchored myself.

And he let me.

But it happened fast.

One second, he was beside me, his hand steady against my back, grounding me.

The next— gone.

I didn't see them coming. I didn't hear them.

But as soon as I closed my eyes, I felt the hit. Hard and sharp at the base of my skull.

The world tilted, as it blurred around me.

And then—darkness.

When I woke, I was on cold stone.

The taste of copper flooded my mouth and as I coughed, blood spattered on the floor.

I slowly breathed through it in measured exhales, making sure to keep my head down.

Let them think I was still out. Let them wait.

The air was damp and thick. Humid.

It stunk of incense and something like ash. The kind that sticks to your skin and gets into your lungs, taking residence there.

I felt them watching me, but I tried my best not to move.

Until a voice came to fill the space and I couldn't ignore it.

"You are not what we expected."

Male. Controlled. Smooth in a way that made my stomach turn. The kind of voice that was used to people listening and not talking.

I opened my eyes. Slow. Deliberate.

And I saw him.

A man, standing in the doorway, with his face half-shadowed.

He stepped forward.

The torchlight caught the edge of something at his throat. A mark.

The same one on Reich's neck. The same one that kept him branded. *All of them branded.*

My pulse spiked. "Who are you?" My voice was hoarse and rough from screaming or disuse. I wasn't sure which.

He tilted his head. There was no warmth in his expression. No life.

"The same as you," he said. Quiet. Calm. But it landed like a verdict. "Not a prisoner. Not a pawn."

He glanced at me. Amused, as he continued, "A piece of something greater."

I wanted to spit at his feet. I wanted to scream but I stayed still, choosing words of defiance instead.

"I'm not part of this," I said.

His lips curved into something cruel, almost knowing.

"Oh," he murmured. "But you are."

He stepped closer and I forced myself not to pull back even though I wanted to.

His fingers grazed the side of my face. Light. Too light.

But I held my composure the best that I could, feeling myself unraveling at the edges.

"Your boyfriend, Reich, thinks he can outrun fate," he said softly. "He doesn't understand that fate has already claimed him... and it looks like it claimed you too."

Me? Why me?

My heart hammered against my ribs. "What did you do to him?"

His smirk deepened like he was waiting for the question and enjoyed hearing me ask.

"We didn't do anything but help him get where he needs to be" he said. Soft and final like he was closing a door.

And then he continued, "It was always inside him and now it's inside you too."

CHAPTER THIRTY-ONE

REICH

SAGE WAS *GONE*.

THE REALIZATION didn't just hit me—it destroyed me.

It tore through my chest like a blade driven straight through my ribs.

The breath that left my lungs was a violent, deep exhale I felt myself choke on.

They took her. I let them take her.

I stood there. I hesitated. And they took her from me.

The feeling that hung heavy in my chest wasn't pain.

It was a hollow absence.

It was the space where she should have been—torn wide open, with nothing left.

No warmth. No breath. No *her*.

I didn't remember falling. One second, I was standing. The next, I felt my knees slam into the dirt hard enough to jar my teeth. But I didn't feel it.

I just felt everything else.

My pulse hammered inside my skull as my vision tunneled.

I clenched my fists. Nails splitting skin. But the bite of it brought no clarity. No focus. Just more chaos. More rage.

And then—I felt it.

The *mark*.

I felt it as I writhed on the ground, unaware of what surrounded me.

But I knew it was *them*.

I knew it, as the pain tore through me—not beneath my flesh but *through* it. I ripped at my shirt with shaking hands, clawing until the fabric gave way. And when I saw it—when I saw the ink blooming across my chest like wildfire—

I knew it was too late.

I was losing this. I was losing *myself*.

A sharp voice cut through the night.

It almost sounded *ancient*.

"You are ready."

I snapped my head up, chest heaving, breath slicing like knives down my throat, as I fought against it.

The forest watched me. The trees didn't sway—they loomed. The wind thickened, letting the dark breathe.

And then—I saw him.

He stepped from the shadows like he had always been there. Like he was waiting for me to *see* him.

White robes. Calm expression.

He was one of them.

My fists clenched. My mark flared, searing hot, but I didn't feel the pain.

Only rage.

Only *her*.

"Where is she?" My voice scraped out—low and broken.

He didn't flinch. Didn't move.

"With us," he said, like it was obvious. Like it was *nothing*.

Then he looked—to my hands, my chest and my mark and smiled.

Smiled like he didn't have to lie anymore.

I didn't think.

I took every last bit of strength and I *moved.*

One breath, I'm kneeling. The next—I slammed him into a tree so hard the bark split. My hands wrapped around his throat, crushing.

But he just *watched* me.

"You feel it, don't you?" he choked, the pressure crushing his voice—but not his certainty.

I tightened my grip. I wanted to break him. Snap his spine. Make him *beg.*

But my hands—somehow aren't mine anymore.

"I will kill you," I snarled, and I meant it. I meant *every word.*

He exhaled and smiled.

"You won't… not yet. Besides…we had to take her away for this part…"

I froze.

My pulse stuttered.

And then—I saw his eyes.

Hazel green, ringed in gold.

Mine.

It was one of them… one of those things Sage and I saw before.

"She was the last thing keeping you human…" he whispered. A breath. A brutal truth. "…And now she's *gone.*"

Something *snapped.*

The world tilted.

The mark burned down my spine, uncoiling like something *dragged up from the depths.*

My skin ignited. Heat in every vein.

And then—he screamed.

Because of me.

Because the thing they carved into me was *real.*

And it was *awake.*

My hands dug deeper—not into his flesh, but into *something else.* Something *underneath* him. Beneath skin and soul.

And I ripped.

He seized.

His mouth stretched, a soundless cry splitting his throat until it bled. His eyes rolled back, whites flashing silver before they *ruptured*, weeping black smoke.

But I didn't stop.

I didn't want to stop.

Because they took her.

And now, I was as gone as she was.

The darkness poured out of me.

From my mark. From my hands.

It stayed wrapped around him like chains.

Completely *devouring*.

And then—he *shattered*.

Not bone. Not blood.

But *spirit*.

I *felt* it. Like glass under pressure.

And when there was nothing left but dust, I was still standing there. Still breathing.

For a long moment, I didn't move.

The blood that once filled his mouth stained the earth, already drying into cracks. The last of it still clung to my fingers.

My chest heaved and my body hummed but the night stayed silent.

Even *the darkness* feared me now.

But I wasn't afraid.

Not anymore.

I stared at where he stood. Where he smiled. Where he screamed.

Like he *wanted* this. Like he *knew*.

I looked down at my hands, as I flexed them. The glow vanished beneath my skin like it was never there.

But I remembered the sounds.

IN REICH AND RUIN

The beat of his pulse dying beneath my grip.
The crack of his wrist when I stopped holding back.
And the shriek that never really left the air.
I told myself to stop.
But something in me never let go.
Because this—*this* was always waiting.
And then came the voice.
Not from him. Not from outside.
But from *within*.
"This is what you were born for."
I stumbled back, as my breath caught like smoke trapped in my throat.
All of a sudden, I didn't recognize my hands. Didn't recognize my arms. My *self*.
Something was *different*.
I was still staring at my palms when the silence pressed in again.
I didn't know what I had become.
Only that it didn't feel human anymore.
And that this thing inside me—this hunger and ruin wasn't born tonight.
It was *always there*.
Coiled. Waiting.
And losing her to them was the final key.
This wasn't about vengeance.
Not really.
It was about *permission*.
And now I had it.
And I knew exactly what I would do, the moment she was taken.
Sage, my wildflower.
She was the last real thing I had.
My tether. My mercy. My reason.
And they tore her from me like it meant nothing.

So, I would burn their sanctuary down.

I would rip open the walls between this world and whatever waited beneath it.

I would unmake every god who ever watched and said nothing.

And when I found her—*what was left of her*—I'd carry her out of that place.

Even if I had to drag the ashes of the world behind me.

Because I was not their weapon.

I was the consequence they never accounted for.

And I was *coming*.

Chapter Thirty-Two

SAGE

IT STARTED WITH DIZZINESS.

Not the kind that comes from exhaustion or the hollow sickness of running for too long on little to no food or water.

This was different. Like something was *wrong*.

It coiled deep in my gut, a slow, twisting thing that pressed against my ribs as if it wanted out.

At first, I tried to ignore the pain. I forced myself to believe it was stress or just hunger. A side effect of the hiding, running, and then capture. Or from watching Reich slowly lose himself right in front of me.

I told myself that I didn't have time to be sick. I didn't have time to be anything but ready and hopeful that Reich would find me... but the feeling wouldn't stop. It built as it crept around the edges of my awareness like a shadow moving just beyond my line of sight.

Always there. Always waiting for me to turn my head.

I swallowed against the thick burn in my throat and closed my eyes, breathing through it, like that would be enough.

And then— the blood.

It wasn't much at first.

A few drops smeared across the floor.

But the moment I saw it, the moment my eyes landed on that sharp contrast of blood against the concrete, it made my stomach knot. Something terrified tightened inside me as I kept my eyes closed and begged for relief through sleep.

The cot on the stone floor beneath me was cold but not just frigid—it felt dead. It took the heat from my skin with every second I laid there like it was drawing the life out of me and wouldn't give it back. Like it had been doing this to others for centuries in this exact concrete box of a room.

The air was damp, and I felt it growing thicker around me. There was a heaviness in my lungs, like I was breathing through a wet cloth soaked in vinegar, adding to the sickness inside.

The silence pressed in hard.

No voices. No footsteps. Just my pulse pounding in my ears.

I knew this was the ENA's doing, even though the man from earlier never said it.

Who else would move in the dark, silent and efficient, while Reich was standing right next to me? Who else could drag me out of the woods so quickly and without a sound?

And if they had me—if they took me— they'd come for him next.

If they hadn't already.

I breathed through the pain and the cold. Through the scream locked behind my teeth.

I breathed and I counted.

One. Two Three. Four...*in.*

One. Two. Three. Four...*out.*

Because it was the only thing I could control.

The only thing that felt like it was still mine.

At least for now.

And then I saw it. Across the room, the faint light of a torch flickered against the far wall.

I didn't know how it was lit. Someone must have come in while I was asleep.

The thought unnerved me but that's when I saw it—a mural.

Paint cracked and worn, eaten away by humidity and aged by time but not enough to erase it. Not enough to hide the face that stared back at me.

A man who looked similar to Reich.

His hazel eyes. That sharp jaw. That mouth I'd traced with my fingertips more times than I could count.

But it wasn't him.

Not *my* Reich.

That version of him—

A burning halo of symbols and scripture carved the stone around his figure.

And beneath his feet, a field of bodies. Hands reaching up toward him. Pleading. Worshipping. Almost *dying*.

I stared at it until my eyes stung. Until the sickness threatened to pull me under again.

This was who they must think Reich is. What they believe he was always meant to become, and they'll burn anything to ash that stands in the way.

Including me.

A voice cut through the thick quiet. Low and measured, like it had been waiting for me to notice it all along.

"He was always meant to return to us."

I clenched my jaw, teeth grinding until it hurt as I forced my hands into fists, even though it sent fire screaming up my arms.

I didn't flinch. I couldn't.

I turned to face the voice.

Cresil.

The woman from back at the bunker.

The one who made Reich kill that boy while I hid.

She stepped out from the dark like smoke spilling through a cracked door. Her white robes gleamed in the torchlight, flowing over stone as if she was gliding.

I swear she looked like a ghost.

Berith, the other one, followed behind her, silent.

Eyes like still water. Empty and waiting.

The two of them together would be enough to send a shiver through anyone but it was the third figure that made my breath lock in my chest. The third who moved through the archway, tall and slow. Controlled.

That same man from earlier.

"High Ordinant Astaroth," Cresil said softly.

As if this was a casual gathering and introduction.

He stood taller than Berith. Broader. His eyes didn't look at you like any normal person would. They measured you. Weighed out your presence.

He didn't move like a normal person either. He moved like a cautious predator.

His gaze slid over me like a butcher appraising meat.

And something in me reacted.

"Let me go. You all are insane." I snapped.

My voice was rough, but it held. Even now as I tried to convince myself to fight and then run and hide.

But I knew deep down it was too late for any of that.

Cresil's lips curled into a smile, like a game she had played too many times, always with the same ending. "That's what he said, too, at first... before he was given his mark. He has been fighting us for so long on this.

But you... You changed him..." she murmured. She glided closer, the hem of her robes whispering across the stone. "You, Sage—" She tilted her head, almost fond. "You were meant to bring him home."

I shook my head before I could even think. The denial was instinctive. "No." But my voice wavered and I hated that it did.

It didn't make sense to me. I didn't do anything. I didn't change him. They did.

"Yes," Cresil said softly. Pitying. Like I was too small to understand the shape of what I had stepped into. "You think it was an accident you found him? That you were drawn to him? That you couldn't stay away?"

I swallowed hard and I didn't answer. Because the questions had already lived inside me. Nights I couldn't sleep. When Reich's skin burned hotter every time I touched him. When his eyes darkened at the mention of the ENA. When his mark—*his pain*— seemed to flare in sync with my heartbeat.

Cresil circled me. Amusement flaring across her face as the others watched.

"Fate isn't something you choose," she whispered. "It's something you surrender to."

Berith shifted behind her but said nothing. He only watched and waited.

For me to break. For me to give up.

Astaroth moved. Stepping forward.

No sound. No rush. Just inevitability. His head tilted slightly as he studied me.

Not curious, but calculating. Measuring how much fight was left. Deciding how much he would need to take.

I glared at Cresil, forcing defiance and anger into my voice. "I didn't bring him anywhere and I won't."

Her smile deepened. Wider now. "Oh, sweet girl, but you already have."

Astaroth crouched in front of me. Close. *Too close*. His knees crackled against the stone beneath him, and he didn't even blink. His breath was cold when it touched my cheek.

"You think this is a choice?" His voice was deep and rough.

I met his gaze and I didn't flinch as I retorted, "Reich isn't your choice."

He tilted his head. "Isn't he?" continuing, "He wears our mark. He'll always choose the mark. In fact, he's on his way towards us now…"

He leaned in, whispering something in a language I didn't understand but I felt it. Low and dark, sliding under my skin like poison seeping deep within the pit of my stomach.

I tilted my chin up in defiance as I stated, "You're wrong. He's not coming because he chooses *you*…he's coming because he chooses *me*…"

He smiled, almost amused, "Cresil, dear, why don't you go meet up with our man of the hour and ask him?"

She nodded but before she left, I felt her fingers tighten on my shoulder. Firm but oddly gentle.

I wanted to tear her hand away but something inside of me wouldn't let me move.

I was stiff and *paralyzed*.

"Whether he is coming to us because of the mark…" she said softly, "Or coming to us because of you…" She leaned close. Her lips near my ear. "It ends the same."

And it was then that I realized— they were doing something to him that they had already planned out.

And we were near the end.

Reich was already halfway gone, but he wasn't yet… not entirely.

And as long as I had breath, I wouldn't let them finish what they started. I would fight even if I had to find a way to drag him back from their hell myself.

CHAPTER THIRTY-THREE

REICH

I WAS FUELED WITH anger and every bit of rage as the lingering dust from the man's shadow settled in front of me. And I knew—whoever I was before this moment...was *gone*.

The mark at the back of my neck seared into my skin like a brand burrowing deeper into my very nerves.

Claiming me.

Like it always belonged.

Something was different. Something had awoken inside me, and it didn't want to stop.

I was still trying to steady my breathing when I heard the whispers.

The *footsteps*.

Like they wanted me to know they were coming and wanted me to have time to think about what came next.

Cresil stepped into view first. She moved like a shadow, gliding over the uneven ground seamlessly as her white robes trailed behind her.

Berith followed. Silent as death itself. His pale eyes were flat and empty like a void.

They both wore the same expression. Patient and certain.

Like they had been expecting this. Like this was all unfolding exactly as it should.

"That was quick," Cresil murmured. Her voice was almost gentle. *Pleased.* Like a mother congratulating a child who finally learned their lesson.

Her eyes drifted to the dust that laid motionless in the dirt where the man I just killed once stood.

No sorrow. No disgust. Only satisfaction.

Like this was something inevitable and written in stone.

They clearly didn't care that I had just killed one of their own, and I knew they had taken Sage... so this meant that there was only one thing left: *war.*

I clenched my jaw. My teeth grinding hard enough to make my temples throb, but I didn't look away. I couldn't.

"Where is she?" I asked. My voice was low and raw but I maintained calculated control.

Cresil's gaze slid back to me calmly and unhurried like she had all the time in the world.

"She's safe," she said. The words were smooth and rehearsed.

A lie that was meant to taste like honey, even though it would turn to vinegar.

Her words meant nothing to me. I knew it and she knew that I knew it. Yet, she still said it like a promise.

Berith tilted his head, studying me like I was a puzzle with a missing piece. Like he was waiting for something inside me to snap.

But the joke was on him because it already had.

Cresil smiled. But it wasn't a smile meant to comfort. It was something sinister. "If you want to see her again," she added, "You'll need to come with us. She's rejecting the shift."

Shift? What the fuck was that supposed to mean?

I drew my knife. Slow and deliberate. The steel gleamed pale in the torchlight, slick with someone else's blood.

Her smile widened. Of course, she expected that.

"What did you do to her?" I snarled and then I moved.

The blade sliced through the space where Cresil stood a second ago—but she was already gone, gliding like fragments of dust wisped up by the wind.

I pivoted hard.

Berith's fist swung toward me, heavy and effortless.

It would have knocked me out had I not dropped low and hooked my arm behind his knee. My shoulder slammed into his gut, driving him back into the trunk of a large fallen tree behind us.

The wood cracked as it splintered but he didn't flinch. Didn't even grunt.

His hands were on me a second later. Crushing and pulling against my face.

He hauled me up like I weighed nothing at all, and I twisted out, while driving the hilt of my blade into his jaw. Bone gave way with a sharp crunch and his head jerked back violently, but he didn't go down.

I moved again.

Cresil was behind me now. Fingers cold as ice brushed against the back of my neck and towards the mark.

Fire exploded through my skull. A burst of blinding white flashed that knocked me to my knees. A guttural noise ripped from my throat, raw and violent.

I couldn't see. I couldn't think. I couldn't *breathe.*

"You can't fight what you are," Cresil murmured. Her voice got under my skin like a splinter that wouldn't give way, "Stop trying."

I shot up. Blind and furious as I swung wild.

My knife caught flesh— her arm.

And I watched as the edge of the blade sliced deep and a dark almost black color of blood spilled from it.

She hissed, enraged, and backed away.

And then Berith grabbed me by the throat with his iron grip. I barely registered it before he slammed me to the ground. The impact rattled my teeth as it knocked the air out of my lungs in a brutal rush.

I gasped and began to cough up the blood coming from my mouth.

"You fight well..." Berith said. His voice was flat and dull, like he was commenting on the weather. "... but it's over."

I spit blood into his face and drove my knee into his ribs.

Once. Twice.

He grunted but didn't flinch. Didn't loosen his grip. His hand tightened, crushing my windpipe until my vision went white.

Cresil stepped closer, wiping the blood from her arm in a slow, bored motion.

Like an afterthought that didn't matter.

"You can't save her," she said. Soft. Almost kind. "You can only join her."

I lashed out one last time. A punch that snapped Berith's head back, but my strength was fading.

I was slowing down.

And I knew. *I knew.* I was losing this.

Berith let me drop and I hit the ground hard. I felt the cold ground against my back as my chest heaved, desperate for air that didn't seem to come fast enough.

Cresil kneeled beside me, brushing my hair from my face with fingers cold as ice. "There's no shame in destiny," she whispered. "It's time."

Berith hauled me upright effortlessly again, like lifting a doll.

Cresil turned, leading the way through the ruins.

Her steps were light and graceful like this was just another day. Just another piece falling into place.

I was dragged after her.

One arm useless, hanging limp at my side and the other still clenched around the knife.

I wouldn't drop it. I couldn't. Even if it was the last thing I held on to.

Because it was the last thing that made me, *me*.

I couldn't move even though I tried. It was like I was paralyzed or held by some invisible chains.

After what felt like hours, they led me to a gate I knew too well.

It was tall and imposing, carved with grotesque, twisting symbols and statues. The ironwork was intricate, almost beautiful in its wickedness, like something sacredly defiled. Time and rot had gnawed at its edges, but its presence still commanded this reverence and dread.

Beyond it loomed the ENA compound.

The place that I got initiated at. Their headquarters for this division of land, that housed: Sanele, Providence and several surrounding cities and communities.

It was once a cathedral, now it was nothing but a corpse of what it was. Crumbling stone spires reached towards the sky, their stained-glass eyes remained intact, but some were long since shattered, replaced by reinforced steel and surveillance camers. The air itself seemed to resist being breathed—thick with smoke, sulfur, and something like decay.

The gate creaked open like a throat clearing before a final judgment.

I knew what waited beyond.

Or rather—who.

Astaroth.

And if he had Sage—if he had hurt her in any way—I'd tear these walls down brick by brick. I'd rip the skeleton from this sanctified hell and salt the earth beneath its foundations and then I would burn it all until the sky choked on the smoke.

But not yet.

I was surrounded and outnumbered. Pinned in place while something inside me clawed at the seams, begging to be let loose.

And when I finally released it—when I stopped fighting the thing that had been waiting beneath my skin?

PAIGE ALEXANDRIA

I didn't know what I would become.
But I knew this much: I'd find her.
No matter what was left of me when I did.

Chapter Thirty-Four

SAGE

THE ROOM FELT MORE like a crypt than a cell, like some forgotten hollow space carved deep beneath a sanctuary that everyone had given up on. The architecture overhead hinted at former grandeur; arches ribbed like the bones of something ancient, but it was barely visible in the ambient light. A single window interrupted the stone: small, set high, and etched with an intricate lattice that let in no light.

Strange markings were painted along the far wall. Symbols. Figures. Things I didn't understand and wasn't going to dare try to.

I retreated to the farthest corner with my spine pressed up against the stone, hard enough to bruise by how tense I was. My knees were drawn to my chest, arms wrapped tight around them—not for my comfort, but as my armor.

Time didn't seem to move here. It dripped and pooled like the moisture down the walls—slow, quiet and unnoticed until it eventually would flood everything. Seconds, minutes, hours... I didn't know what I was counting anymore.

The kind of dark this place held spilled through every crack, every thought.

My shoulders ached, probably from being dragged here. My joints screamed in protest when they finally let me collapse and still, I could feel Cresil's hand on me—like a phantom brand she had seared into my flesh. Her fingers were on my shoulder, as she spoke down to me with that sickeningly sweet tone.

But it was nothing compared to *his*.

Astaroth's voice... was even worse than hers. It was in my head now, crawling along my thoughts like a sickness I couldn't shake off. Whispering things that I didn't want to understand and then repeating them until they started to sound like truth.

I didn't know where Reich was. I didn't know if he was even still alive.

And if he was— I didn't know if he was even still Reich.

That was the thought I tried not to have but seemed to stay there regardless. Buried deep like a splinter I couldn't pull free. Every time I moved, I felt it and I bled.

And then— the screams started.

They caused me to wake from the pathetic fragments of sleep I tried to indulge in.

I jolted upright as my pulse spiked, pounding in my throat and against my chest. My body screamed to run, but there was nowhere to go.

Nowhere but here.

Footsteps scraped over the stone.

Heavy boots. Deliberate and unhurried as they made their way in front of my cell.

The clang of iron followed. Then the groan of the cell door as it creaked open, spilling thin streaks of a bright LED light into the dark. It cut across the floor in a narrow strip, almost blinding after so much black. I squinted against it, as I blinked hard trying to regain my focus.

Two men who looked like guards stepped inside. Their faces were blank beneath bone-white masks.

Emotionless and voiceless.

But they stood with sheer purpose.

They didn't need to speak. I already knew they were taking me somewhere.

They moved toward me like machines. One of them grabbed my arm, his grip bruising, fingers locking around my bone like he meant to crush it. The other hauled me to my feet, the sudden movement yanking a cry from my throat I couldn't stop. Pain shot up my arm and into my shoulder.

I stumbled as I felt my legs grow weak. My boots scraped against the floor as they dragged me forward.

I tried to ask where they were taking me.

My lips parted but my throat was too dry, and no sound came out. Just air and what felt like the hollow shape of fear.

We moved through corridors that pulsed with damp rot. Walls sweating. Stone darkened by something I didn't want to name.

Every step echoed like a warning. Or a countdown.

And then we reached it.

A heavy iron-banded door with hinges shaped like a contorted rib cage.

One of them shoved the door open. The hinges didn't make a sound.

It gave me pause at first, but it was quickly masked by what waited beyond it that made my knees buckle.

A courtyard. Wide and open to the sky, but it felt like a tomb. Torches lined the walls. Flames twisting and writhing in the wind. Their light threw wild shadows against cracked stone and broken statues. Figures and symbols that I started to recognize from the book Reich had back in Providence, the *Eiloud Naphal Ascendancy*, the ENA.

Something I was never supposed to look at but I still always wondered what they meant.

What was their story.

I staggered as they dragged me forward and that's when I saw him.

Reich.

He was on his knees in the center of the courtyard. Head bowed, his shoulders heaving with ragged and broken breaths. His shirt was torn open, blood slicking his ribs, painting his arms in sharp, vicious lines and his eyes...

They were dark.

Not that perfect shade of hazel green.

Not the ones I used to know.

But something else.

They were nearly black, yet they pulsed with something deeper.

I attempted to take a step forward and stopped.

Because in front of him— a crushed body laid in the dirt contorting itself.

It was bent wrong and unmoving, with pale skin beneath a smear of blood.

The hands hung limp at his sides, fingers twitching and moving oddly like they were caught on puppet strings.

And then the body jerked, a sharp spasm ripping through it.

The mouth opened in a scream, but it was silent.

Blood started to tear from the eyes and dripped down the face in thick rivulets, staining the throat like something inside was tearing itself loose.

And Reich— Reich didn't stop it.

He wasn't fighting. He wasn't resisting what was happening to the body that was helpless right in front of him.

I staggered back, boots scraping against the stone. My hands shook, fists clenched at my sides so tight my nails cut into my palms. I couldn't look away and I couldn't move.

And then— his head snapped toward me.

"Sage." He breathed my name like it was the only word he remembered like he was pulling it out of the wreckage of himself, but it didn't sound right anymore.

It was his voice— but something else was wrapped around it. Wearing it.

He rose slowly. The movement was fluid and too smooth. His feet didn't even scuff against the dirt. The air around him wavered against him. Like heat rolling off a desert road.

He took a step toward me, and I took one back. My heart slammed against my ribs so hard I could barely breathe.

"What did they do to you?" I choked.

His expression shifted. Flickered. Like the question confused him.

"Nothing," he said with confidence.

I felt it before I saw it. The shift in the air that was cold and heavy like a storm rolling in without warning.

Reich went still beside me. His head turning toward the dark archway at the edge of the courtyard, shoulders locked. I watched as his hands flexed once and I knew he felt it too.

A cold, familiar voice followed.

"You cannot run from fate."

I reached for Reich without thinking. My fingers brushed his hand, and it hurt, because it burned. Pain raced up my arm, but I didn't let go.

I wouldn't.

Because if I did...I didn't know if I would get him back.

If I'd get any of him back.

His hand tightened around mine, and for one fractured heartbeat—I felt *him*. The man I love.

I felt Reich.

CHAPTER THIRTY-FIVE

REICH

WHEN THEY BROUGHT ME into the courtyard, I didn't know what to expect.

They said it was the only way that I would be allowed to see her.

Sage.

Then they placed a man in front of me.

He began to writhe beneath my stare—trembling, unraveling.

And I couldn't stop it. All I could do was watch.

And when Sage finally stepped into view, my breath caught.

Relief flooded me, but it was short-lived because there was fear in her eyes.

And not just fear—but hesitation.

At me.

Like she was looking at a stranger.

Like she didn't know who I was anymore.

And I wasn't sure I knew either.

Cresil looked at us like she knew a secret—like she had been waiting for this moment where everything was about to break.

I had always belonged to them, ever since that first initiation years ago, but this felt different.

This felt final and *damning.*

She stepped forward out of the shadows, with this calm and certain look plastered across her face—like she had been orchestrating every move that led to here. And now she was just ready to watch the wreckage.

And she probably had.

The pieces probably were falling just as she and the elders had planned.

"Reich."

Cresil said my name like I was good friend she'd taken pity on, like she wasn't someone who knew they had power over me and abused that power over and over again.

She was good at that. Better than anyone. And now she was looking at me like this—like Sage and I standing in this courtyard was inevitable.

Her gaze shifted, slow and deliberate, until it landed on Sage.

And something in me stiffened.

Cresil's eyes softened. Almost pitying. Like she already knew whatever was coming was worse than anything we could have imagined—and like it was already too late to stop it.

"You're both to come with me now," she said. Her tone was clean and polished. Too controlled.

There was no pretense of threat because she didn't need one.

She never had.

She gestured with an elegant flick of her wrist.

Behind her, Berith waited silently, not moving a muscle. A shadow that didn't need permission to become its queen's teeth.

"Astaroth is expecting you," Cresil added. Like it was an invitation and not some fucked up form of sentencing she was announcing.

But I knew better.

I knew the punishments... I knew that this is where Sage and I would burn together.

Because Sage was an outsider, and they didn't take kindly to outsiders.

Cresil's gaze lingered on Sage again, and I felt the shift in the space around us before she continued, "He has something you both need to hear."

The way she said it made my pulse thunder behind my ribs and I felt Sage tense at my reaction while she stood beside me. There was a spike in her pulse where my fingers wrapped around hers.

I glanced down at our hands. At her fingers that were cold but strong, clenched tightly around mine like she was scared to let go. So, I did the only thing I could do and gave her a small, deliberate squeeze.

A steady one.

A touch that said, *"Stay calm. Stay close. We'll get through this."*

I looked back at Cresil, my expression probably carved from the same stone this place was built from.

"Then what are you waiting for? Take us," I said, trying to keep my voice even and controlled.

Like it was a choice. Like Sage and I had any control at all.

Cresil's mouth curved at the corner into a vicious smile. Not kind. Not even cruel. Just *knowing*.

Berith stepped forward and for a second, I felt Sage shift her weight— a moment so brief it almost slipped by but I felt it.

The tight coil of muscle like she was ready to fight them and run for our lives. But that wasn't the right move here, so, I tightened my grip again.

A wordless command.

Not yet. Stay with me.

She stilled.

But I could feel her heart racing and I hated this, putting her through this. I hated all of it.

But we followed. Because we had to. Because this wasn't a fight we could win.

I didn't know what was coming—only that it wouldn't be good.

Whatever it was, it was going to change us. I could feel it in my bones.

I brought a stranger into their territory. This had to be about that. This had to be my punishment.

But if it was—then so be it.

I'd take whatever was coming and I'd do everything I could to protect her through it.

And I wouldn't go down without a goddamn fight.

The corridors inside of the main hall twisted around us like a throat closing in.

Narrow and slick with condensation.

Every step sounded louder than it should. Boots scraped against damp stone. Breaths came too fast and too shallow. My own pulse was counting down to something I couldn't stop.

They led us deeper into the compound.

Past places I'd been once upon a time.

Past the familiar rooms where I had been initiated and taught to serve the ENA in.

And then further. Down into places you didn't go. The ones I had never seen and never been allowed to see.

Even during my first years when I wore their mark with pride, I was kept from this.

Even when I was the knife they pointed at their enemies, they never let me get this close.

Not to these halls.

They were reserved for the elders. The place where, from what I understood, legacy families traded in bloodlines and fate.

Where Astaroth ruled over all of it. Like a god.

But to me he was more of a corpse propped up on a glorified throne.

I felt Sage watching me out of the corner of my eye, carefully as we moved. Like she was still searching for something in me.

I didn't know if she was afraid for me—or of me and I didn't know which one was worse.

They took us to a chamber carved from black stone. The walls were smooth and polished, regal like, in their glossiness. The floor glowed faint beneath our feet, runes embedded and burned into the checkered flooring.

Fire burned in sconces along the walls but they didn't give off heat. Their light was cold, just like that massive room. And the smell—sickeningly sweet incense littered the air, thick enough to choke on.

I felt Sage's breath hitch beside me as we entered. Feeling her fingers flex in mine like she was already pulling away, but I wouldn't let her because it was too late.

It was too late the moment we were both dragged to this compound.

And I was going to beg for their mercy on her if it came down to it.

A set of twelve eyes watched me, as they sat high and mighty at their crescent table pointed inward towards us.

They told me to kneel, but I didn't move.

I didn't flinch and I hardly even blinked.

They didn't force me. They just watched. Like they were waiting for something to click. For something inside me to snap back into place. Like they already knew it would.

My eyes moved to Cresil who stood off to the side as Berith lingered behind her. Pristine in her robes. Calm as ever. Like a statue waiting for its next offering.

But it was the others who mattered now.

The elders seated in front of Sage and I, like a court order. Shrouded in white robes, with hoods that kept their faces half-shadowed and eyes gleaming slightly like knives catching a glimpse of light in the dark.

They studied me like a weapon. Like a thing they once forged and left to rust. And were now wondering if I was still sharp enough to be useful. Or maybe dangerous enough to need destroying.

Astaroth stepped forward.

His movement was slow and measured as he took deliberate steps towards us.

His voice was quiet when it came but it sliced through the chamber in merciless echoes.

"Blood recognizes blood."

My jaw locked and I didn't move, as I felt Sage go rigid next to me, like the phrase meant something to her.

His gaze shifted past me, as he turned towards Sage.

My heart pounded behind my ribs and I kept her close.

Ready to tear him limb from limb if he came anywhere close to her.

Astaroth's mouth curved. It wasn't a smile. It was something cold and assured.

It made my mark burn and I couldn't help but flinch.

But when he didn't actually make any move towards Sage.

That's when it clicked.

This was always part of it.

Somehow, she had always been a part of their plan.

Then...

"She carries the next," Astaroth said, almost casually—like it was nothing.

But it hollowed me out.

The air thickened, pressing down on my chest until every breath felt weighted. Even the shadows seemed to lean in closer, listening.

I looked at Sage.

She looked at me.

And in her wide eyes, I saw it—the flicker of realization. Like something ancient had just stirred awake inside her.

My voice caught before it could form the question, but she beat me to it.

"How?" Her voice trembled. "How do you know?"

No one answered.

Astaroth's smile didn't move, but something behind his eyes did—a slow, knowing gleam.

Then Berith spoke, low and calm:

"Blood recognizes blood."

Sage took a step closer to me, her hand hovering near her stomach as if she could somehow protect what they claimed was there. Her breath hitched, and I could feel it—the tremor running through her body as it reached me.

I wanted to tell her they were wrong. That this was just another mind game. That we could still leave, still fight.

But my throat burned.

Because part of me—the part I didn't want to admit existed—wasn't sure anymore.

Astaroth studied us like a proud creator admiring his work. "You were always meant to return, Reich," he said smoothly, each word deliberate. "And she was always meant to bring you home. Together, you will bring forth the next of your generation. A prophecy has been born. Congratulations. We'll be speaking with you soon. You're dismissed."

His voice lingered long after he finished speaking, curling around the room like smoke.

The prophecy. The purpose. The chains they'd been forging since the beginning.

They ushered us out of the room within seconds.

And I didn't know what to do.

So, I obeyed, even as I seethed inside.

Chapter Thirty-Six

SAGE

They separated us the second we were dismissed. The second I thought maybe—*just maybe*—Reich would take my hand and we would make a run for it.

But the moment never came.

The guards peeled him away from me like it was already done. Like everything had already been decided for us.

And I let them. I didn't even speak out because I knew that I no longer had a choice and neither did he.

But I watched when Reich flinched as they pulled me from his grasp.

He mouthed something to me I couldn't quite make out.

And I hate that I couldn't.

The guards brought me to a different room, one that actually had a bed, leaving me to wonder where they had taken Reich and why we were being separated.

All I could see was the pained look on his face as they escorted me away, the silent plea in his eyes for me to go quietly, to not make a scene.

I sat on the stone bench in the middle of these new chambers.

My back was pressed hard against the cold stone wall like I was holding myself together with the pressure alone. My knees were drawn up tight, arms wrapped around them until my hands ached from gripping so hard.

The room was silent, but it wasn't the kind of silence that was empty. It hummed with something old and weighted like the bones likely buried underneath this floor. The torchlight flickered against damp stone. A low, imperfect flame that brought shadows that moved even when nothing else did. They danced on the walls like they had their own rules.

And my heart— it was pounding so hard I swore they could hear it.

After what seemed like hours, a woman came in and hovered in the corner across from me along with a man that looked like a guard standing like a sentry against the door.

They were staring but I ignored them all the same. What was the point when all hope seemed lost? I knew that the moment I walked into that massive room with all those leaders.

Reich and I weren't ever getting out of this.

We were stuck.

And now they thought we were holding their prophecy.

The sickness coiled in my gut again, even heavier now, but it wasn't just nausea anymore. It was this deep feeling inside that knew. The terrible, irreversible knowledge that I didn't want to admit. Not even to myself. But it was there, and I wasn't sure it was ever going away.

The woman sat across from me and watched with the kind of stillness that made my skin crawl. Like she didn't have to do anything else but wait. Like she had already seen how this whole thing ends and was just here to witness it.

She was older, mid-fifties. Her face was lined, but there was a softness about her. Her ceremonial-like white robes were pristine and bright.

I always found that amusing.

They wore white, the color of purity, yet nothing about them was pure.

It was *corrupted*.

Yet, every fold of fabric fell exactly where it was supposed to, with no blemish on the white canvases they paraded around in.

She reached for me without warning. Her hands steady as stone, fingers cool as they curled around my wrist. As if it was the most normal thing in the world.

I didn't pull away. I let her. And I didn't know why.

Maybe it was because I had already lost hope.

"I know you must be wondering how we know about the baby," she said, voice smooth and calm. "We do not need to test you."

Her thumb brushed over the skin where my pulse pounded wild. Out of control and frantic. And she felt it. I knew she did. I could tell by the way she looked at me with pity.

"Blood recognizes blood." She whispered.

Those words. They had meaning now.

I wanted to tear my arm from her grasp. I wanted to fight.

Scream. Shatter something— her fingers, my bones, the entire world.

But I didn't. I just sat there. Frozen.

Her fingers pressed more firmly against my pulse— not hard, not cruel. But with a tenderness behind her touch like she deemed me precious or sacred in some way.

"This is ridiculous," I whispered. More to myself then to her. I heard the lie in my voice before I finished the words, and I knew she heard it too.

She smiled, like she was happy and it made my stomach knot.

"This is all a superstition..." I said, as I stared back at her with disbelief. ".... This place's sick delusion. You can't know I am pregnant... I've barely been with Reich for two weeks and even if I was, Reich and I aren't a part of some prophecy."

She continued to smile at me faintly. A small, controlled expression that didn't reach her eyes.

"No," she said with finality and a sharpness to it, like what she spoke was gospel. "You knew before we told you, didn't you? It was fate. Always fate." she said.

Her tone was gentle. Almost kind. But I didn't trust it.

Her gaze held mine and caused my breath to stutter, as my whole entire body stilled.

I contemplated what she said...

No, I couldn't have known.

Could I have known?

But deep down— somewhere in the dark— maybe I did, that first day I woke up nauseous.

No. Maybe. What does this mean?

The man continued to stand nearby. Like a dog waiting for a command that it already knew was coming. He didn't move until I forced myself to look at him.

And when I did— he looked human. That was the worst part because he didn't look like a monster. None of them did.

They looked like ordinary people, lost in this.

But I had learned better. And I didn't want to fall prey to that trap.

Monsters didn't wear masks. They wore human faces. Soft eyes. Gentle smiles. They spoke of mercy while they sharpened their knives.

"You all keep talking about fate," I said. My voice was steady, but everything inside of me was shaking. "... About prophecy."

I breathed in slow holding the man by the door's gaze. "But Reich isn't yours."

He tilted his head like he was listening to a child. Or a fool.

As I continued, "And I sure as hell am not either."

There was no fear in my voice. Not now. Only fire and I made sure he heard it.

But instead, he just watched me amused, almost patient, like he was waiting for me to finally come to terms with my new reality they had handed me.

"You misunderstand," he said softly. As if it was a kindness. "It isn't about a prophecy."

His gaze flickered down to my stomach then back up as he held my eyes in his, "It's about destiny."

I scoffed and the sound tore out of me sharp as I spoke, "I don't give a damn about destiny."

His lips twitched. Just once. Like he was waiting for that. Like he expected it.

"And yet," he said, "You carry the next piece of it."

My stomach knotted. The sickness surged. Not from nausea or fear but from fury. A kind of rage I didn't know what to do with. I curled my hands into fists, digging my nails into my palms until I felt skin split, and it stung.

I wouldn't let them see me break. I wouldn't give them that. Not now. Not *ever*.

They wouldn't take that ownership over me.

"I don't believe in whatever purpose or destiny you have," I snapped.

The man stepped closer in, measured and controlled steps. Like he had already won, as if merely having this conversation was a formality before cashing in his winnings.

"That doesn't matter," he murmured. "Because it believes in you."

The words settled cold into my spine, as he and the woman turned back around and left me to myself.

Or maybe they just left me to think I was.

Either way, I sat there on the stone bench, arms wrapped tight around my stomach as my body curled in on itself.

I didn't know how much time passed because I swore it felt like time moved different in places like this. Or maybe it stopped altogether.

But eventually— I heard the scrape of the door again.

Footsteps that were steady yet heavy all at the same time.

They were familiar and I didn't look up because I already knew who it was.

Reich stopped in front of me, but he didn't say anything at first. All he did was stand there, silently but his presence was heavy, and it commanded the attention of the room.

It was the same presence he gave when he was carrying something too big to set down.

He knelt down in front of me slowly. His hands resting on his thighs like he was fighting the urge to reach for me or maybe he already lost the fight hours ago and just hadn't found his way back yet.

But he stayed there, eyes fixated on the ground with his head bowed like he didn't know where to start.

Neither did I.

The silence stretched and I couldn't bear it, so I spoke first, even though I didn't want to.

"I'm still not afraid of you," I whispered.

And it was almost true. I wasn't afraid of him. Not really. I was afraid of what was happening to him. What they were turning him into. This so-called prophecy they think we are a part of. That I might be pregnant.

Reich's jaw tightened. His fingers twitched and then curled into fists. He looked away from me. Down. Anywhere but at my face.

And when he finally spoke—his voice was low, broken in a way I had never heard before.

"I'm sorry wildflower," he said.

I stared at him, frozen. Not sure I'd heard him right.

"Sorry?" I repeated, my voice small.

For what?

But he didn't answer, and I hated that I expected that.

Because I didn't know what was in his head anymore and that scared me.

Still, I waited. Because that's what love does—it waits even when it knows better.

Even after years apart, I still loved him.

And beneath that love was something uglier, something I didn't want to name— the fear of losing him again.

He stepped closer for a heartbeat, like he might reach for me.

Then he stopped and pulled back.

The space between us felt like punishment.

"I'm sorry that you got involved in this," he said finally. "That I didn't protect you... again."

The word *again* hit me.

I rose to meet his gaze, shaking my head. "Reich... you couldn't have known. I don't blame you for this."

He exhaled, jaw tightening. "I blame myself," he said. "All I ever seem to do is the wrong thing but I'm going to keep trying to make it right."

Before I could answer, before I could tell him that I didn't want redemption—I just wanted *him*—he was gone.

Just like before.

Leaving me with nothing but the echo of his apology and the hollow space where he should've stayed.

CHAPTER THIRTY-SEVEN

REICH

I SHOULD HAVE BEEN dead.

By every law that governed that place.

By every decree they had handed down for less than half of what I'd done.

I should have been gutted on their altar in front of her.

But I wasn't.

I was standing there. Alive and breathing.

And they wouldn't touch me even though they should.

God knows they have executed men for less.

But they wouldn't.

Because I wasn't just a traitor anymore.

I was also a prophecy.

And it made every part of my skin crawl.

I had to know. I needed to know. I wasn't going to settle for a "Congratulations you're pregnant and part of a prophecy...see you later."

So, after I left Sage, I asked for the guards to escort me back to the elders' chambers.

I stood back in the center of the chambers. A hollowed-out cathedral of stone and fire.

The elders sat in their carved stone chairs like relics dug out of the dirt. Their robes hung heavy around them, thick with power they didn't earn and history they didn't survive.

Their eyes watched me. Measuring and calculating.

Astaroth spoke first. "Reich... good and loyal servant. What brings you back to us so soon?"

I hesitated but I knew that I had to speak, I had to know, which meant I had to ask. "What is this prophecy that Sage and I are a part of? Why did you choose us?"

He paused as I watched the elders around him sit in a sort of indifferent silence before continuing, "We didn't choose you. The higher power chose you at birth. Your bloodline must continue."

I clenched my jaw until I heard the faint grind of my teeth.

"And she ensures it," he added, like Sage's existence was just another line in their scripture.

Like she's some kind of sacred vessel they can hollow out for their use.

They owned me. They weren't supposed to own her.

My hands curled into fists at my sides, and I forced the words out through clenched teeth. "What does that mean for her?"

The question wasn't soft. It wasn't polite. I knew they could hear the edge in my tone and I wanted them to.

One of the elders tilted their head. A slow, deliberate motion and I caught the faintest glimmer of amusement in their eyes like they'd already seen the end of this story and were just waiting for me to catch up.

"She is untouchable," one of the elders said.

Like that was meant to reassure me. But it didn't and it never would.

Untouchable.

I knew exactly what that meant.

It meant she was some artifact.

Like something preserved under glass.

Like a relic they didn't intend to worship but instead to be kept on a shelf, locked away. Something valuable enough to guard, but never free again.

"You will live, Reich," Astaroth said, stepping forward. His voice was smooth and practiced but also as hollow as an empty grave. "And so will she... because what she carries is our next most valuable soldier for the coming generation."

Soldier?

The burn at the back of my neck flared again. The brand. The mark they gave me. It seared hot like an ember pressed into flesh, giving me a silent warning or perhaps a promise of what was to come. I'm not sure which it was anymore but I could feel it.

I took a slow breath, controlling every inch of my breathing.

And I asked.

Because I had to.

Because I needed to hear it from them and because deep down I already knew, but I needed it spoken aloud to make it real.

"What about my mark? Why does it burn now? And if my bloodline is so important then what happened to my brother?"

There was a silence that followed that was heavy. Like a door closing or more like a tomb being permanently sealed shut.

Astaroth's gaze settled on me.

Flat. Unflinching. Almost dead.

Just like the corpse that I had always thought him to be.

"So many questions..." He said. "Your mark is fate doing its job and it isn't your job to ask until the time comes... You are transforming into something magnificent, be grateful you and Sage have been chosen to see the light."

See the light?

I stared at him. At the calm stretched too tight across his face. At his certainty.

And I wanted to tear it away. I wanted to see if he bled just as black as Cresil did.

"As for Castor... he is serving his purpose now, just like you," he continued simply. A hint of finality to his voice like it was already done.

I saw Cas in my mind. He was standing in front of me. Alive and smiling, cracking some unhinged joke.

But his eyes were gone and hollow.

I knew before I asked. I knew. I just needed to hear it. Needed to drag it into the light so I couldn't keep lying to myself.

They took him and Sam.

Just like they took Sage and I.

"You were always meant to return," Astaroth said, like this was a homecoming that I should be grateful for.

And then he gestured towards the exit as he finished, "....and she was always meant to bring you home."

His eyes stayed glued to the door, as he dismissed me.

And everything hit when that door shut.

The inevitability they believed in like they thought they wrote this story and we were all just playing our parts.

Two pawns finally back where they belong.

They believed they owned us now.

Me, her, and their supposed soldier.

They already buried us beneath their prophecy, and the truth was—I was part of it. No matter how badly I didn't want to be.

I *did* belong to them. Not by choice, but by blood. By the brand that was burned into me all those years ago.

There was no escaping it.

I knew it even then.

But Sage—

She was still reaching for the edges of something free.

And maybe that's why I refused to let go of her when I got her back and why it was so hard to leave all those years ago.

I remembered her face when she saw me for the first time in here. The fear in her eyes. The fire burning underneath it. And I held onto it.

Because it was still there.

The fight. The refusal.

She wouldn't let me slip. She'd keep fighting with me.

I took it in like a promise and made one of my own.

Right here. Right now.

In this place that wanted to break us both.

Whatever happens next—I was going to find a way to unravel this all from the inside out.

Quietly. Precisely. Permanently.

And I was going to find my brother and his girl.

But first, I had to get us out.

Chapter Thirty-Eight

SAGE

I FELL ASLEEP AFTER Reich came by to say sorry and basically vanish again into thin air.

When he came the second time, it startled me. The door shut behind him with a heavy, deliberate click.

Reich didn't move at first and neither did I.

He stood there in the silence, our breaths lingering, as if the walls were holding theirs and waiting, listening for what happened next.

I stared at them—the walls. At the old damage that was carved deep into the stone. Damage someone survived. Or maybe didn't.

I wondered which ones we would be.

I wondered what pieces of us would survive this place.

If we'd leave anything behind when this was over for this 'prophecy' or 'destiny' we didn't ask for.

Reich exhaled slowly behind me. Like he was catching his breath. But I could feel his eyes on me, their weight a pressure at my back, steady and familiar even when I couldn't bring myself to meet them. At least, not while I was still holding myself together with broken hands.

My arms stayed wrapped tight around my ribs, as if I could hold in everything that was trying to tear out of me, but it still felt like I was unraveling. And he knew it.

I felt the way his attention sharpened— not pushing. Not demanding. Just aware and present.

"Come here," he said quietly.

It wasn't a command. It wasn't an order.

It was a *plea*.

And it slipped into my heart before I could stop it.

I moved toward him. Because no matter how many times this world has cracked open beneath us, no matter how terrified I was of what I might find in his eyes, some part of me was always reaching for him.

Even when I was afraid.

His hands found my shoulders first. Slow and steadily. His fingers settling like they were afraid of hurting me and were cataloging all the ways I might break.

His grip tightened—just slightly—his thumbs brushing along the slope of my shoulders in quiet reassurance, but it was careful.

"I'm going to get you out of here... both of us," he said. His voice was low and rough around the edges.

I closed my eyes. Just for a second. Because I wanted to believe him.

"We're going to figure this out," he added, his voice a little steadier now like he was saying it to convince himself as much as me.

When I opened my eyes again, he was already looking at me.

Not just looking but *seeing*.

And it was the same look that made me weak. The one that made me feel like I was the only thing tethering him to the world. Like he needed me.

But there was still something heavier behind his speech. Something dark and afraid. And it was that fear that gutted me the most.

His hands slid from my shoulders to my arms, his fingers curling around my elbows like he was keeping me steady. Or maybe it was for him.

"I should have talked to you about what was happening to me sooner" he said suddenly, the words catching in his throat. His thumb brushed along the side of my neck, a slow drag of skin on skin, like he needed the contact to ground himself as he continued.

"I didn't know how to cope or what was even happening to me," He exhaled harshly. "... I still don't."

There was an ache in his voice I had never heard before.

"I thought if I didn't say it," he goes on, quieter now, "if I didn't let it be real, I could—" He stopped. The words choked off like they cost too much to finish. His hand dropped away from my neck, falling useless at his side. He shook his head, jaw clenched tight against something sharp.

"I'm sorry... every time I am close to happiness... something tears it apart and when you came back into my life, I was so happy. I didn't know how to trust it. I didn't know how to trust that it wouldn't get ruined again... and in some ways it still is... ruined." he said.

I leaned into him closer. Close enough that our breath mingled in the small space between us. I pressed my forehead to his, closing the distance because I needed to. Because we both did.

And I believed him. I did.

But it still hurt.

Because even though he was scared, I had been carrying this weight alone. Believing he didn't trust me. Believing I wasn't enough for him to let me in. But it wasn't about trust.

It was about fear. The kind of fear that gets under your skin and hollows you out from the inside. The kind that makes you think if you name something, you'll lose it.

His hands found my waist like they had always belonged there, like they never left. He pulled me in, not rough, not desperate—just there and ready.

And I let myself fall into him deeper because I needed this as much as he did. Maybe more.

His hands trembled against me as he pulled away, but they didn't seem fearful. It was more like a simmering anger. It hummed through him like a low-grade current, contained but lethal.

"They aren't keeping us alive for us," he said, his voice biting, sharp enough to wound.

"They're keeping us alive for this—for whatever cursed *soldier* they believe is inside of you."

I flinched. I tried not to, but I did. The words cut deeper than they should. Deeper than he meant them to.

He saw it immediately and I watched it flicker across his face— the realization and immediate regret.

"Sage—" he started, but I cut him off before he could finish.

"Why would you call it cursed?" I said. "This isn't a curse, Reich. It's— well we don't even know what it is or if it is even true. It's not a curse. It's—"

I couldn't finish. I couldn't name what it was. But I knew it wasn't that.

How could it be? Wasn't a baby supposed to be a blessing?

His gaze darkened. Something feral flickering there. "You don't know what they'll do to you... me...," he said, glancing at my stomach, "You don't know how they are going to control everything."

And he was right. I didn't. But neither did he because this had never happened to him and they didn't make a guidebook for how cults deal with people they deem to be part of their prophecy.

And the truth of it hung between us like a noose.

"What if they're right?" I asked, sharper than I meant to be. But I needed him to hear it. I needed him to understand. "What if this was always supposed to happen?"

He goes still. Completely still. Like the words had knocked the air out of his lungs.

The silence that followed was heavy and I swallowed hard. Forcing the next words out even though they hurt. Even though they feel like betrayal.

"What if I always was supposed to be the one who brought you back here? What if we are really a part of some prophecy?"

His jaw clenched so tight I could see the muscle jump. His breath came ragged, uneven. Like he was holding back something he knew he couldn't stop and then I saw it.

The pure, unrelenting fear in his eyes.

Not for himself. But directed at me... like I was one of them.

I thought for a moment he was going to push me away, but he pulled me in closer instead.

He pressed his forehead to mine, as his hands tightened at my waist like he could anchor me there.

"No," he said, his voice firm. "We are not them. I won't ever let us become them."

I closed my eyes again. Just for a moment. Because I wanted to believe that too. And because I still loved him. Even if I wasn't sure who we were becoming anymore.

But I knew who we were going to have to be.

I sighed deeply as I spoke, "You're right. We aren't them." I said. "But it's who we have to be now because if this is real..." I clenched my stomach. ".... Then we can't let it become one of them either."

I held onto Reich, and I felt him flinch beneath my touch.

His breath hitched—just once—like he was about to say something. Like there was still time to undo whatever this was turning into.

But he didn't speak.

He only looked at me, eyes heavy with that familiar look that told me what his next move was.

And sure enough, he stepped back.

Out of my arms. Out of the moment. Out of reach.

The door creaked open behind me and I turned away, curling myself up on the bed, so I didn't have to watch him leave.

I just listened.

Once again, to the soft drag of his footsteps across the floor.

To the quiet click of the door as it closed.

And to the silence that followed, heavier than anything he could've said.

For once I wished he would just stay.

Chapter Thirty-Nine

REICH

SHE TURNED AWAY FROM me, and I watched as she drew her knees up to her chest and wrapped her arms tightly around herself like she was holding everything in—her fear, her hope, whatever tiny thread of trust she still had left for me.

I watched her for a second longer than I should have. Long enough to know I hated walking away from her right now.

But I had to do this. For her. For the chance at a future that felt less like survival and more like something we could actually live.

We had two options, find a way out of here and risk death or play by their rules.

And I knew the decision I was going to have to make.

Because every decision I had made up until this point never worked.

So I was doing the opposite of what I thought was right.

I didn't know if it was the correct decision, but Sage was right, we had to play their game.

I just knew that this was the only way through.

And I needed answers. I needed more than what Astaroth gave me in the elders' chambers.

I turned away before I could talk myself out of it and let the doubt swallow me whole.

Walking through this whole compound felt like one massive mausoleum. Every breath tasted like dust and something older. Like history that refused to die and for a moment, I wondered if that's what they had been shaping me into this entire time— A history relic of their war. A monument to their control.

I shoved the thought down and kept moving.

No more thoughts of prophecy. I would figure that out later with Nael.

As I turned my focus from the things Astaroth and the elders' said, my mind kept circling back to what Sage said.

This isn't a curse.

Her voice was in my head.

This isn't a curse.... but it didn't feel like a gift either.

It felt like they had carved open our future and left us bleeding in it.

They had given us life, and they were holding it over our heads like a weapon.

But I needed to know.

Because it wasn't that I didn't want a future. I wanted it. I wanted it with Sage.

But not under their terms.

I wanted a life where no one was watching us through a scope. Where I didn't have to sleep with a knife under my pillow. Where Sage didn't flinch every time the door opened.

But I guess neither option really offered us that kind of mercy.

But if the one where we lived meant I had to make a deal with a devil like Astaroth— then so be it.

After I left Sage, I had the two guards that were tasked to 'guard me' take me to where I found Cresil near the lower chambers. She stood with her trusty Berith by her side, silent and still like a statue. He watched me like he was calculating how many bones he could break before I took my last breath.

I stared right back, giving them nothing, because I wasn't here to play games with either of them.

Cresil didn't seem surprised to see me but then again, she never was. Her expression said that much.

There was no satisfaction in it. No triumph. Just indifference.

She lifted one hand in a lazy gesture and Berith took a half-step back. Not far.

"I need to speak with Astaroth," I finally said. My voice was even and flat, giving away nothing.

Cresil's brow lifted slightly, the faintest crease between her eyes, but she didn't argue. She knew why I was here. She knew from the second I walked up to them.

"Follow me," she said, shooing the guards who had escorted me, and turning without waiting.

The corridor stretched long and narrow. The further we walked, the colder it got.

And then we stopped.

Cresil pushed open a door and gestured me inside with a small flick of her fingers. Like I was stepping into a confession I was too late to avoid.

Astaroth was waiting.

He sat at the head of a long table but it didn't feel like a throne room. It felt like a crypt.

The walls were stone, cracked in some places, with mortar splattered within the creases. The light was low, casting long shadows that looked too much like teeth.

He gestured to the seat across from him, but I stayed standing.

My small act of defiance, but he didn't care. He already knew I wasn't here for respect or to cower at his feet.

"I need to know," I said, keeping my voice steady. Not because I was calm but because I had to be. Otherwise, I was going to lose it and risk everything.

But God, did I want to smash his face in.

"What do I have to do?" I swallowed, the words cutting sharp. "To keep her safe. To give us... a normal life. You say I am important, and we are raising your next greatest soldier... we have to be safe... for the prophecy."

The words tasted bitter like something I wasn't allowed to say but said anyway. Because they mattered. Because *she* mattered.

Astaroth studied me for a long time. His gaze was cold and measured like he was cataloging the final pieces of me before he filed them away.

Then he nodded slowly, as if he has finished deliberating.

"Reich... you have always been so impatient but a good and faithful servant. So, I'll give you this kindness and tell you what I will arrange. We will have you moved to a remote area," he said. "A new settlement. Rural. Hidden. New identities."

He paused like he was letting that sink in.

"You will be protected," he added. "The child will be shielded from the outside world."

Protected meant hidden. Shielded meant owned.

"No outside contact will be allowed unless it is from ENA-approved members. You will have limited duties outside of your inhabitance. And when the boy comes of age, he will begin his duties just like his father." He concluded.

A boy? How would they know?

God, I hope it's a girl.

I kept my expression blank but inside, everything tightened because I heard these rules for what they were.

Control. Isolation. A slow death painted up like *mercy*.

They didn't want to protect us. They wanted to keep us *quiet*. Tame and docile because I've become too problematic for them. We *all* have.

Something inside screams at me that he knows about what me and the guys have been up to.

He knows about the plan.

Somehow, He does. I could see it, but he was keeping quiet.

He wasn't gutting all of us... *why?*

Why leash the wolf instead of putting it down?

I nodded tightly like I had any choice.

"And Castor..." I said.

Astaroth didn't blink. "What about him?"

"Where is he?" I kept my voice flat but I needed this answer like I needed air.

"He's here taking care of a few things for the elders. Some experimentation and training." Astaroth said.

Experimentation? What the fuck was that supposed to mean?

It felt like he was lying, and I was sure he saw the skepticism etched on my face, but he didn't elaborate and I wasn't stupid enough to push.

But I could put it together. They took Castor because he was too close. Because he found something in the files he wasn't supposed to and was working with us to take them down.

And I wasn't sure I was ever going to get him back. Not the way I knew him and maybe not at all.

Astaroth stood like he was getting ready to dismiss me.

But I interjected because I needed to ask, "Sage and I saw something in the woods, it tried to summon us to you."

"Ah yes! The mephistos... don't worry about them. They are just our messengers. Think of it as a type of special messaging from the ENA. You and Sage are now a part of the light. You will perceive what others cannot."

He had mentioned that before... "*the light*". That Sage and I could '*see the light*' and now we were '*a part of the light*'.

"The light?" I said.

"It's not your job to ask so many questions."

I could tell he was getting irate by his tone.

I didn't push but I wanted to. I wanted to keep pushing until he broke. But I kept restrained. Leaving me feeling so fucking helpless.

He dismissed me with a glance, but not before twisting the knife one last time. "You will have time to say goodbye to those within the ENA," he said. "To make your peace but after that... you'll need to submit any visitations for approval. Not that you'll get many based on where you'll be located."

Then Sage and I will be gone. Hidden away.

They had officially stripped me down to something simple. A man with something to lose, who now had to be dependent upon them completely and that was the point.

I had been too close to breaking their hold. Too dangerous to let run loose. But chain me to a family— and they knew I'd chain myself for them.

They were betting on that and maybe they were *right*. Maybe they had finally found a leash that worked.

When I stepped back out into the cold hallway, I stood there for a long time. Listening. Thinking. Letting the weight of it settle into my bones and I couldn't stop but think about my brother and wonder where he was in this place right now. What he would say to me in this moment. How we'd find a way out of this. How he'd never let me succumb to this kind of defeat and how he would then remind me of who I am.

But I knew who we were now.

We were Ovitts. Or maybe I was one and he wasn't.

I didn't know. But he would never stop being my family and I needed to get him the hell out of here.

But I couldn't right now.

Not without risking Sage.

And I hated that.

I dragged my hand over the mark at the back of my neck as it burned—steady and familiar now. A reminder of what I was. What they had made me.

I pressed my fingers to it, like that might dull the sting. It didn't.

And I wondered if this was what Castor felt before they broke him. If he was still fighting somewhere inside or if everything Astaroth said was just a lie and he was already gone.

Chapter Forty

SAGE

I HEARD THE SOFT metallic click of the door before I saw him there. Subtle and controlled.

But the sound still seemed to cut through the stillness of the room, and my body reacted before my mind could catch up. My breath hitched in my chest, as my spine stiffened instinctively.

And then I looked up and saw Reich as he stood there across from me in the low light. Framed by the doorway, his broad shoulders tensed beneath his shirt, his hands flexed loosely at his sides. He was standing still—*too still*. Every muscle braced. Like he was waiting for a hit or about to deliver one.

For a long second, neither of us moved. It felt like I had stopped breathing the moment he looked up at me. Because for a moment there was something about the way he was looking at me that was *different*.

But then it softened back to him.

And I breathed.

The air dragged in slow and rough, but it filled my lungs. Because it was him.

And no matter how much of him that I felt like I was losing. I seemed to always find him again.

He crossed the room slowly, every step deliberate and measured. Like he wasn't sure how close he was allowed to get. And like he was waiting for me to decide.

"We're leaving," he said quietly.

I blinked. Once. Then I waited.

Because it couldn't be that simple.

It was *never* that simple.

He sunk down in front of me, lowering himself to his knees like it was the only place he could be. His hands came to rest on my thighs, steady and warm, his thumbs brushing slow circles into my skin like he was grounding himself. Or me. Or maybe the both of us.

"They're letting us go to one of their sanctioned areas," he said, voice low. "Out in some rural nowhere. Hidden. New names. New lives."

The words hung heavy like a sentence disguised as freedom.

A breath stumbled out of me and caught in my throat.

Protection. I'm sure that's what they were calling it, but it sounded like exile, and I was sure it would feel no different than this current prison. For both of us.

My fingers twisted together in my lap. The edges of my nails dug into my palms until they hurt but I needed to feel something. Something *real*.

At least it was out of here. I told myself.

"Did they say anything about Castor?" I asked.

Reich's throat worked as he swallowed. The flicker of something in his eyes—guilt, maybe. Regret.

"Yes, but I don't know," he said quietly.

"And Sam?" My voice was softer now. Smaller.

He didn't answer right away. His jaw tightened, a hard line that cut through his otherwise careful expression. He breathed out through his nose, slow and rough.

"*I don't know.*" he said finally. But there was something decisive in his tone. Something finished. Something that said there was nothing left to do right now.

And I didn't push because I knew that edge in his voice too well. I knew what it cost him to admit there was nothing he could fix.

His hands slid higher on my thighs, slow and sure. His thumbs still circling in that steady rhythm. Comforting and anchoring.

"I'm not going to fight it because I'm choosing this," he said. His voice was rough now. Low and raw, like he was afraid it would break if he spoke any louder. "You... and..."

His gaze dropped to my stomach, just for a heartbeat, then lifted back to meet mine. Clear and steady but also, certain.

"I didn't know where I stood for a while," he admitted. "I didn't know how to handle it. How to... cope." The word was heavy in his mouth. "Hell... I honestly thought we were dead the moment we walked through these gates and into that chamber... but somehow we are here. And the smartest thing for us to do... is exactly what they tell us to...until we can figure out a way around it."

I nodded slowly. And my hands found his.

I threaded my fingers through his, lacing them together. Tight. Secure.

"I was worried... when you left... I'm still worried about what's happening to you." I whispered.

More than worried but it's the only word I could say.

"I know... I am too." he said, as he leaned in, his forehead resting against mine and for a moment, we just breathed. Together.

In and out. Slow and steady.

"But for now, I'm here," he murmured. His voice was steel and softness all at once and I couldn't help but believe him. *Trust him.*

Even if everything else felt broken.

Even if nothing else made sense beyond this moment.

He lifted me down onto his lap without asking like he already knew I'd let him. Like he knew I needed this as much as he did. Maybe even more.

His arms slid beneath me, hands warm under my thighs as he lifted me gently, standing with me against his chest like I was something fragile.

He carried me up and lowered me down onto the bed behind us with a tenderness I'm not sure I deserved but he gave it anyway.

And I took it.

Reich hovered over me for a long moment. His gaze dragged over my face, tracing every line like he was memorizing it all over again. Like he was afraid he would forget.

"Somehow you've become everything to me, wildflower," he murmured. His fingers brushed my cheek, featherlight, like he was testing to make sure Iwas real.

My throat tightened. I wanted to speak. But I couldn't and I wasn't sure that I needed to say anything in this moment.

He leaned down and kissed me, softly. Slower than he ever has before.

It wasn't a claim. It wasn't desperation. It was something else. Something deeper. Like he was giving me something I didn't ask for but needed anyway.

His mouth moved over mine with quiet patience, coaxing, careful.

He undressed me with maddening patience—every button, every layer shed treated like a secret he'd been aching to unveil.

His eyes never left mine, even when his fingers skimmed down my arms and over my ribs, tracing the shape of me like I was something fragile.

By the time his lips found the curve of my neck, I was already trembling.

Not from nerves—

But from anticipation.

From the unbearable slow burn, he'd ignited with nothing but reverence.

It didn't take long for him to lose control and when he did, his mouth explored me like he was starved.

But not for release—for *connection*.

He sucked a bruise into the hollow of my hip, as he pressed his palm flat between my thighs, and I gasped, already aching beneath his touch.

He didn't tease. He parted me with his fingers, slow and deliberate, watching the way my body responded like he was memorizing it for the end of the world.

When he sunk into me, it was slow, deep and *perfect*.

I gasped his name like a plea, and he shook—like hearing it wrecked him.

He held my face in his hands as he thrusted, rolling his hips with an aching precision that left me shaking and *clenching*.

Every movement was a vow, every stroke angled to ruin me and rebuild me in the same breath.

My eyes fluttered but he didn't let me lose contact.

"Look at me... I want to see your eyes when you come undone," he said—voice wrecked, low and raw.

And I did because I *couldn't* look away.

He didn't stop. It was like he was drowning in it.

Like the only thing that would save him was being here with me, like this, breath to breath.

I clawed at his back, dug my nails in, trying to keep him tethered to this moment.

But he was already there.

Already *lost* in it.

Moaning against my mouth, whispering broken promises into my throat, telling me I felt like heaven and sin wrapped into one.

We fell apart together—

My legs wrapped around his waist, his hands gripping my hips like I was the only solid thing he'd ever held.

I came with a cry that said I didn't care what any nearby eavesdroppers thought.

And he followed immediately, releasing into me as he buried his face in my neck.

After, he didn't let go.

One arm locked around my waist, the other splayed possessively over my stomach.

His body still sheathed inside mine, as if pulling away would undo everything we just built.

He kissed my shoulder. My spine. My temple.

"You're mine," he murmured, voice hoarse. "Even if we are exiled... even if they change their minds and decide to kill us tomorrow."

I didn't answer because I didn't have to.

Because my body curled into him on instinct, and the world outside couldn't touch us here.

Not on this beat up little bed.

Not tonight.

I wouldn't let it.

And as I drifted, held tightly in the arms of the only man who's ever *seen* me, I let myself believe we survived.

Even if just for one night.

Even if just in each other.

CHAPTER FORTY-ONE

REICH

S AGE WAS ASLEEP.

HER BREATHING was soft and even, each slow exhale feathered against my skin in delicate pulses. Her fingers were curled tight in the sheet between us, like she was holding on to something she was afraid to lose.

Like if she let go, she wouldn't get it back.

And I couldn't blame her for that because I felt it too.

The uncertainty.

The slow pull of something that was slipping through our fingers no matter how tightly we held on.

I watched her chest rise and fall, steady. Still peaceful even though her body language told a different story.

But at least for now… she was *safe*.

For now… we were *together*.

And I would take it. Even if it felt like we were living on borrowed time.

I couldn't fall asleep, even though she could. I tried but eyes refused me rest. All I could do was stare at the ceiling like it might give me answers or assurance that the decision I made was the correct choice. Hoping that Castor was out there, safe but I hated not knowing for myself.

I continued to observe the cracks in the ceiling above, tracking the way the shadows shifted as the light gathered in from the tiny window and brought forth dawn.

But none of it calmed me. None of it settled the weight in my chest. Because I didn't know how to do this.

To stop scheming. To just live. To be a *father*.

I got up and made my way back to the room they'd kept me in before they allowed me to be with Sage. I still had one last piece of due diligence to handle—tie up what I could for the cause by seeing if I could dig up anything useful for Nael in the process.

Something on the families, at least. It wouldn't be much, but it was the least I could offer before being sent off to my next prison.

And while I wasn't exactly eager to step into whatever new life they'd laid out for me, I *was* in a hurry to get the fuck out of this place—and out from under their watchful eyes.

Not that it would matter on the outside. I knew they'd be checking in on us no matter what settlement they dumped us in.

As soon as I got back to the old room, I sat there on the cot, contemplating heavily, wishing I could just talk to my brother and hoping that this wasn't the end.

The door clicked softly, and I was on my feet before the latch finished turning. Silent. Steady. Years of training snapping through my spine before I could think or take a single breath.

I stood there, my weight balanced, my hands loose at my sides—but ready. *Always ready.*

The door opened slowly, and Cresil stepped inside, framed by the dead light in the hall.

She was wearing that same look she always did. Like none of this mattered and we were all wasting her time. Smug and bored, her expression polished so smooth like there was nothing left to read.

But there was something different now. A flicker in her eyes. Amusement. A new kind of knowing that made my skin crawl.

She stepped aside without a word and to my surprise, Castor walked in.

Smiling like he'd only been on a supply run instead of disappearing into the black for a goddamn week.

He grinned and it was familiar, almost easy. Like none of this was wrong. Like this was all *normal*.

"Miss me?" he said, flashing that same cocky smirk that used to drive Sam insane but somehow kept us both alive.

Cresil didn't wait for my answer or our reunion. She just turned and left as the door clicked shut behind her like a nail being driven into a coffin.

And then it was just us.

Me and him.

Neither of us moved.

I watched him. Carefully. Like I was seeing him for the first time.

Because I was.

He was still Castor. But he wasn't. Not exactly. Not like this or in this place. Not after everything I knew now.

Like the things he'd been keeping from me.

The truth about the Ovitts and who we killed.

All hidden. But why?

"You look like shit," he said, stepping closer. His tone was light. Teasing.

But his eyes—there was something there. Something sharp but off.

"Funny," I said flatly. "You look like you went on vacation."

He snorted. "Yeah, the spa services at the ENA's death camp are top-notch. You should try it sometime."

I should laugh. He wanted me to. It was the kind of line that would have pulled us both out of worse moments than this.

But I didn't. Because this wasn't Castor. Not really. And I could feel it.

There was something too smooth about him. Too casual.

His body language was perfect. His smile was intact. But the space between his words—it was too measured.

And then his eyes went wide for half a second.

Almost like a tell. The smallest shift.

But I saw it. Because I was trained to.

Because I trained him to.

It was a *warning*.

Not here. Not now. Play along.

So, I did. I relaxed my shoulders on purpose.

He would see it. They would too.

And I settled back into the chair behind me, arms loose at my sides like this was fine. Like I wasn't dissecting the entire situation apart in my head. Like I wasn't counting the exits and running every possible outcome while I sat there.

"What are you doing here, Cas?" I asked.

He shrugged like he hadn't just delivered a loaded message in the smallest flick of his eyes.

"Thought I'd check in," he said. "Congratulate you. Kid on the way." He grinned again, the sharpness of his teeth glinting in the low light. "I didn't think you had it in you."

"Neither did I but that's not what I was asking." I said almost halfheartedly but everything about my demeanor screamed of my skepticism.

He chuckled. Thin. Almost hollow.

And his eyes flicked again. Once. Fast. Urgent.

I sat with it. Because he did it again and I knew what this was.

He was telling me not to ask. Not to push.

And I couldn't help but trust him. More than I trusted anyone. Even if he was hiding something.

Even if he knew about the Ovitts and didn't tell me.

I still trusted him because he was my brother, and he always would be. And I was starting to think he didn't tell me because if he had— I wouldn't be alive.

And neither would Sage.

So, I let the conversation drift. I let it fall into old rhythms.

He asked me about the guys... how everyone was doing.

He said some backhanded jokes and brought up old stories that felt like they didn't belong to us anymore. How Keenan was really the one who had the worst—most unhinged—sense of humor. How Sam could outshoot all of us if she ever stopped flirting long enough to learn and aim. How Nael was so rigid he was eventually going to physically crack under the tension in his shoulders.

All of it felt normal in a strange sort of way. Though all we were doing was avoiding the conversation I wanted to have.

I smiled where I was supposed to. Laughed once or twice. Just enough to make it believable. Just enough to buy us time.

But underneath it all, I was calculating. Watching. Waiting for the next tell. For the next slip.

Because I already knew. The second Sage and I were in that new settlement— wherever the hell they were sending us— I was going to have to pull this apart.

I needed to find out what Cas was hiding and why he was hiding it.

What deal he made and what it had cost him.

Because whatever it was—it had to be life or death for him to end up in here.

I knew how Sage and I got here. We were forced and dragged in by the ENA for some prophecy.

But for Cas and Sam? It couldn't have been the same. Another prophecy? That didn't seem likely...

Astaroth said experimentation... why wouldn't he have said the same? And wouldn't us blood bound brothers be exiled together...

No, that couldn't be it.

And Cas wouldn't have come here willingly and he sure as hell wouldn't bring Sam ...would he have?

I leaned back in the chair, arms crossed loosely over my chest as I watched him.

My brother.

Cas was my family and I was going to get him out of this.

Even if he didn't think I could. Even if he didn't ask. And even if I had to do it in the middle of nowhere.

But I wouldn't move just yet.

I would let him keep pretending. I would let him play the part.

Because that was what he was asking me for in those moments he signaled. And because I owed him that for now.

But this war wasn't over. Not even close.

Cas glanced toward the door like he was already halfway gone.

He shifted on his feet, restless in a way I had never seen from him before. Not even when we were neck-deep in fire with nothing but each other and bad odds. There was something new now. Something hesitant. Like he wanted to say more but knew he couldn't. Or knew it wouldn't matter.

"I should go," he said finally, scratching the back of his neck like the movement might soften the moment. "Just stopped in to say hi. Make sure you weren't dead yet."

"Not yet," I said. "Give it time."

He huffed a short laugh, but there was no heat in it. No joy. Just familiarity. That same broken rhythm we always fell into.

He nodded toward the door. "I'll check in once you're both set up. Wherever they drop you two. Then we can *talk*."

I studied him for a moment, committing the details to memory. The careful stance. The weight in his jaw. The way his eyes hadn't stopped scanning since he walked in. He was already miles away.

"Be safe, Cas," I said. And I meant it more than I could let on. "You and Sam."

His gaze flickered once, just briefly.

"You too, brother... enjoy the quiet side of the ENA." he said.

Quiet meant watched. Quiet meant leashed.

Then he stepped back. One foot through the door. One hand braced on the frame like it was the only thing keeping him from disappearing entirely. "And Reich—"

He paused.

"Don't waste it."

The door latched shut before I could ask what he meant.

I stood there in the silence after, letting the weight of those words settle into my chest like they were meant to stay. Like maybe that was the real message. The one buried beneath all the others.

Don't waste it.

Don't waste *her*.

Don't waste *this*.

I stayed rooted in place, staring at the empty doorway like it might still give me answers. Like if I waited long enough, he'd walk back through it and say what he couldn't.

I sunk back into the chair, my elbows on my knees, hands laced tight like I could hold the moment still. Like I could stop whatever was coming next if I just sat there long enough and breathed through the ache.

The air felt heavy with everything left unspoken. With warnings and promises and the weight of a thousand things we couldn't say out loud. And even though I couldn't name them all, I knew this much:

Cas was still fighting. Still shielding me from something bigger. And it was on me now to figure out what the hell it was.

I pushed to my feet, the scrape of the chair legs sharp in the quiet.

I paused, one hand on the doorframe, and let the silence settle one last time.

Because whatever this life was about to become—it started now.

And I had to be ready for all of it.

Even the parts that felt impossible.

Then I turned, the weight of Cas's warning pressed deep into my ribs and made my way back to her.

To the only peace I'd ever known.

And I swore—I wouldn't *waste* it.

Not this time.

Chapter Forty-Two

SAGE

THE WARMTH WAS THE first thing I noticed when I woke.

It clung faintly to the sheets, tangled around my body like the ghost of his arms. The air still carried the heat of his skin, subtle but present.

But he wasn't here.

And sadly... I had gotten used to it.

My hand drifted over the empty space beside me, fingers searching instinctively, tracing over the indentation his body left behind on the bed.

Still warm. But cooling fast.

He couldn't have been gone long.

And Reich was not the kind of man who would leave without coming back. Not anymore. At least, that's what I told myself. That's what I had to believe now.

I breathed in slowly, forcing the air deep into my lungs. Steady. Controlled.

But the quiet in the room was heavy. *Too heavy.*

The stone walls that surrounded me felt closer than they did last night. Pressing in. Silent and suffocating.

Without him, this place felt smaller and colder.

It was a cage. Polished and clean, but a cage, nonetheless.

No matter how many times I told myself that we were getting out. That we would at least be away from them. This place made me doubt.

And I hated it. I hated what it seemed to be turning me into.

Someone who was losing hope.

I had fought too hard these last few years to let that happen again.

I sat up slowly, the sheets fell away from my skin, the chill in the air biting at my legs as I moved. I pulled his shirt tighter around me, the hem brushing my thighs as I settled back against the wall.

It still smelled like him. Cedar and smoke. And something dark but comforting underneath.

I breathed it in anyway because it grounded me. Because it reminded me that he would come back. And it was all I had right now.

I rubbed a hand over my stomach, slow and careful.

My body hadn't physically changed.

But I could feel that it was different. The quiet shift of something alive inside of me. Something new. Something *ours*.

The sound came softly.

Barely there. A faint scrape against stone, just beneath the door.

I froze. My breath hitching in my throat as my body went still, just listening and waiting.

No footsteps. No warning. Just that faint drag of something being slid across the cold floor.

Slowly, I pushed the blankets back and swung my legs over the side of the bed. The floor was freezing under my bare feet, but I didn't hesitate. I moved toward the door, careful and silent.

And there it was, through the gap at the bottom of the door.

A ribbon.

Deep red, its edges frayed and worn, like it had been handled too many times and carried too far to get here. It lied flat against the ground, unmoving, waiting for me to notice it. Like a message left by something that didn't knock.

I stared at it for a heartbeat. Then another before kneeling. My fingers closed around the fabric, lifting it slowly, carefully.

It was softer than it looked. Thin and old.

I turned it over in my hands and my stomach knotted when I saw the words. Small. Precise. Etched deep into the weave of the cloth, with ash.

GET OUT.

My breath left me in a sharp exhale, and I went still. Cold sweat beaded along my spine.

The ribbon... the writing...

Sam.

My pulse pounded in my ears, drowning out everything else as the room narrowed and shrunk.

Sam was here.

Somewhere in this place. And she was warning me.

I folded the ribbon carefully, the fabric trembling in my hands as I shook. I slipped it beneath the mattress, hiding it before I could talk myself into something reckless. Before I made a move, I couldn't take back.

The door opened a few minutes later.

Quiet. Careful. Like always.

Reich stepped inside, his movements smooth and practiced but his shoulders were tense. His jaw tight but his eyes— they softened when they landed on me.

Like I was the only thing that could ease whatever war was still raging behind them.

He crossed the room without a word, his hand brushing over my shoulder as he sat beside me on the bed. His thumb lingered against my skin with a warm and reassuring touch.

"You okay?" he asked quietly. His voice was low and steady but there was something under it. Something hollow.

Something that made me hesitate about telling him immediately about the ribbon.

I nodded. A small, forced gesture.

"Where were you?" I kept my tone casual even though my chest was wound tight.

He shrugged like it was nothing. Like we were talking about the weather. "Had to clear my head."

I studied him. Every line of him. Every shift of his expression. And I knew he was lying.

"Have you heard from Castor?" I asked, keeping my voice light, though my heart was pounding too hard in my chest to match the ease I was pretending.

Reich stiffened quickly. It was barely noticeable. But I saw it.

"Why do you ask?" he asked.

I shrugged again, mirroring him. "Just wondering."

His gaze held mine. Sharp. Searching. Like he was waiting for me to confess something.

Like he was expecting it.

But I didn't give him anything because I wasn't sure I could. But then he spoke.

"He came to see me," Reich said after a moment. The words were measured.

I waited, holding my breath before I prompted, "What do you mean? What happened?"

He exhaled through his nose as he leaned back against the wall like he was contemplating what to say.

"He's fine," Reich said. "Sam's fine."

My pulse didn't believe him. The ribbon burned in my palm even after I'd hidden it.

No, she's not.

But that's all he offered. Like it was supposed to be enough. Like I was supposed to believe it.

But I saw the tension in his jaw. The stiffness in his shoulders. I felt the distance like something was already slipping away and I knew that he wouldn't elaborate.

But the thought wouldn't leave me alone.

Her. Sam.

"She's not fine, Reich," I finally said, the words slipping out before I could swallow them down.

"What do you mean?" He turned toward me, a crease forming between his brows—confusion, worry, maybe even fear.

Instead of answering, I got up and dropped to my knees beside the bed. My fingers slid beneath the thin mattress until they brushed against the frayed ribbon I'd hidden there. When I pulled it out and held it up, his expression shifted—something tightening behind his eyes.

He didn't speak right away. He just stared at the ribbon like he was staring at a warning written in blood.

And when he did speak, his voice was low, urgent.

"We need to go. First thing in the morning."

"What? No." My voice cracked. "How can we leave when Sam is still in here? Clearly something's wrong. She's in danger, Reich. We can't just walk away."

"Sage... we have to."

"What do you mean, 'we *have to*'?" My chest burned, panic rising again.

"We. Have. To." He swallowed hard, his voice barely holding steady. "Because we can't... not right now. Not with everything stacked against us. If we move too soon—if we get caught—there won't be anything left to save. Not Sam. Not us. And not our child."

That stopped me. Just for a moment.

I reached for him, needing the grounding more than I wanted to admit. My hand covered his; he turned his palm up and laced our fingers together instantly, like muscle memory. His thumb brushed my knuckles—slow, and steady.

Like a silent promise. A plea. A tether.

He was here. He was trying. And he was scared too.

When he laid down beside me and pulled me close, I let myself sink into him. His arm wrapped around my waist, his hand splaying over the small curve of my stomach.

His warmth seeped through me. His breath steadied mine.

But my heart wouldn't stop racing.

I wondered if he could tell—if he felt the tremor beneath my skin. If he sensed the battle happening inside me, the part of me that wanted to believe in safety and the part that knew better.

I covered his hand with mine, pressing down gently.

Holding him to me. Holding us together.

But Sam's voice still echoed in my mind, sharp and urgent:

GET OUT.

And suddenly everything felt more fragile.

Him.

Me.

The life growing inside me.

The thin little future we were going to try to build in the middle of a nightmare.

The world was closing in again. I could feel it—like walls shifting, tightening, rearranging themselves with each breath.

I didn't know who I'd have to fight when everything finally snapped.

I didn't know what I'd have to become.

Chapter Forty-Three

REICH

I KNEW FROM THE moment she told me about the ribbon that she wasn't buying my story.

She knew there was more to what happened with Castor.

I could feel it in the quiet way she nodded, slow and deliberate, like she was humoring me. Like she was giving me the response she knew I wanted, even though we both understood there was more.

She was waiting for me to crack. To give her something real. And I would eventually.

Just not here. Not now. Not when the walls might still be listening. Not when there was still a chance they could take this—*her*—away from me if I let my guard slip.

But her silence cut through me. It always seemed to.

I brushed her hair back from her face, the strands slipping through my fingers. I let my hand linger along the side of her neck, feeling the steady thrum of her pulse beneath my thumb.

Warm. Alive. *Here.*

That should be enough. It should be.

But it wasn't.

Not when there was a hollow piece inside me that wouldn't quiet.

Not when I could feel her slipping away, even while I was holding her that close.

"I never thought this would be us," I said, keeping my voice careful and controlled.

Like I wasn't hanging on by a thread.

Her eyes flicked toward me, catching mine. Her brow lifted, just slightly, as she asked, "This?"

I smirked because that was what she expected. And because honestly it was easier than telling her the truth right now. About the uneasiness and battle that raged within my mind.

About everything...

The light... The mephistos... The ribbon...

And the one too many things that seemed to be aligning too perfectly. The ENA never made things easy. If they were helping us now, it was because they wanted something worse.

But I forced the thoughts into the back of my mind.

I couldn't do anything about right now.

Hell... I didn't even know what it all meant.

She looked at me for an answer. But I didn't give one to her just yet.

Instead, I let my fingers trail lower, slow and deliberate, sliding down the line of her throat, tracing her collarbone.

I followed the same path I felt like I had memorized a thousand times but still never got tired of learning.

And then I gave her the answer she was asking for.

"Suburban dreams..." I murmured. "White picket fences... Babies... Dogs..."

Her mouth twitched at the corner, like she was caught between smiling and pulling away. I could feel the hesitation in her body. The tension that never fully left her anymore. The part of her that was still waiting for me to walk out the door and not come back.

If she looked at me like I was one of them, even once, I wasn't sure I'd recover from it.

So, I pushed because I needed to drag her back to me.

Any way I could.

"Maybe a house with a porch swing," I continued, tone lighter, even as something sharp twisted in my chest. "You can sit on it while I mow the grass shirtless."

That earned a soft snort. A breath of something close to amusement. But it wasn't the laugh I wanted. Not the one I needed.

Her walls were still up. Braced. Waiting for the impact.

I couldn't stand it. I tilted her chin up with two fingers, my thumb dragging across her bottom lip, feeling the faint tremble in her breath.

The words almost slipped out—the real ones—but the way she looked at me made the lie easier.

"You know, I was serious about the dog," I said quietly.

Her lips parted slightly under the press of my thumb.

"A big, one that the neighbors mistake for a wolf." I continued, as my mouth quirked up, "Name him Navren."

Her eyes softened. But there was still something hiding behind them. Like she was waiting for the moment I let go. Like she knew it was coming and she was already trying to guard herself from it.

And I was so tired of her looking at me like she was bracing for another scar.

"So, we do all this... we look for answers... and no matter what we find out, no more running?" She asked.

"No more running." I whispered.

I leaned in close, letting my breath trail over her ear, knowing what it did to her. The way it made her breath catch and her pulse skip beneath my fingers.

"When we finally get wherever the hell we're going, wildflower," I murmured, my voice low and rough, "I'm going to claim you the way

I should have three years ago—every inch of you will be mine the way it should've always been."

Her body jolted and I felt it. The shiver. The sharp intake of her breath as her fingers curled against my chest like she was drowning in me.

I pulled back just enough to meet her gaze. Her pupils were blown wide, her lips parted as she stared at me like I'd stolen the air from her lungs.

I tilted her face toward mine, holding her still.

And I kissed her. Hard. Possessive. No softness this time. No pretending. No indecision.

I took her mouth like it was mine because it was. *Because she was.*

She opened for me immediately, her hands fisting in my shirt, dragging me closer like she couldn't stand the distance anymore.

I was done pretending I could wait. I wanted her undone. I wanted her wrecked. And I wanted her to know it was me who put her there. That I was the only one who ever would.

I pulled back just enough to speak, my breath ragged against her lips.

"Clothes off," I told her, voice low and calm. The command didn't leave room for hesitation. Her breath stuttered, but her hands moved. Quick. Sure.

I sat back on my heels as she stripped, her eyes never leaving mine. She peeled off my shirt she was wearing first, slow enough that I could savor every inch of skin as it was revealed. Her skin glowed faintly in the low light, smooth and perfect, marred only by past scars I'd kissed over and over again.

When she moved at her underwear, I shook my head, giving her pause. "No..." I said low, "Leave them on."

Her brows lifted but she obeyed.

And *fuck*... the sight of her standing there, bare but for that thin scrap of fabric, nearly undid me. She was a weapon like this. A prayer. A goddamn promise I wasn't sure I deserved.

I let my eyes drag over her slowly, "You looked good in my shirt," I murmured. I watched the flush of her skin creep up her throat. "But you look even better when you're desperate for me."

Her breath hitched again, her chest rising faster, her fingers twitching at her sides. She wanted to reach for me.

But she waited.

Good girl.

I reached out, my fingers hooking into the waistband of her underwear. I pulled her to the edge of the bed, parting her legs with a firm grip on her thighs. I could feel the heat radiating from her.

I ran two fingers over the damp fabric, painfully slow. She shuddered, hips jerking toward me, but I pinned them down with my free hand.

"Patience," I warned.

She whimpered, low and needy in her throat, but she listened. She always did for me.

I dragged the soaked fabric aside, sliding my fingers inside of her. So warm. So perfect. I groaned softly, leaning in to brush my lips over the inside of her thigh.

"So perfectly ready for me," I murmured, voice rough with need. She shivered, her hands clenching the sheets. I pressed two fingers inside her, slow. Feeling her clench around me, hot and constricting.

"Always so incredibly tight," I said against her skin. My teeth grazed her thigh as she arched toward me, desperate for more but I kept the pace slow. Almost cruel in its taunting.

I curled my fingers inside her, finding that spot that always makes her gasp and I stayed there. Rubbing. Pressing. Until she was shaking, her body fighting to stay still even as she clawed at the bed.

I watched her. Memorized her.

I owned this. I owned *her*. And I was not giving her up. Not ever.

When she was close—*too close*—I pulled back, licking my fingers clean as I watched her fall apart at my removal. Her breathing was ragged. Her thighs trembling. Her eyes wild.

I stood, stripping off my clothes slow enough that she squirmed. By the time I was back over her, her pupils were wide, her chest heaving. She was wrecked already and I was just getting started.

"Hands behind your head," I told her. She obeyed without hesitation, fingers lacing together. Her obedience made something vicious twist in my chest.

Something protective. Something feral.

I smiled dark as I leaned down to kiss her again with patience this time. Deep. Claiming every inch of her mouth like I'd never taste it again.

"Such a beautiful wildflower," I murmured against her lips. She moaned, and I felt her body tremble beneath me.

When I pushed inside her, I took my time, moving painfully slow as she took all of me. *Every inch*. Her nails dug into her wrists to keep from straining against her pinned hands, but I felt the fight in her body.

"Reich," she begged, voice rough.

I pressed my mouth to her ear. "I know," I murmured and I moved slower. Watching every reaction, every gasp, every shudder that wrecked through her body.

"How is it that you feel like you were made for me," I whispered, biting gently at her neck.

By the time I set a rhythm, we were both shaking but I wouldn't go faster. Not yet.

Not until she was begging for it.

Not until I said she could release.

I scraped my teeth along her jaw. "You're mine... now say it," I instructed.

Her whole body arched into me. "I'm yours," she gasped and that was all I needed.

I let her hands go as I grabbed her hips, pulling her harder onto me, driving into her deep and fast now. She shattered first, crying out my name. Her body convulsed around me, draining me as I followed, groaning against her mouth. Holding her tight. Like I could lose this.

We rode it out, hips grinding, mouths nearly bruising and hands gripping tight enough to leave marks.

I didn't move for a long time. I stayed connected to her.

Her hands were soft stroking my back. Her breathing was calm against my neck as I brought my hands to her face and kissed her temple.

"We'll figure this out," I whispered.

She nodded against me but neither of us said anything else.

Not because we couldn't but because deep down we both knew that words were easy.

That was never our problem in the first place.

It was that everything else was hard.

But still we stayed tangled together, wrapped up in something that felt like it might actually be ours.

And I kissed her like the ENA might take her from my hands at any second—because I knew that at any second, they could.

Chapter Forty-Four

SAGE

HIS HANDS WERE STILL on me. One draped heavy and sure over my stomach, the other curled beneath my ribs, holding me steady. His body was warm against mine, his breath slow and even where it ghosted over the back of my neck. I could feel the faint drag of his eyelashes as they brushed my skin every time he twitched.

I laid there in the dark, counting each of those breaths. Memorizing them and letting them attempt to anchor me.

His palm shifted slightly, splaying wider over the curve of my stomach. It was protective. But gentle in a way Reich almost never seemed to let himself be.

And it should have been enough. It felt like it should be enough.

But it wasn't.

There was a hollow ache lodged behind my ribs that wouldn't go away. No matter how close he was. No matter how tightly he held me.

It was there, gnawing at the edges of everything we were about to embark upon.

And it made me ask the question...

What if he was already slipping away into whatever they were turning him into—and I was the last one who hadn't noticed it yet?

I already knew there was something wrong but what if Sam's warning was about *all* of them, including Castor and Reich.

I stared at the ceiling. The dark beams above us, weathered and cracked, blurred at the edges by what little light seeped through under the doorframe.

I counted the seconds as they passed. Each one stretching longer than the last.

I told myself not to think too hard. Not to spiral. Not to go there. Because I trusted him. I did. But trust wasn't the same as certainty. And it was the uncertainty that was killing me right now.

I kept replaying it in my mind. The ribbon. Sam's handwriting. The way her words were scrawled jaggedly across the fabric like she wrote them in a hurry.

GET OUT.

It echoed, again and again, carving lines into the walls I kept trying to rebuild around my heart and then there was Reich's carefully controlled answers when I asked about Castor. When I asked about *anything*.

How he avoided my questions with the same ease that he used to kiss me breathless. How I let him. Because I wanted to believe him.

Part of me wonders if it's the ENA. If he couldn't say anything because we were still surrounded. Because Cresil and Berith always seemed to be watching from some unseen place and Astaroth's reach didn't end at the gates or borders.

It was *everywhere*.

And maybe Reich was carrying the weight of that silence because he was protecting me. Just like he always had tried to do.

I told myself that's what it was. That as soon as we were alone, truly alone, he'd explain everything. He'd tell me what was going on. What was really happening with Castor.

With Sam.

With *us*.

But there was another part of me—the part Sam's warning pried open—that whispered something different.

That maybe he would be as he had always been, keeping me in the dark, because he had already made his choice. That maybe this future we kept talking about wasn't something he could give me.

Maybe he was going to let me go.

Or worse— maybe he was going to become one of them.

I closed my eyes, willing the thoughts away, but they just twisted deeper.

I pressed my fingers against my stomach, grounding myself in the weight of what we'd created. This life inside me. It was real. It was *ours*.

And it mattered. Enough for me to stay. Enough for me to fight. Even if part of me was terrified of what that fight was going to cost.

I breathed slowly through my nose. Trying to imagine it— this new life he kept talking about. The one we might still have.

A quiet house. Reich sitting on a porch, his boots kicked up on the railing, watching the sun set over the lake while our child plays in the dirt at his feet. Me planting something in the garden. Maybe roses. Maybe something that won't die when winter comes.

And him smiling at me the way he was starting to.

Before all of this. Before the bloodlines, the scars and the marks that won't ever fade. Back when he gave me that playlist and I saw a different side of him.

I wanted to believe in that life. Desperately. But it was fragile and thin like a sheet of glass easy to break. And I was terrified we wouldn't survive long enough to live it without that illusion shattering.

I didn't know when I fell back asleep, but I knew exactly when I woke.

The soft sound of the door opening. The hush of boots on the floorboards. The shift of cold air hitting my skin where Reich's body used to be. I blinked and realized he was no longer beside me.

I sat up quickly. Heart pounding.

The room was quiet, but the tension was immediate.

Reich stepped back inside; his expression unreadable. His face carved from stone. But there was something different in the way he moved. Something final and certain.

He gestured to the two backpacks he had slung across his shoulder.

"They gave me everything we need," he said quietly.

The door clicked shut behind him.

His voice was low and controlled but there was an edge.

"We can leave," he added and the air in my lungs caught.

I nodded slowly, my pulse quickening. "Now?" I asked, my voice rough from sleep.

"Whenever you're ready," he said.

I stood. My legs steady under me, even though I didn't feel steady inside. I crossed the room slowly, grabbing the pack Reich handed me. My fingers trembling as I opened it and slipped the ribbon Sam gave me deeper inside.

Reich was still as he watched the door and didn't say anything.

I squared my shoulders and forced a breath out of my lungs that didn't want to release.

"Let's go," I told him.

He nodded once but he didn't smile and neither did I because I still didn't know what we were walking toward and I wasn't sure he did either.

But I took his hand anyway. I intertwined my fingers through his, feeling the roughness of his skin, the steadiness of his grip.

Because for now, that was all I had, and it had to be enough. Even if everything else fell apart.

Right here. Right now. We were still together, and I held onto that like it was the only thing left keeping me alive.

Even if my doubts told me a different story.

Reich walked silently beside me down the quiet corridor, our footsteps echoing faintly against the stone walls. I thought about what our life would look like for a brief moment but the image was still filled with uncertainty.

Suddenly, Reich halted, his gaze fixed sharply on a door left ajar. He tilted his head slightly, suspicion tightening his features as he looked around to make sure no one was coming. "That's strange. They don't usually leave things unsecured."

We peaked through the opening, and I glanced over, noting a file left on top of a filing cabinet drawer. Curiosity tugged at me, mingled with unease. "Reich... these look like the same files I found at the Bloodwine."

"They keep files everywhere, Sage... but they don't keep them left out in the open like this." Reich muttered softly, moving forward cautiously. His hand lingered instinctively near the holster on his belt as we stepped into the room together.

Inside, shelves crowded the walls, filled with meticulously labeled files and boxes. Yet, conspicuously, a selection of documents laid spread out across the central table. Reich's eyes narrowed, skepticism etched clearly on his face.

"It's like they wanted us to find these," he said quietly, with the distrust evident in his voice. "The question is why."

I watched as Reich pulled out a folder. His eyes blown wide.

"What is it?" I asked.

"A piece of the puzzle... but I don't know what it means. At least not right now." I peered over his shoulder and saw faces with blacked out eyes and ancient writing that looked like it came out of that ENA book I came across in Reich's old library.

The images in that book seemed to keep popping up but they didn't make any sense.

"What is it, Reich? Who are these people?"

He quickly folded and slipped the piece of old looking parchment into his pocket.

"We need to go." He muttered.

My eyes scanned the other papers on the table, landing abruptly on a folder marked with handwriting I immediately recognized. My breath stilled, heart hammering in my chest as I reached forward, drawn irresistibly to what looked like my mother's handwriting.

Reich watched quietly, his presence reassuring as I sunk into a chair, hands trembling slightly as I opened the faded folder.

Inside were letters and notes—more pieces of this never-ending puzzle I'd spent this last year trying to solve.

And then there was one... it stuck out because it was addressed to... *me*.

"Reich... this letter has my name."

I held it with trembling hands...

My throat tightened painfully as I read:

"Sage,

I knew someday you'd find this. If you're reading this letter, I've failed to protect you as I'd intended. Joining the ENA was never about me—it was always about you. Every decision, every sacrifice, was meant to save you from the altar I never wanted you near. But clearly, I was not strong enough. Do not repeat my mistakes. Choose the life you want, filled with love and freedom. Trust the family you create—not the one that claims to own you.

Your Mother"

Reich stepped closer, gently resting a hand on my shoulder. "Are you okay?"

I nodded slowly, wiping my eyes as clarity settled within me. "She was trying to protect me."

He exhaled softly, caution still evident in his voice. "Even if so, it doesn't change the fact that they wanted us to find these. We need to be careful, and we need to get the hell out of here."

I looked up, finding his steady gaze comforting. "You're right. But at least now I understand. It at least gives a small ounce of closure that I never knew I needed. Enough to hold onto as we try to start something in the midst of all of this."

He offered a faint, reassuring smile, taking my hand in his. "Good. We deserve a fresh start even if it isn't quite right yet... But right now, wildflower, we have to go. So... lets go before I drag you out of here myself. We have a life to build."

I hesitated for a moment, curious of what other answers might be hidden in this room.

But Reich was right... something was wrong and we needed to get as far away from here as possible.

Together, we stepped back into the corridor, leaving behind the ghosts of the past and moving toward a future we might never survive, but one we still had to try for.

Chapter Forty-Five

REICH

The gates of the ENA compound opened slowly.

Slow, like they didn't want to let us leave. Like they were dragging their feet through centuries of blood and bone just to remind me we were only walking because they were letting us.

The grinding screech of the iron carried in the wind, slipping under my skin.

They could have opened them faster. They could have been quiet about it, but they weren't.

This was theater.

Every inch of that gate swinging wide was a performance designed to remind us of what we already knew. We were only free until they said we were not.

Sage stood silently beside me. Still and stiff as a board. Her hand was warm in mine, but there was no weight behind her grip. Her fingers just rested against the back of my palm, like holding on was merely a reflex and letting go was just as easy.

And maybe it would have been. I couldn't tell anymore. She was withdrawn but still watching. I could feel the space she put between us—not in distance, but in her silence. Like she was waiting for me to say something that would make this right. Something that would make sense of what happened while we were in here. What we had discovered.

But there was nothing I could say. Nothing I trusted myself to say. Not yet at least.

I didn't blame her for pulling back. I didn't blame her for the distance. If anything, I blamed myself for not finding a way to stop this all from happening in the first place.

Cresil stood at the threshold. Her pale eyes flicked between us, dissecting every inch of us. She didn't smile. Her expression was carved from stone, as cold and unmoving as the compound sitting tall and proud behind our backs. She gave us our final instructions in that same clipped, clinical tone she always used. Like we were just another task on her endless list.

Berith stood beside her. The same guard dog expression waiting for the order to bite. His hand rested on the grip of the blade strapped across his chest, fingers flexing like he was hoping for an excuse to use it. I didn't spare him more than a glance and I didn't say a word to either of them.

Nothing was worth saying here. Not when they had already made it clear this wasn't over. Not when I was too busy holding Sage upright with the only thing I had left—my presence, which I am not sure was even enough for her anymore.

I took the map. The coordinates. The key to our new house. Our new life.

If you could even call it that and I got Sage the hell out of there.

Step by step. Across the threshold. Through the iron gates and out on the road.

The path out of the compound was quiet. No guards tailing us. No patrols shadowing our steps. Just the low crunch of our boots on gravel and frost-bitten earth.

But I could feel it. Eyes watching from their ivory towers. Scopes trained on our backs. Every move dissected and catalogued in some report Cresil would probably read later over tea.

We were alone but we really weren't because I knew better.

Sage hadn't spoken since we left. I kept waiting for her to. Waiting for her to say my name in that quiet, sharp way that always cut through my noise but she didn't.

And I didn't push her.

I didn't need to hear her voice to know the weight she was carrying. I could feel it rolling off her in waves, settling in my shoulders, wrapping around my ribs like a vice. Like a chain.

And it killed me that I couldn't fix it right in that moment. Not until I knew we were out of their range. Even though I knew that we never would be completely.

They told us to make it to Keenan's first. To gather up supplies that we would need. Keenan's place was their midway point. An hour or so outside of the compound by walking. We would stay and rest for a day. Just long enough to remind us that this wasn't freedom. This was their leash. One with a longer chain than the last place they kept us.

And when we got to Verena... the place they'd chosen for us, that chain would get even shorter. Tighter. Collared right around our throats.

Verena.

The name stuck in my head like a splinter I couldn't dig out. A rural town northeast of Providence. Tucked into a mountain range that swallowed people whole and forgot their names. It overlooked a lake that froze over half the year. Warm a few months at best. Quiet and most importantly, isolated.

The kind of place where you either melted into its structure and became part of its story ... or you rotted inside it and disappeared.

They'd given us new names, new identities. A new life, stamped and approved by the same people who carved the old one out of our backs.

The pictures of the house looked nice, though it was more fortress than home. High walls. Thick locks. And what looked like barred windows that didn't open.

Sage hadn't asked me about it.

Not directly but I sensed that she already knew and expected what we would be walking into.

And that look in her eyes back at the compound— the one that said she was waiting for me to leave.

Or worse— waiting for me to stay but never really be there...it was still behind them. Right under the surface. And I didn't know how to tear it out without tearing both of us apart.

The trek to Keenan's didn't take long.

He was the only one of us in the group that had been assigned an actual house, with a shed and a field... even a car. He was their maintenance man of sorts.

Lower in rank than the rest of us. He didn't have much of a job except to monitor the area, which was almost always vacant.

I never knew why. It was almost like the ENA didn't trust him. And part of me wondered if it had to do with what happened with Blythe all those years ago.

Sage kept pace beside me, step by step, her silence louder than any scream. Her boots moved steady in the frost-covered dirt. Her breath came out in faint white clouds, catching what little light the gray sky had left to offer.

She hadn't let go of my hand.

But it brought me no comfort.

Not really.

I could say something. Tell her it was going to be okay. That I would fix it and make it right.

But I didn't. Because there was nothing I could say.

I didn't understand it.

There was so much unanswered that made my mind feel like mush. I was convinced I was an Ovitt and I was convinced the ENA knew that too.

That was the file Keenan had found at Castor's and immediately after I was captured.

The parchment in my back pocket held faces that looked too familiar—first the five men I'd accidentally hunted and then the five I actually shared blood with, the Ovitts.

Did they know? That I killed all those people and that I was after the Ovitts in the first place?

Maybe Keenan had something he could give me if I couldn't reach Nael.

Because I needed answers. I needed something. I hadn't felt that strange pain on my mark since we left the compound. It was a relief but also unsettling at the same time.

Because I didn't know if it would come back.

I still couldn't figure out why it did that. I wondered if it only happened when the ENA was close. It seemed like that was the case. But what was it?

And what was the light and prophecy they kept talking about?

It was all starting to feel deliberate—like psychological torture designed to keep me just confused enough to be controllable.

And that's what I was—*controlled by them*.

Even though I didn't want to admit it.

Chapter Forty-Six

SAGE

REICH DIDN'T SPEAK.

Not after the gates shut behind us with that low, grinding finality that still echoed in my mind.

Not after Cresil's parting words faded into the cold, brittle air, leaving nothing behind but a hollow feeling that settled somewhere beneath my ribs.

There was nothing to hear out here. Just the wind cutting between narrow ravines, carrying the ghosts of all the things we didn't say and the things we did.

Reich kept walking. Shoulders tight. Head down. Focused on the ground in front of him like the path was the only thing keeping him tethered to the earth. And to himself.

I didn't press him. Part of me wanted to. To demand something—*anything*. A word. A look. A sign that he was still here with me and not spiraling into that place he sometimes goes. The one he never talks about. The one I can't reach him in when he falls too deep.

But I still didn't. Because I knew him better this time.

When Reich fell silent like this, it meant he was holding everything inside. Holding it back. For me. For himself. For whatever was left of the person he still hoped to be when this was over.

And I hated it, but I understood it.

So, I silently followed. One step after another, the cold seeping into my boots, biting at my toes and causing my fingertips to go numb inside my gloves.

And I waited. I waited for him to be the first to break. And I prayed that when he did, I'd still recognize the man who'd been holding my hand through hell.

By the time the house appeared through the trees, the weight in my legs was a dull, constant ache. My lungs were raw from breathing the sharp, freezing air for too many miles. And my head— my head was full of too many thoughts, tangled and sharp, half-formed questions circling themselves into knots I didn't know how to untangle.

The door was already open when we approached. I tensed automatically, my fingers twitching toward a small pocketknife that was in my pack.

Reich noticed and his thumb brushed over mine as we stepped forward, a small, wordless reassurance. His skin was rough, but his touch was steady. And for just a second, I let it ground me. I let him hold me there.

We stepped inside. The heat hit immediately, a stark contrast to the cold pressing against my back. It smelled like old metal, dry wood and cigarettes but none of it did anything to thaw the chill working its way deeper into my chest.

Nael was here, seated at the long table, spine straight, hands folded like a man waiting for judgment or war. His sharp eyes flicked up as soon as we entered. No smile. No greeting. Just a nod and an expectation.

"We need to talk," he said. His voice was always calm. Always controlled. But this time there was something harder under it. A weight I could feel almost pressing between my shoulder blades.

I waited. I waited for the look that usually comes next.

The one from Reich that silently tells me to go into the other room and be out of sight and out of mind. To sit this one out. To let them handle it.

And when Nael glanced at me, that familiar flicker of distrust in his eyes, it was like a knife twisting under my ribs.

I braced for it. For Reich to say it. To tell me I needed to give them space and then try to convince me later that it was safer that way. That it was *better* that way.

But he didn't.

Instead, he slid his hand across my back as he stepped forward. Steady. Firm. Certain.

"She stays this time," Reich said as if he was already anticipating the dismissal. His tone leaving no room for argument. No room for anything but agreement.

Nael's jaw tightened, the muscle ticking once as he held Reich's gaze. But after a long beat, he smiled and relented. A clipped nod. "Fine."

It shouldn't have felt like a victory. But it did.

Nael leaned forward, his eyes moving between us like he was measuring something.

"I found out what happened quickly after you two disappeared. Fit some of the pieces together but first... how are you both holding up?"

The way he said it made me wonder if he already knew the answer. If he already saw the cracks in us.

Reich's response was low and controlled.

"We're fine."

It was a lie.

And I could tell that Nael knew it. But he didn't argue. Didn't call him out. He just exhaled slowly and continued.

"And I'm surprised you are. They knew you'd never go to them willingly." Nael's gaze sharpened as he watched us. So, they gave you something to run from and someone to run for," he said.

Then his eyes flicked to me. And lower. To my stomach.

"And they knew you'd come for her... and that you'd be willing to do whatever it takes to protect her."

The chill that spread through me had nothing to do with the cold outside. I pressed my hand flat against my belly, instinctive and desperate, as if that would somehow shield what was inside from words that felt too much like that prophecy.

Nael didn't stop. "I am pretty sure they also knew she'd be carrying your child when you did. They already made the announcement. Everyone knows you're to be in Verena."

His gaze cut back to Reich, like this was something he should have figured out already.

Something he should have known. "They know you're an Ovitt... they have to. That's why they think your bloodline is part of their future in some way. The Davidians never held a place in their ranks."

"Soldier..." Reich murmured. "That's what they called it. They kept saying that this was all a part of some prophecy and that we were part of the light."

"Prophecy? Light? What do you mean?" Nael asked, a puzzled expression across his face.

"They kept talking about 'the light'—like some higher level of initiation. Said we were part of it now. Said that's why we could see the mephistos. Their messengers."

Nael's face turned sideways almost completely as soon as Reich said *mephistos*. He stared at Reich like he had two heads.

And I felt Reich go tense beside me. But it didn't stop him from continuing.

"And now they're sending us to Verena." He said in defeat.

Nael sat back, folding his arms across his chest like he was about to deliver some final blow but all he did was repeat what was said.

"They're sending you to Verena…"

He said it like it was inevitable because it was.

For a long moment, there was only the sound of Reich's breathing. Rough. Measured.And then—

"Cas."

The word scraped out of his throat, hoarse and strangled.

I snapped my gaze toward him.

His face was pale, tight, but something raw flickered behind his eyes—something I hadn't seen in a long time. Fear. Or recognition. Or both.

"I saw him," Reich said quietly. "At the compound."

Nael's head lifted sharply. "You *saw* him?"

Reich nodded once, the motion stiff. "He was… off. Different."

A heavy, uneasy silence settled over us.

"That doesn't make sense," Nael muttered. "Why would he be there?"

Keenan leaned against the far wall, arms crossed, silent as Nael spoke. He hadn't said much since we walked in, but his eyes were sharp. Listening.

He shifted his weight. Just slightly. But enough to make his sudden presence known. His arms were crossed over his chest in a tight, guarded fold. His expression smoothed into something almost too neutral.

Reich's eyes slid to him immediately.

"Keenan."

Not a question. More like a pressure point being pressed.

Keenan blinked. "What?"

His tone was light. Too light. Casual in a way that felt like a performance.

Reich watched him like he was trying to read a language on Keenan's skin.

"You didn't know he was there?" Reich asked slowly.

Keenan shrugged, brows lifting. "I mean... no? Last I heard, he and Sam went dark. Disappeared. I figured they were laying low. I don't know anything past that."

His voice stayed even, but the muscle in his jaw twitched. A small tell. Barely there. But Reich caught it—I could *feel* him catch it.

Nael frowned. "You think something happened to them?"

Keenan shook his head quickly, too quickly. "I don't know. I don't know anything."

He lifted his hands as if to show they were empty. But they trembled. Just a fraction. His eyes didn't meet Reich's.

Reich's stare sharpened.

Quiet. Calculating. Hurt in ways he didn't voice.

He didn't confront him. Not directly.

But the silence between them turned thick and sharp, like it could cut.

I reached for Reich's hand, threading my fingers through his. He didn't pull away. His grip tightened like he needed something—anything—to hold on to.

He exhaled once, a shuddering, exhausted sound.

"I need some rest," he said, voice barely above a murmur.

And he walked out of the room without looking back.

CHAPTER FORTY-SEVEN

REICH

I PACED THE ROOM, unable to settle myself, as my thoughts spun in tight, frantic circles.

Nothing landed. Nothing made sense.

I wasn't angry at Keenan.

Not exactly.

But something about the way he looked at me—

the way his voice sounded too steady, too practiced—

the way his eyes flicked away when I pressed him...

He was keeping something from me.

Just like Cas.

And I didn't know what it was, but I felt it.

A shift. A hesitation.

Like there was a truth sitting behind his teeth that he refused to release.

And that—combined with everything else—made my chest feel too tight to breathe.

But the real anger?

That was for Cas.

Because he should've told me *something*. Anything.

We never used to hide from each other.

We never used to be afraid of the truth between us.

When did it change?

When did he start building walls I didn't notice until they were already too high for me to see over?

He didn't tell me about the Ovitt line. About the research on the brothers.

He disappeared and went dark.

And now I saw him again and he was just as dark as when he went missing.

I never kept anything from him.

Not once.

But it felt like that was all he did now.

Secret after secret.

Distance after distance.

And Keenan—whether he realized it or not—was sitting on a piece of that distance too.

The ache sat low and heavy in my chest.

But my thoughts were interrupted when Sage stepped quietly into the room. She didn't speak. She just wrapped her arms around me, like she could feel the way everything inside me was unraveling.

She didn't try to fix it.

She didn't pry.

She just held me—arms tight, steady and certain—and the silence in her embrace felt like the first safe thing in hours.

I let myself breathe into her. Just breathe.

After a long moment, she gestured softly toward the bed. Not pushing. Just offering.

We laid down together, the room dim and still. Her hand found mine beneath the blanket with a touch that was warm, grounding and patient.

And I let myself rest, even as that uneasy feeling about Keenan lingered at the back of my mind like a shadow I couldn't yet name.

When we woke, I knew something had shifted.

She was scared. I could see it in her eyes—undeniable, unspoken. The ache. The weight. She was exhausted in a way that lived beneath the skin—bone deep, soul deep—but still, she watched me like she was waiting. Waiting for more than I'd given her. More than I could give right now, no matter how badly I wanted to.

Because I didn't know anymore.

Not after all the secrets.

And especially not after the way Nael looked at me when I told him what had happened.

I reached for her hand. It was cold in mine, her fingers smaller than I remembered, fragile in a way that ripped through me.

I lifted her hand slowly, pressing her palm flat against my chest—right over my heart.

It was still beating. Slow. Steady.

And it was hers, whether I was here or not.

"You should get some more rest before we have to leave" I murmured. My voice was softer than it should be. Rougher than I wanted it to be, but it was honest.

She looked like she was about to protest but retreated when I spoke.

My thumb brushed over her knuckles, back and forth, lingering there because I wasn't ready to let go yet. "For you..." I added. "... And for him."

Her other hand lifted, almost unconsciously, resting over her stomach like she was protecting something precious. Because she was. It was instinctual.

"Him?" She asked.

I almost winced at the word as it left my mouth. I already knew the gender. Another thing they'd stolen from us and turned into a weapon.

"Just a guess." I lied.

I saw the way her throat worked as she swallowed. Saw the way her jaw flexed when she fought to keep her expression neutral. But it was all there in her eyes. The fear. The longing. The fight to stay strong when I knew she was running on nothing but hope and willpower.

She nodded, slow and heavy. But she gave it to me. Even if it cost her. And that made me hate myself a little more.

I watched her leave the room, into the adjoining bathroom. Every step she took was quieter than it should be. Like she was walking away from something she wasn't ready to say goodbye to. And maybe she was. Maybe we both were.

The door clicked shut behind her, soft but final and I laid there in the hollow space she left behind for too long.

When I finally got up and turned back down towards the hallway to the living room, they were waiting.

Nael. Keenan. The last pieces of family I had left.

Keenan leaned forward where he sat, elbows planted on the table, his hands folded loosely in front of him.

Nael stood beside him, arms crossed, posture deceptively relaxed but I could see the tension in his shoulders. The tightness in his jaw.

As he spoke, "You and Sage should be getting to Verena soon."

"I should be searching for answers... not running off to Verena," I grinded out. My fists curled at my sides as I paced, boots hitting the cold tile floor with too much force. Each step echoed in the empty space like a hammer striking steel.

They watched me. Silent. Calm. Like they had already made peace with something I was still ripping myself apart over.

Keenan was the first to speak, voice low, rough around the edges but steady. "You've never been able to walk away before." He shifted forward slightly, his eyes dark with grief and resignation. "Trust me, we get that."

I stopped pacing long enough to glance at him, but he didn't flinch. He never has. Even though I knew he was hiding something.

"But this," Keenan said, his jaw clenching around the words, "this isn't about you anymore."

"This isn't the way," I snapped. I rounded on him, pacing the same line again because it was the only thing keeping me from exploding. "You know it's not."

"It's the only way," Keenan said evenly. And that was the part that made me want to scream.

"No." It came out sharper this time. Harder. "Don't ask me to run."

Nael's voice cut through then, low and quiet, but sharp enough to draw blood.

"We're not asking you to run," he said. His steady eyes found mine, unyielding. "We're asking you to protect what you've spent your whole damn life fighting for."

He took a step closer, pinning me in place with that look. The one that didn't allow room for anything close to rebellion.

"You've spent the last ten years fighting for other people's families by our interventions during the ENA's transport..." Nael's tone was even and measured, but there was a steel edge beneath it. "Now you finally have one of your own, and you're still trying to die for everyone else first?"

The words hit. A clean shot between the ribs.

And I felt it. I flinched. It was slight but Nael saw it.

I'd always known how to die for strangers. I'd never learned how to live for myself.

I dragged in a breath, slow and ragged. My lungs felt too tight in my chest. The walls felt too close. I didn't say anything. Because there was nothing to say. Because he was right. And we all knew it.

I'd spent my life tearing things down. Breaking them. Destroying them. That was what I was made for.

But this...this was *different*.

For the first time, I had something worth building. Something worth keeping alive. And I was terrified I'd ruin it.

That I'd ruin *them*.

It wasn't in me to sit back and wait for the war to come knocking at my door. I was made for the frontlines in the battlefield. It was written into me.

And yet...when I thought of Sage—of her hand resting on her stomach in her sleep like she was already cradling something fragile, something breathing— I knew.

I couldn't leave her behind. Not this time. Not for this.

"But Cas is still in there... " I muttered, more to myself than to them.

Keenan shifted in his chair. His fingers flexed once against the table.

"We'll find him," he said quietly.

Keenan met my stare without blinking, but his hands didn't lie—they flexed once against the table, the tiniest tremor. He knew something. He just wasn't saying it.

"How can I trust you both to actually do that?" I bite out.

Keenan met my stare without blinking. "Because all of us have always been brothers, even without bloodlines. We help each other. We keep each other's secrets. And we *save each other*." he said it simply, like he was encoding some message to me in his words.

And I believed him.

Just like I believed Cas.

I stopped pacing as I stepped in close to the table, setting my hands flat on the scarred surface, feeling the rough grain under my palms.

I met both of their gazes in turn and held them there.

"This isn't the end," I said.

It wasn't just words. It was a fact. A promise.

Nael nodded slowly.

"No, it isn't. But it *is* your break."

I narrowed my eyes. "And after?"

Nael shrugged. "That's up to you."

I forced myself to breathe. In. Out. Somehow, my pulse steadied. But it still felt like a hollow victory.

I pushed off the table and headed for the door where Sage was hidden behind, jaw clenched tight enough that it ached. I needed to get back to her. I need to feel her close before I lost my nerve.

We would leave at first light. If I stayed here any longer, I'd talk myself into staying for good. Into fighting. And I wasn't sure I'd make it out of that alive.

The door creaked when I opened it.

She was lying on the bed, half-curled on her side, her hand resting over her stomach the same way it always did now. Her breathing was slow, measured. But she was not asleep.

Her eyes flickered open as soon as she sensed me. Like she'd been waiting.

I crossed the room in three long strides. Sliding down beside her, boots and all, and pulled her close. She came willingly, her body fitting into mine like she was made for this. Like she belonged there.

Her head settled against my chest, and I could breathe again, as if I was drowning this whole time without her.

This was why. She was why.

I pressed my mouth to her hair and closed my eyes. I could do this. For her. For them.

Tomorrow, we would leave.

But tonight...we stayed.

And I held on to her. To this. To what we were, even when everything else was falling apart. Because I didn't know how to do anything else anymore.

And because this...this was the one thing in my control that I still had left worth saving.

Chapter Forty-Eight

SAGE

WE LEFT AS SOON as I woke.

I watched as Reich handed Nael the folded up parchment that we had found at the compound.

Nael just nodded and said he'd be in touch.

Reich stayed quiet as we said our goodbyes to him and Keenan, but there was something different about Reich—something lighter.

The cold bit at my skin as I stepped outside.

My breath fogged the air in front of me in pale clouds that vanished almost as quickly as they formed. The sky above was overcast in gray—an endless stretch of muted light, flat and dull, without warmth. The type of light that made it impossible to tell how much of the day we'd already lost... or how much time we really had left.

Reich was already waiting for me at the bottom of the steps, adjusting the strap of his pack across his shoulder with one hand. The other lingered at his side until I reached him. His fingers brushed mine—hesitant at first, rough and calloused—before they wrapped around my hand in a slow, steady squeeze. It was possessive and grounding. And maybe a little reluctant to let go.

"You ready, wildflower?" His voice was low and quiet like he was asking something deeper than the obvious.

I nodded. But it didn't feel like readiness.

It felt like we were standing on the edge of something vast and dark, staring into a bottomless place we couldn't see the end of and knowing we were going anyway because there was nothing left behind us.

Still, I squeezed his hand back and let go as we started to walk.

The trail out of Keenan's house wound north through the mountains. The path was narrow, cut between sharp ridges and old pine forests that swayed stiffly in the wind. The trees up here didn't grow like normal. They leaned sideways at strange angles, their trunks marked by the years they spent weathering things even storms couldn't navigate. It was steep in places. Treacherous. Frost still clung to the ground even this late in the season, slick patches hid beneath the dead leaves and brittle grass. Each step forward was careful and deliberate.

Reich glanced back at me what seemed like every ten seconds. He kept checking and observing. Making sure I was close.

It was sweet, in its own stubborn way...and a little annoying.

"I'm pregnant..." I muttered after the twentieth time he slowed down, letting his pace ease just enough for me to catch up. "...Not broken."

He snorted, but he didn't stop. "That's debatable."

I rolled my eyes and gave him a shove, palm braced against the space between his shoulder blades. It didn't move him, not really.

But it made him smile and that made me smile in return.

For a little while, we walked without saying much. The silence was companionable this time even though it was heavy. Like we were both carrying too many things we hadn't figured out how to talk about yet. The weight of what had happened. The weight of what we knew was coming.

But as the sun rose higher, as the sky shifted from flat gray to something bluer than I'd seen in months, Reich started talking again. Little things at first.

He pointed out animal tracks in the dirt—deer, he said. Maybe elk.

"Their numbers are returning, slowly." he'd say.

He'd tell me where he'd set a snare if we needed additional food, how to follow the slope of the land to find water if we ran out. "Basic Survival 101." he called it.

But I could tell that having these talks made him feel normal. Like this was any other day. Like we were any other people. And somehow, it made me feel a little more normal too. Or at least less like we were walking targets.

Then out of nowhere he asked— "What do you think it'll be?"

I glanced over at him. "What?"

He nodded toward me, toward my stomach beneath the heavy coat I was wearing.

"It. The baby. I already told you what my guess was."

I blinked at him for a second. Then I smiled. Slow. "I don't know," I said, drawing the words out like I was really considering it. "An assassin, maybe."

He laughed, rough and genuine, the sound curling warm in my chest despite the cold.

"Sounds about right."

"Although I think it's more likely to come out stubborn and brooding." I grinned. "Then we'll definitely know it's yours."

His lips twitched, but there was a spark in his eyes now. "The brooding part, sure. But stubborn? That's all you, wildflower."

I shook my head, but the smile lingered this time. Longer than I expected. Longer than it had in months.

We stopped by a stream around midday, where the water ran clear and cold over smooth rocks. The sound of it filled the air, soft and constant. A small thing, but it reminded me we were still in a world that moved. That breathed. Even if we were not sure where we fit in it anymore.

Reich crouched by the bank, refilling our canteens.

I watched him for a moment. The hard lines of his shoulders. The way his jaw tightened even when he was at rest, like his body didn't know how to be still. Like he was always bracing for the next thing.

His reflection shivered on the surface of the water. Broken but there.

He glanced up at me suddenly, catching me staring. One brow raised in silent question.

"What?" he asked.

"Nothing," I said quickly ... but it was not nothing.

It was *everything*.

I was carrying our child. We were walking into a future we didn't ask for, toward a life we didn't know, and I was terrified, but I wasn't alone.

I had him and that made me so damn happy.

In the distance we saw smoke curling through the trees in the direction we'd just come from.

I asked Reich about it... he said it looked like it was coming from the compound.

The warning ribbon from Sam was burning a hole through my pack.

I couldn't help but think of her. Wonder if her and Cas were still there.

I told Reich about it... but all he said was that we would figure things out once we got to Verena safe.

We were halfway there when the trail flattened out. It opened onto a ridge that overlooked a valley and field of wildflowers that stretched wide beneath us.

They swayed in ragged clusters, stubborn and bright, growing in a place that should've choked them out this time of the year.

It was quiet. No birds. No wind. Just us.

Reich stopped walking. I almost kept going. But then his hand wrapped gently around my wrist, pulling me back.

He turned me toward him. His eyes searched mine for a long, heavy moment. Like he was still waiting for me to vanish. Like if he looked away, I'd be gone.

"Come here," he said softly.

I stepped in closer without thinking. Without needing to.

His hands slid over my waist, steady, rough palms settling on my hips. He held me like I was something fragile and he was afraid he might break me... but was still not willing to let go.

His mouth found mine. No rush. No desperation. Just need. And something deeper.

It was different out here.

Out of the compound.

No eyes. No cameras. No gods in white robes waiting to judge every breath we took.

Just me. Just him. And a field of wildflowers.

I threaded my fingers into his hair, tugging gently until his body pressed closer.

"Reich," I whispered, everything in me unraveling into that single word.

"Wildflower," he breathed. "I told you I'm going to make this right... and that includes whatever mess my brother has gotten himself into... we'll find her. I promise," His voice was hoarse, but certain.

And I believed him when he said it. Even if neither of us knew how yet. Because for the first time, neither of us was running when there was a problem.

We were staying right here to face it headfirst together.

EPILOGUE ONE

REICH

Seven Years Later

THE WIND ROLLED OVER the valley, heavy and low, dragging with it the scent of dry earth and the faintest trace of rain that would never come. It kicked up dust along the worn path that snaked its way through the fields toward the house—a path carved by old footsteps and older memories.

The sun hung low in the sky, swollen and red, casting long shadows that stretched thin and sharp across the horizon. Shadows that reached like hands, skimming the wildflowers that had begun to grow again.

Stubborn things. Bright. Fragile.

They shouldn't be here, not in this soil. Not after everything. But still, they pushed through.

A haunting melody sifted through my memory and to my ears as I sat on this empty porch overlooking this even more barren field.

I'm in the middle of nothing and it's where I want to be.

It was true, although I didn't like to admit it to myself.

It always had been true.

I kept my boots planted solid against the old wood, my knife balanced easy in my hand. The rhythmic drag of the whetstone along the blade filled the silence, a steady, familiar sound.

I didn't need to carry a weapon anymore. Not really. But old instincts died slow deaths. And some never did.

The edge was already sharp—razor-thin, gleaming faint in the dying light—but I kept going. Not because it needed it, but because I did. The movement settled something in me. Anchored me. And gave my hands something to do when the rest of me wouldn't stop watching the horizon.

Behind me, the old door creaked open on its rusted hinges. It was a quiet sound, but not quiet enough to slip past me unnoticed. I went still, listening.

There I heard them, small footsteps. Light. Hesitant. Careful in a way that made my chest ache.

Then— "Dad?"

I paused, the whetstone stilling in my hand. Exhaled slow and steady as I let the air out of my lungs before I turned.

Rune stood in the doorway, framed by fading sunlight, his hands loose at his sides. His dark hair fell into his eyes that were hazel-green, just like mine. His hair had grown too long. I should cut it. He never lets his mother do it.

He was six now. Just tall enough that when he crossed his arms over his chest, it almost looked like a decision instead of a habit. And when he frowned, like he was doing now, I saw every piece of myself I never meant to pass on.

Our dog, Navren, came up beside him and they both stood and watched me for a long moment. Silent. Rune's expression caught somewhere between curiosity and fear. I knew that look.

It was the same one I used to give Castor. The same one I wore when I was small and still believed answers could fix things.

"What is it, Rune?" I asked, setting the knife down carefully by my side, blade angled away. My voice stayed low and steady despite the knot forming in my throat.

I set the whetstone down beside the knife, laid both hands open on my knees, and tilted my head down toward him.

He hesitated on the threshold, his bare feet shifting against the wood. Then, slowly, he crossed to me. Small fingers found the hem of my sleeve. Curled there, gentle at first, then tighter before he spoke.

"Mom says I shouldn't ask."

I felt something tighten behind my ribs. Not anger but fear.

"Ask anyway," I told him.

His fingers twisted harder in the fabric of my shirt, like he was afraid I'd disappear if he let go. He shifted from one foot to the other, restless energy shivering through him the way it always did when something was digging at him. His eyes flicked toward my neck—toward the place where my mark still stained. The place I couldn't cover, no matter how many years passed.

When he spoke again, his voice was quieter. Like he was afraid someone else might hear.

"The men in my dreams," he said slowly, "the ones in white... they know my name."

The world tilted under me. Only slightly. But enough.

The mark at my neck stayed quiet. That almost scared me more.

"What do they say?" I kept my voice level, but it shifted ever so slightly.

Rune's brow furrowed, his mouth pulling thin like he was thinking too hard for someone so young. "They tell me I'm supposed to come home."

I didn't move. Didn't blink.

I watched him as he said it. Every word landing heavier than the last.

The ENA was gone. We ended them. We burned it all down and salted the earth. We left their bones to rot beneath a sky that doesn't remember them anymore.

But some things... some things didn't need to exist to be real.

Their faith was older than cities. Older than wars. Older than Rune. Older than me,

And my son— my son was always going to be part of it. Born with blood he didn't ask for. Carrying a prophecy, I swore I would die to keep from him.

But I was still here. And it found him anyway.

"Dad?" His voice broke through, soft.

I placed my hand on his small shoulder, fingers firm, grounding him the way Sage had always done for me.

"Yeah?" I said. Because I couldn't say no. Not to this.

His other hand curled tighter into my sleeve, tugging like he was holding on to something fragile.

He swallowed, glancing toward the fields like he might see them there. The ones who call his name in the dark.

"The men in white," he whispered, "they said I'm next."

The air around us stilled. Even the wind died. Like the world was holding its breath.

I heard the blood rushing in my ears, a dull, familiar roar.

Next.

They said he was next.

I forced my jaw to unclench. My grip stayed steady, but my other hand came up, resting over his where it gripped my sleeve. I covered it completely almost as if to shield it.

"Don't listen to them," I said, voice low. Steel under quiet.

Rune hesitated, his gaze flicking back to mine. And then he nodded. Slow. But the weight didn't lift. His fingers stay curled tight in the fabric of my sleeve, like he was trying to anchor himself to something solid.

IN REICH AND RUIN

Like he knew— even if he was too young to say it.

And I sat there, watching him. Feeling the shape of a fear I thought I buried with the bones of the men who made me.

But it was back. Older. Stronger. Wearing my son's face.

For the first time in years— I was afraid again.

And this time, I didn't think I could stop what was coming.

EPILOGUE TWO

SAGE

I WATCHED THEM FROM the window.

Reich and our son—standing on the porch, their dark hair pulled back and tangled by the wind. The same wind that always came before a storm. It stirred the loose strands around their faces like a warning, whispering through the skeletal trees that lined the property.

The sky was heavy. Low and bruised. The kind of sky that didn't just promise rain but reckoning with it as well.

And still, they stood there. Father and son. Reich with his hand resting on Rune's small shoulder, steady in a way that looked effortless. Rune watched the distance with eyes too old for his face. Eyes like his father's.

I pressed my palm flat against the glass, the cool surface shocking against my skin. My fingers splayed instinctively, as if I could reach through the window and pull them both back inside where it was safe. But there was no such thing as safe. Not really. There never had been for us.

I knew something was wrong. I knew the moment I woke up. Before the light shifted in that quiet, eerie way that signals the world is about to change. Before I found Reich already awake, already dressed, standing silent by our son's bed, watching him breathe like he wasn't sure he still could.

I knew. Because I had the same dream our son had.

And I knew he was telling his father about it.

I pulled my hand away from the window and rested it over my stomach instead, fingers grazing the soft fabric of my dress. The wind outside gusted harder, rattling the panes, and I could feel it inside me.

Another child.

I remembered Reich's face when I told him. The line of joy but also fear.

I exhaled slowly and shakily with my throat tight.

Outside, Reich kneeled in front of Rune, lowering himself carefully, hands braced on our son's small shoulders. His fingers were steady, but I could see the faint tremor in his jaw. The way his throat worked like he was swallowing something sharp.

I couldn't hear what he was saying, but I knew the way his lips moved. The same tone he probably used with me on the worst nights. When my skin burned and my hands wouldn't stop shaking. When I woke screaming from dreams that weren't only dreams but memories of the past.

He gave our son that same comforting look.

Rune nodded, though his brows looked drawn together in confusion. He was too young to understand. Too young to carry this.

I took a step back from the window, closing my eyes for a moment. I already knew the truth. This wasn't over.

I pressed both hands to my stomach now, as if I could shield this new life from what was coming. As if I could hold it inside me long enough to make a difference.

But I couldn't. I knew I couldn't.

But I would do everything to make sure there would be no war today. No fires in the fields. No men in white robes waiting outside our door with their pale faces and their black mouths, chanting their endless liturgies.

Not today.

I slipped on my boots, and tugged my shawl tighter around my shoulders, and pushed the door open. The wind hit me like a breath held too long.

Rune darted past me as I stepped outside, his footsteps light as he ran toward the house. His cheeks were flushed from the wind, his dark hair wild across his forehead. He flashed me a grin as he passed—quick and bright, because he didn't know that there was a world that was still hunting him.

I crossed the porch slowly, each step measured. Deliberate. Reich was still standing at the edge of it, his arms crossed, his gaze locked on the horizon. The storm clouds hadn't moved. They sat there like a wound that refused to close.

His fingers twitched against his sleeve, subtle. Reflexive. Like he was reaching for a weapon he no longer carried. Like his body didn't know how to stop waiting for the next fight.

I came up beside him, close enough that my shoulder brushed his. He didn't flinch.

But he didn't look at me either.

"You felt it too," I murmured.

A muscle in his jaw jumped, and he exhaled through his nose. It wasn't agreement. But it wasn't denial either. The silence was answer enough.

I pressed my hand to my stomach again, slower this time.

Reich dragged his gaze from the horizon long enough to look at my hand. His brow furrowed.

His throat worked like he was trying to speak and couldn't find the words.

"We won't let anything happen to either of them," he said finally, his voice rough. I nodded, though the gesture felt hollow. Because even as I stared out at the horizon, at the unmoving storm clouds stitched across the sky, I couldn't shake the thought worming its way through my ribs.

Was it already too late?

It was that thought that kept me awake long after Reich was asleep. It was that thought that followed me into dreams that weren't dreams.

Where I saw our son standing alone in a field of ash. White robes at his back. A mark burned into the skin at the base of his neck.

When the time came—*because it always did*—he would have to choose. Just as we once did.

About Paige Alexandria

I write stories that live in the shadows—where love is tangled, passion burns deep, and healing comes with scars. With a background in mental health, I understand how heavy the past can feel, and I weave that weight into characters who are raw, flawed, and achingly human.

Music is often my refuge and my muse, fueling the rhythm and intensity of my words. My hope is that each story draws you in, offering both escape and connection—reminding us that even in darkness, there is beauty, and within every broken piece, the possibility of redemption.

When I'm not writing, you'll find me lost in music, wandering through new ideas, or savoring the quiet moments that inspire the chaos on the page.

Instagram - @authorpaigealexandria
Paigealexandria.com

Sneak Peek

Castor Away
Book Three of
The Black Sigil of Naphal Series

After three years on the run, Castor Davidian knows the ENA's reach is endless. Every step forward is a battle against the chains that made him, and every choice threatens to drag him back into the shadows he's spent his life trying to escape. But Sam Vandella changes the rules. With her beside him, survival isn't just about staying alive—it's about holding onto something he was never meant to have.

What begins as another mission spirals into something far more dangerous. Castor isn't just a protector—he's bound to secrets carved in bloodlines and betrayals that stretch back centuries. The deeper they're pulled into the ENA's web, the more the truth threatens to destroy them both.

In Book Three, Castor and Sam face the ultimate question: what are they willing to sacrifice—for freedom, for the truth, and for each other?

The fight against the ENA isn't over.

For Castor and Sam, it's only just beginning.